PENGUIN E
ONCE UPON A TI

Carl Muller completed his education from the Royal College, Colombo, and has served in the Royal Ceylon Navy and Ceylon Army. In 1959 he entered the Colombo Port Commission and subsequently worked in advertising and travel firms. Muller took up journalism and writing in the early Sixties and has worked in leading newspapers in Sri Lanka and the Middle East. His published works include *Sri Lanka—A Lyric, Father Saman and the Devil, Ranjit Discovers where Kandy began, The Jam Fruit Tree*—for which he was awarded the Gratiaen Memorial Prize for the best work of English Literature by a Sri Lankan in 1993; the prize was endowed by Booker Prize winning author, Michael Ondaatje—and *Yakada Yakā.*

Carl Muller lives in Kandy, Sri Lanka, with his wife and four children.

Books by the same author

Carl Muller

ONCE UPON A TENDER TIME

The Concluding Part of the
Von Bloss Family Saga

PENGUIN BOOKS

PENGUIN BOOKS
Published by the Penguin Group
Penguin Books India Pvt. Ltd, 11 Community Centre, Panchsheel Park,
New Delhi 110 017, India
Penguin Group (USA) Inc., 375 Hudson Street, New York, New York 10014,
USA
Penguin Group (Canada), 90 Eglinton Avenue East, Suite 700, Toronto,
Ontario, M4P 2Y3, Canada (a division of Pearson Penguin Canada Inc.)
Penguin Books Ltd, 80 Strand, London WC2R 0RL, England
Penguin Ireland, 25 St Stephen's Green, Dublin 2, Ireland (a division of Penguin
Books Ltd)
Penguin Group (Australia), 250 Camberwell Road, Camberwell, Victoria
3124, Australia (a division of Pearson Australia Group Pty Ltd)
Penguin Group (NZ), 67 Apollo Drive, Rosedale, North Shore 0632,
New Zealand (a division of Pearson New Zealand Ltd)
Penguin Group (South Africa) (Pty) Ltd, 24 Sturdee Avenue, Rosebank,
Johannesburg 2196, South Africa

Penguin Books Ltd, Registered Offices: 80 Strand, London WC2R 0RL,
England

First published by Penguin Books India 1995

Copyright © Carl Muller 1995

All rights reserved

14 13 12 11 10 9 8 7

ISBN   9780140249910

This book is, as the author claims, a work of 'faction' and, while fixed both
historically and chronologically, remains fiction, based on fact, embroidered
and distorted in order to protect the characters herein. All names, save
where obviously genuine, are fictitious, and any resemblance to persons
living or dead, is wholly coincidental.

Typeset in Palatino by FOLIO, New Delhi
Printed at Repro India Ltd., Navi Mumbai

To the memory of Anuradhapura,
a place of incredible enchantment and woodland beauty,
where I spent the happiest days of my own boyhood.

ACKNOWLEDGEMENT

A toast to memories of childhood, boyhood, various history masters in various schools, a box of ball point pens and . . . Sastry Ravichandran, a computer print wizard who typed this book with lightning efficiency. Memories may fade but my friend Ravi, who is over six inches taller than me, will always stand tall in my mind.

CONTENTS

AUTHOR'S NOTE

Now in the honey pot, now in the acid jar—it's these Burghers of old Ceylon playing silly buggers . . . the eight-to-eighteen of third generation Carloboy and his kin—in and out of the garbage pails of life, love and lunacy.

The saga continues in the best (or worst?) Burgher traditions. School days, fool days, one foot in the cabbage patch, the other in overripe manure.

You will meet many old favourites: the redoubtable Sonnaboy von Bloss of *The Jam Fruit Tree* and *Yakada Yakā* and his host of brothers, sisters and cronies. That was the second generation. These, the sprat-brat days of Carloboy von Bloss get too, too complicated for words!

I guess I'm a glutton for punishment.

FOREWORD

The story of Carloboy von Bloss is a story which has been 'factionalized' from many lifetimes. This message of the tender years is based on the real experiences of many, not one, and strung together, not compartmentalized, to create a single experience of child abuse, growing up, first loves, experiments and experiences.

The backdrop is fact, the centre stage fiction, sometimes exchanged, transposed. The author exhorts readers not to get involved, and confused, in the exercise of picking fact out of fiction or fiction out of fact. Many true to life characters pop up to mix with the fictional. All very Pink Pantherish and Roger Rabbity. A strong skein of fact runs through this tale but even this unravels, dissolves at times and the reader may find real people they know and recognize in a fictionalized classroom or a real school with boys or girls who do not exist.

It is a writer's responsibility to protect the living, honour the dead. It is also an urgent matter, in the times such as these, to shout a warning to the adult world. Children need love, support, understanding, protection. Carloboy von Bloss had small measure indeed.

Carloboy von Bloss is a lesson, an example of all the things a child could experience, the good, the bad and the ugly. He weathered every careless brush stroke of life and eventually found a desolation that demanded that inner strength of mind to help him overcome.

This is not a happy book but it does not dwell on agony or ecstasy overlong. It just goes on, like its hero, a procession of good and bad, better and worse. A cloud nine over a cesspit.

And it's true . . . up to the point where fact embraces fiction and lives, hopefully, most satisfactorily ever after.

CHAPTER ONE

'Yeeeach!'

Beryl von Bloss, twiddling the big cloth-covered buttons of her housecoat in the grey-orange light of the smoky kerosene lamp, knew what that squelchy cry from the next room was all about. She was going to give up on the buttons anyway. There was absolutely no sense in latching together the front of a housecoat and climbing into bed. Not with husband Sonnaboy in it—in bed, I mean, not in her housecoat. She reminded herself that this was not regular nightwear. At twenty-three, a young wife should be wearing something more diaphanous. Trouble is she had two nighties in the bathroom tub and one that needed mending. Also, as she wisely pointed out, what with baby Marie in her cradle and daughter Diana's constant bed-wetting and son Carloboy's midnight tantrums and the servant-girl, Poddi, maintaining a sort of night watch, thin nightdresses were definitely not on. Night and day made scant difference in the von Bloss household. Infants, children, servant-girls, things stirred vigorously whatever the hour.

Sonnaboy considered buttons, zips, press studs and the frustrating world of textile fasteners in the trying category of impedimenta. Getting into bed was not in itself an end. He had, ritually, to get into Beryl too, and these damn buttons were, to his urgent loins, an obstacle. He had tried them earlier and sworn. 'What the hell, men, damn buttonholes you're stitching so small. And the size of these buttons. What for you're putting them so big?'

'So get off, will you, and let me take out,' Beryl hissed, 'how to do anything when you're on top . . . there, can't wait a little while. Now don't make too much noise. Children are sleeping never mind, but that Poddi is not a small one. Sometimes just sitting on the mat and waiting. Must be listening.'

The von Bloss sleeping arrangements were simple. Sonnaboy and Beryl in one room; the children in the other. Carloboy and Diana in one old, low bed, Marie in an ancient cradle swathed in a dingy mosquito net. Poddi spread her mat between bed and cradle.

Poddi was twelve, had a sergeant-major's appetite, a headful of lice, dirty feet and a missing front tooth. That was the debit column. To her credit, she was maturing alarmingly and had developed a frontispiece which was of intense interest to the servant-boy next door. That worthy, as black as sin and with piano-accordion teeth would sidle up to the low side wall and bob his head knowingly. Poddi would give hers a toss and ply her eekel broom, then stop raising the dust to demand: 'At what you're looking?'

The scamp would slyly reach over the wall.

Poddi would move back. 'Wait, I to *nona*[1] will tell.'

'So tell.'

'I'll go and tell.'

'So tell.'

'If telling, you'll get for you good whacking.'

'*Apoi*,[2] as if you don't like. Little to squeeze only I'm asking.'

'For what?'

'Just. You near come a little. My one you want to see?'

'*Chee!*'

'Little close come will you?'
'Can't, can't, if *nona* suddenly call—I going.'

So Poddi, coming along very nicely, thank you, lies on her mat and listens to the old bed creak rhythmically in the next room and realizes that there are more things on earth than she has been privy to and this, she tells herself, is a most unsatisfactory state of being.

Her fantasies are punctured every night by Carloboy who gives voice to utter boyhood disgust with a long drawn out Yeeeeach! Poddi knows the reason why and rises to minister. Beryl, too, abandons the last two buttons of her housecoat and rises, muttering. At least her son's timing was better tonight. Sonnaboy grunts, snaps on his short pajamas and strides to the lavatory. Carloboy, shedding the befuddlement of sleep is seated in bed and pummelling Diana furiously. Diana, clouted into wakefulness ripens the air with perforated bagpipe squeals while her tormentor justifies himself to all and sundry by crying: 'Again doing pippie all over me!' and hurriedly scooting down the bed as his mother bears down, housecoat flapping and in a mood that is far from indigo.

It's the nightly ritual. Diana, everybody knew was a perfect little 'pisspot'. She peed the bed with ardour. It was a big bed and Diana, to say the least, remained in her sodden corner against the wall, growing soggy in the small hours and soggier by cockcrow. Six-year-old Carloboy had this penchant to roll. Bedtime crackled with repartee.

'You stay there,' the boy would say, 'and I'll sleep on this side and don't come to pippie near me.'

'Mummeeee, see what this Carloboy is telling.'

'Pisspot, you're a real pisspot!'

'Mummeeee!'

Beryl from the hall: 'Shut up you damn wretch and go to sleep. You wake the baby to see. Put you out and close the door!'

Silence. Five minutes later Beryl comes to the bed. 'Devils are still not sleeping? Close your eyes and sleep! Not a hum!'

and the devils decide to call it a day because being little devils is a tiring business and they are only six and four and very small and Mummy is very big and smacks very hard and dislikes them intensely.

Each night, Carloboy tries to keep awake until Poddi comes in. Trouble is Poddi's washing plates and scouring the cooking pots with a *polmudda* (the pointed tuft of husk that covers the eyes of the coconut—makes an ideal scrubbing brush) and scraping the ashes out of the hearth and performing all manner of chores. Some late evenings, however, she gets through early and carries in her mat and pillow.

Carloboy, dozing off with a frown was dragged awake on the last such occasion by the slap and sussuration of Poddi's mat being unrolled. Usually he would give a small treble snort, turn on his belly and bury his face in his pillow, but this time he just lay, watching the girl in the dim yellow glow of the railway signal lamp.

Carloboy liked to muck around with that lamp. There was a thingummy at the top which you yanked on and this freed the inner mechanism. By turning the handle, a three spot cylinder would revolve: first click, open slot for the wick that was lit inside and a yellow-white light. Next click and a green glass spot masked the burning wick. Next spot was red. Railwaymen carried these tricolour lanterns. Guards would wave the green spot at nights so that drivers, leaning out of their cabs and looking back were assured that all systems were 'go'. Sonnaboy used his lantern as a night light at home.

It was in this light that Carloboy, six years old and 'knowing damn too much for his age', as Beryl would insist, saw Poddi taking off her clothes. It had never occurred to his child mind that Poddi could so transform herself to become a creature of special interest. He stared. Why, Poddi did not wear knickers! The girl bent down, took up a length of cloth and draped it around her waist, then slung on a sort of blouse which she extracted from inside her pillowcase, then lay down with a small, complaining sigh and scratched her head.

For that tiny instant of eternity, Carloboy had seen Poddi—her brown buttocks, short, fat thighs and the little black beads of her nipples which caught the yellow lantern light. The boy stared at the foot of the bed. If he raised his head a little, moved it a little to the right, he would be able to see the girl on her mat. The yellow light would be flowing all over her, but she was now in a cloth and jacket and be the old ordinary Poddi of the daytime. It had been too shadowy to see much else. Poddi had turned when draping her cloth, depriving him of her facing nakedness and he now screwed tight his eyes and tried to imagine what that would be like. Carloboy was quite familiar with the way girls were. Wasn't Diana smacked, stripped and propelled a dozen times a day to the bathroom, howling like a sorely tormented cat? Didn't Poddi bathe them in the little bathroom, in the big metal tub with one handle? Carloboy would be made to sit under the running tap and warned not to splash water all over the place (which he always did) while Poddi soaped Diana, and he would say, 'Put lot of soap in her pippie place, everytime pippying, no?' Funny, he hadn't the word for it. He had a birdie and—what did that Uncle Ebert say one day? Ah, yes, that was the day an ant had bitten his birdie. A big red ant. It must have been in his shorts. He was frightened then. The ant bite was fierce and as he scratched and scratched the tip of his foreskin had swelled into a red, curling lump. Beryl had laughed and dabbed butter on it. He was sobbing when Uncle Ebert had come in, chuckled and asked: 'What happened? Ant bit your fly?'

Later he had asked his mother, 'Why is Uncle Ebert saying fly?'

'Fly? What fly?'

'Why he asked if ant bit my fly. Don't even know the word birdie.'

'Shut up!' Beryl raised the hairbrush.

So he had a birdie or a fly and because Diana was quite different, it had to be a 'pippie place' for want of anything better—or worse. He would have seen Poddi's pippie place also but the girl had twisted away as she wore her cloth. So, he tried to keep awake and the effort would daze him into sleep and that was rather a disappointment.

Carloboy was too precocious for words. Also, he rolled in his sleep and, despite the usual rigmarole about keeping to his side of the bed and Diana to hers, he would tumble against her, sometimes throw a leg across her and Diana, an obliging girl, would turn on the waterworks.

Which brings us full circle. Beryl hauls Diana out of bed, gives her son a wallop, Marie wakes to howl and grow very red in the face, Poddi is hustled to see to the baby and Diana is pinched and pushed to the bathroom.

Sonnaboy rumbles from the next room: 'Why don't you put that wretch into the bathroom tub to sleep? Everyday washing sheets, drying pillows and see the stains on the pillows. One cake of Sunlight not enough for a day in this house! Otherwise put on a mat, will you?'

'Damn nonsense,' Beryl storms, glaring at Carloboy, 'you also! Can't sleep in one place. Going to roll! Having such a big bed must go to roll on top of her? Go on! You also go and wash!'

Poddi reminds: '*Aiyo*! Everywhere pippie have been doing.'

It takes time to propel the family once more into the celebrated arms of Morpheus, and when the new day breaks it is Poddi's task to wash the sheets and pillowslips and carry the folding clotheshorse to the rear garden where the damp and smelly pillows are dried in the sun. The stains don't go away. They are creamy yellow at first, then darken to brown and rust-brown. Through the years, Beryl made a lot of pillows. The *pulun*[1] man would come to the door carrying his large gunny sack of 'tree cotton' and Beryl would buy pounds and pounds of the stuff, and sneeze, and stitch covers of longcloth and stuff them (and sneeze) and scowl and push Diana away from the sewing-machine.

'Pillows, pillows, pillows!' she would bark. 'Useless beast, only know to piss on everything. You piss on these to see.

---

1. Kapok

Give you properly!' And Diana would make mournful eyes and shrink away.

She was a scarecrow of a child, sharp-featured and lank-haired. She knew, even at four, that home held many terrors. She disliked her brother, feared her mother and was overawed by her big, brawny father who came and went at the most ungodly hours. She also detested the baby, Marie Esther Maud, who did pippie all the time and was never smacked. Nobody yelled at Marie. Indeed, Marie did all the yelling, and her full-blooded wails were enough to drive anyone up the wall. There was a pink oilcloth in her cradle and a tub of soiled diapers in the bathroom. Poddi would change the squares of cloth after the ritual sponging, cleaning and powdering, and Beryl would warn, 'You don't go and the child with the safety pin prick, did you hear?' and Poddi, who heard, would stick her tongue out fiercely at the baby because she had no one else to vent her spleen on.

CHAPTER TWO

1941 was a queasy year. Ceylon of old had to weather the consequences of many and sometimes quite violent changes caused by hordes of uninvited guests who forged in, upset native applecarts and then swept away leaving such a shambles that the situation begged for another spirit of change to barge in with mop, squeegee and bucket.

The chronicler may as well lay the ground now, elaborating on what has been covered sketchily in his previous books.

The Portuguese, who arrived in Ceylon in 1505, looked dimly on the island's feudal system. There simply had to be a superimposition of European authority. This actually happened thrice in four centuries which left the natives in that silly position of not knowing whether they (and these other foreign infestations) were coming or going. It destroyed their faith in the permanency of things.

The Portuguese came . . . the Dutch came . . . the Portuguese went. The British came . . . the Dutch went . . . everybody else, at least, seemed to know when to come and when to go or be run out, but the natives found these many exits and entrances bad for their nerves. They got quite dizzy and overexcitable. And where, they must have wondered, could they go? Take to the hills, or jump into the sea? This is an island, for Chrissake!

Trouble was, what the Portuguese did, the Dutch undid; what the Dutch set up, the British thumbed down. In Bambalapitiya, the Portuguese built a church to Senhora nostra dos Los Milhagros—Our Lady of Miracles. The Dutch tore it down and raised a 'Reformed' church on the site. The British took it over and made it a Presbyter of sorts. Eventually it became St Paul's and a large girl's school was built behind it and the chapel stayed in business while the entire complex and the area around it was called Milhargiriya—a bastardization of the Portuguese 'Milhagros'. And Milhargiriya it is to this day and the miracles are, of course, the girls in the school who are the magnet of every schoolboy in Bambalapitiya. The Sinhalese were quite happy with the name. It had a nice Sinhala ring to it. After all, there are lots of Sinhalese place names with the 'Giriya' ending (meaning throat or gullet).

All quite confusing, to be sure, and another thing: what about loyalty? No, there was no relying on anything.

When the Portuguese, after lobbing lots of cannon balls and skirmishing up- and down-coast, became the rulers of Ceylon's maritime provinces, they were determined to make the island a part of Portugal. The King of Portugal was proclaimed sovereign of the country, but the natives, who were simple souls and picked their teeth sixty-seven times a day, could not relate to some pot-belly in Lisbon who could be, as far as they knew, in some other plane of existence. Rather, they adopted the Portuguese Captain-General as their king. At least they could see him, hear him and comfort themselves that he was among them. Later they even called him the King of Malwana, which is a sleepy hollow in the hinterland where the best rambuttans are grown.[1]

The Dutch who wore long faces and tramped in in 1658, belonged to an armed merchant company with an eye for

---

1. One can never be sure about native humour. Malwana grows lush, red rambuttans, which, because of the appearance of the fruit, are aptly called 'hairy balls'. To dub the Portuguese Captain-General as King of Malwana could have been the waggish Sinhalese way of calling him 'Big, red, hairy balls'. This, of course, is pure conjecture.

heavy dividends and the main chance. They found Ceylon in a chaotic state with the Portuguese-fashioned local administration in the hands of a bunch of sleazeballs. Also, there were a lot more sergeants than privates.

Native converts to Catholicism rode roughshod over the common, unbaptized herd. There were titles galore, and the only way an ambitious Sinhalese could go places was to accept baptism, latch a saint's name to his and join the brigand's brigade.

The Dutch found this whole boiling administrative jungle too, too complicated for words. The generals had native officials who were known as Basnayakes and Mohottiars,[1] and there were judges called Ouvidors who called the shots and sent out their sidekicks, the Maralleiros on perambulating assizes with instructions to bring back, by way of fines, as much dressed and raw provision as could be wrested from hapless native peasants who were completely overawed by the system and submitted, tamely enough.

The Vendor de Fazenda collected taxes. He prepared a thombo (Lands Register) and, with the connivance of Factors, Secretaries and Sub-accountants, went around like the Sheriff of Nottingham's scurvy band, collecting royal dues in cash and kind. Naturally, nobody took kindly to them and once in a while a better constituted native would slip a knife between a Factor's ribs. This, of course, was frowned on.

In the Forts, there were Captain-Majors and Captains of Forts and Captains of Divisions. They rode Malaga horses and wore thigh boots and bodkins and inspected pikemen and drank too much sweet wine.

The dour-faced Dutch found the whole Portuguese edifice a hopeless mess . . . and as confusing as a wrongly laced corset. There were, for example, a lot of pompous birds with some sort of fluffy cushions on their heads and pillows tied to their middles, called Disavas (the head of a unit of territory called a disavani.) These stuffy fellows controlled gangs of Lascarins, the local militia, and were assisted by

---

1. It is not my intention to identify any of these officials or describe what they did not do. May I ask my readers to just ride along with the names?

gung-ho types called Mudaliyars, Muhandirams, Aarachchis and legal bimbos called Basnayakes and Mohottalas. To rub in the salt, each disavani was made up of smaller units called korales which were in the tender hands of the headman of the korale.

This bloke could summon, in a pinch, sundry minor Mudaliyars and Muhandirams, and in overview it was a seething, sorry picture of a lot of people swaggering around and playing silly buggers and chucking their importance under each other's noses. The Portuguese even took the humble village headman and called him a Mayoral, which made the said headman think no end of himself, and all these little tin gods went on a binge, so to say, and became recklessly arbitrary and were imbued with the greedy Portuguese ideas of profit and be damned! What was formerly tribute and fees degenerated into open, naked bribery. Oppression followed. There were vicious punishments. The sudden desertion of villages, the break-up of lascar contingents as the natives went 'awol' and rebellion rumbled everywhere.

The Dutch stuck a governor in charge and set about cleaning up. The Portuguese had made a mistake. They had imagined that, in baptizing a native and giving him a saint's name, the convert would think, act and behave . . . well, like a Portuguese. On the contrary, the Sinhalese took the water, the Sign of the Cross, the Chrism of Salvation (which was simply a dab of salt on the tongue) and went on to be converts of the best sort. Hah! now to convert all the assets of the village!

The Dutch Governor set up a Political Council and divided Ceylon into the Commanderies of Colombo, Galle and Jaffna. Dutchmen took on the role of Disavas and kept a few native aides who rejoiced in the name of Ata Pattu Mudaliyar—glorified headmen. (Ata Pattu was Mudaliyar of the eight pattus. That's the eight subdivisions of a korale. Likewise we have Atu Korale—eight korales which make up a disavani. This should give readers a hazy idea of the administrative pecking order.) The outstations had some half-and-half fellows called Lieutenant Disavas. All good fun, actually with *hoi polloi* looking on, shrugging, spitting blobs of betel juice and wondering when the circus would come to an end.

The Dutch reduced the native machinery. The Basnayakes and Mohotallas ceased to exist, went back to their villages with their tails between their legs. Some tried to brazen things out and were, if village lore is accepted, set upon and soundly belaboured. The Mudaliyars, however, scraped through. They kowtowed to such an extent that the Dutch Governor, quite impressed by their pretensions of loyalty, even upgraded some of them to Maha Mudaliyar (Great Mudaliyar) status.

Soon the Mudaliyars wormed their way into the korales, booted out the Vidanes and became Mudaliyars of the korales. This put paid to the Atu Korales too, who were the Vidanes' assistants.

Thus did the Dutch cut the native 'nobility' to size, and those who made protest were told to make themselves useful, promote the interests of the VOC (Veeringdee Oost-Indische Compagnie—the Dutch East India Company) and stop being so bloody pompous and a general pain in the ass. To spur them on, the Dutch also dangled ceremonial gold chains, medals and land grants. Get cracking, they were told and you'll get a medal and a chain and a tract of areca nut land.

The British who came in singing 'Rule Britannia' were appalled. Also, they found the central kingdom of Kandy thumbing a nose at Europe in general and blithely carrying on as in the days of yore with all manner of palace-bred Adigars, Disavas, Rate Mahattayas, Atu Korales, Atu Pattus, Lekams, Vidanes and Muhandirams rabbitting around in weird costumes and being exceedingly ceremonial and scheming against each other as in a sort of highly immoral obligation.

The British would have none of it. They were determined that all Ceylon must be theirs. Can't have Her Imperial Majesty tilt her head, wobble her double chins and ask: 'And what, my lords, are we doing ahbaht Kandy? We are h'informed in dispatches that Ceylon is ours. We h'arsk assurance. H'all of Ceylon, we h'arsk. H'and we are told h'almost all. 'Ow is this, my lords? H'ar we then sovereign offer h'almostall country?'

So the British struggled up the mountains and captured Kandy as well. It was a tough campaign. The Kandyans kept rolling rocks down on them and using the mountains to carry out all manner of ambuscades, guerilla tactics and vicious stabs in the back. But, with the services of a few self-serving souls, they triumphed and so was the island truly and completely under foreign yoke . . . and in came a new infestation of white sahibs to structure a Civil Service along the lines of the 'covenanted service' of the British East India Company.

It was the British belief that the Empire of India rested on European superiority. The Britishers moved into India, each with the intention of returning to England some day with sufficient loot—sorry, means—to live out the rest of their lives in comfort, laced with tea, crumpets and gin. In Ceylon, too, this was pretty much the case. Blighters from Blighty swarmed in with the sole intention of making a fortune and returning, 'nabob' style to Dorset, Pearson Road, N.E., Beaumont Road, Plymouth or wherever. Soon British administration at ground floor level was simply all manner of ginger-moustached square pegs bunging up all manner of round holes.

This was a pyramid of sorts. The British sat, bandy-legged at the top. Below sat lesser Brits who were brought in for decorative purpose. Below sat the local Portuguese and Dutch settlers, the Burghers, who were, in a sense, 'western' and deserved such recognition. At the base scrabbled the Sinhalese and Tamils, with the Tamils pushing harder for recognition and promotion to a sort of mezzanine floor which was as far as the natives were allowed to get. But they clung to their positions with great fondness while the Tamils exhibited a great measure of hardheadedness and a near insane fervour to rise, oust the Burghers by hook or by crook and get into the middle.

The chronicler craves his reader's indulgence in quoting a Minute by Englishman Robert Hobart. It puts, in a nutshell, the problems the British countenanced. On 9 June 1797, Hobart said that:

> . . . the precariousness of our position, the short period the whole of the Dutch settlements have been in our hands, the difficulty of obtaining information, the distrust of the natives, the indisposition of the Dutch, were obstacles to a successful management.

Yes, the British found it a hard nut. Civil servants from Madras, well schooled in their work, were shipped in . . . and this caused more problems. It is an age-old story, actually: wherever one Indian goes, others quickly follow. With the coming of the Madrasis, south Indians flocked in and soon, the Madras bureaucrats picked Malabaris to take over the duties of Sinhalese Mudaliyars and Headmen. The Tamils, through the good offices of the Madras government, began to ride the wavecrest. The Burghers continued to be 'looked after'. The Sinhalese, tragically, were left out in the cold . . . and this, tragically too, was their land. The Malabaris became the tax collectors and called the shots in the villages. The Sinhalese fretted and fumed. Open revolt was their only recourse.

When revolt came, the British realized that they were losing their grip on the country. Clearly, Indian forms and administrative methods had proved disastrous. The usual things happened, just as they happen today. A Committee of Investigation was appointed, and in the proceedings we find this sad-faced mea culpa:

> The habits and prejudices of a nation can only be changed by one or two means—gradually, by mildness and a clear demonstration of the superior advantages they will derive from the proposed alterations: or violently, by the compulsive efforts of superior force . . . mildness and persuasion, it appears, were not the distinguishing features of

our change of system, and our force was inadequate to compel obedience.[1]

And so, things got better and by 1801 it was decided that Ceylon would be turned into a Crown Colony and the dust began to settle . . . and through it all the Burghers went blithely on, quite happy in the fact that they were the only section of an explosive citizenry with no axe to grind and being quite content with whatever rung of the ladder they stood on. They brought into the world large broods of handsome children who were looked upon lecherously and sought after to adorn office or wear uniforms and be pressed into marriage at the first hint of ripeness. Of them, Sonnaboy von Bloss drove a railway engine and wife Beryl bore his children (and aborted those that were not) and son Carloboy, who was a very imaginative child, spent the first six years of his life firm in the belief that sisters did nothing but urinate alarmingly and that Mummy was there to beat him, sew clothes, read *True Confessions*, sing, and make funny noises at night when Daddy was with her.

It was best, Sonnaboy said, to put Carloboy into a 'proper' school. St Lawrence's School in Wellawatte, run by the Pouliers, was all very well for a little boy with a *Radiant Way* and a box of well-chewed Parrot crayons, but where was the 'serious' education? Sonnaboy had been startled at the Lower School demands: cartridge paper, plasticine, a primer, coloured paper, tracing paper, pencil, eraser, gum and scissors, a big pastel drawing book, crayons, scrapbook . . . He went to the school one day, looked in and came away muttering.

'Holding hands and singing "Three Blind Mice" and some nonsense and building blocks all over the floor and all,' he growled. 'Just paying the fees to go and play? Sending to learn, no?'

Beryl was young enough to know how nursery schools

---

1. Proceedings of the De Meuron Committee. Mentioned in dispatches from the Secretary of State to the Governor and marked Colonial Office 55,2.

operated. 'So never mind. And anyway he is reading much more here, no?' she would say. 'Just let be for now.'

'Kindger garden!' Sonnaboy snorted. 'No wonder no one studying when sending to a garden! Fine bloody school, just to go and play and come!'

'So never mind, men,' Beryl said again, 'threeanaharf hours peace in the morning now. Otherwise just fighting with Diana and no rest for anybody.'

Sonnaboy grunted. Beryl had a point. He liked to take a turn in bed with her on his mornings off. It was easy to get rid of Poddi and Diana and the baby. Just tell Poddi to keep the children in the veranda. But Carloboy was another matter. He would scuttle around the house, bang on the bedroom door, demand to know why it was locked. One day he had shinned up to the window and Beryl, luckily, had seen his shadow against the blind. 'My God,' she hissed, 'that damn child is going to look through the window! Get up! Quickly! Put a towel or something!'

It was close. Carloboy clutching at the window bars, saw his father's thunderous face and Mummy breathing heavily on the bed. There was a sheet and two pillows on her but one leg, from mid-thigh lay uncovered. Sonnaboy roared so loud, so long, that the boy fell off his perch into a bed of balsams and screeched. Mummy rushed out, slapped him, slapped Poddi too, for not keeping an eye on 'the devil'. The window was closed thereafter and Carloboy would remark on this.

'There, can see? Now door closing, window also. Don't know why.'

Poddi would snap, 'For that never mind. You just come here and play, will you.'

'I can't.'

'Last time saw, no, what happened.'

Carloboy considered, 'So what there they are doing?'

'Just being there, must be.'

'For why?'

'I how to know?'

Life had too many mysteries for an imaginative six-year-old.

CHAPTER THREE

Sonnaboy was an 'old Joe'—having schooled, albeit sketchily, at St Joseph's College until that institution had grown so crowded that the Roman Catholic Bishop of Colombo (who was later made Archbishop and made his Borella residence a 'palace') decided to create another school to ease the strain. Thus was St Peter's College set up in Bambalapitiya and Sonnaboy and about 200 other junior schoolboys transferred to the new school. He was, thus, a Josephian turned Peterite. Soon, the schools developed a rivalry (as most schools do) and met in an annual cricket encounter (also as most schools do) and hordes of Peterites to this day carry blue, white and gold flags and jeer the Josephians who brandish their colours of blue, white and blue and call the Peterites Shit Pot Carriers because the initials S.P.C. also stand for St Peter's College. This is a pattern zealously followed to this day.

As said, this was a queasy year. In Europe, civilized people were priming to kill each other *en masse*, mothers found Hitler useful in getting children to bed and Sonnaboy was going to spread suburban unease by planning a move to Wellawatte. Last year his father, Cecilprins, had died, putting paid to the family Christmas as effectively as if he had used a flame thrower and with the coastal towns rapidly emptying as families headed for the hills for fear of air raids, old Pheobus came bearing glad tidings. Sonnaboy could move to

34th Lane, Wellawatte—to his old house and pay much less rental too.[1]

Carloboy, like all small boys, was self-centred and couldn't relate to death. Also, it was Christmas, and why did Grandpapa have to die anyway? He had stared, and wondered at all the hullabaloo and demanded to make his jigsaw puzzle, and had crept into the storeroom to stamp his foot and scowl at the old cupboard with the torn mesh, after Beryl had clouted him and snatched the box away.

'Damn little brute!' she had stormed. 'Your grandpa is dead, do you hear! Just see, will you,' she told Anna, who was heaving like a whale who didn't fancy Jonah, 'time like this he's taking the jigsaw puzzle. Not a tear in the eye.'

Anna gave a low moan and slumped on the settee which immediately released a protesting spring.

Beryl warmed to her theme. 'Next time ask to take the batanball and go to the cemetery. Get out of here! Can't even cry in peace!'

Carloboy was annoyed. He couldn't understand what all the frenzy was about. Daddy had given him a jigsaw puzzle. His Christmas present. He was entranced with the big box and the picture on the cover—a Greek temple, cypresses, blue hills, stone columns and a mackerel sky. One thousand pieces, the box proclaimed. Sonnaboy had also given him a penknife. That, too, was utterly scrumptious. Two blades, a corkscrew, and another flat blade with a cut-out slot for opening crown corks, and a spatula-like projection which was ideal, he thought, for prising objects out of wood or plaster. The blades were marvellous. The main knife, notched at the top to be drawn out by the application of a fingernail, was a shiny thing of pure venom. It caught the joy light of the boy's eyes, and both shone together in a constellation of belonging.

Beryl was angry. 'Nice thing to give,' she had scolded, 'now will take and cut something or cut himself or do something devilish, you see, will you. Don't come to say

---

1. See *The Jam Fruit Tree* (Penguin 1993) pp. 190 and 191-192.

anything afterwards. That a thing to give? And . . . and you're not to take that thing to school, you heard?'

Carloboy heard and nodded dumbly. The longer he lived the more he was convinced that Mummy hated him. Daddy, he reasoned, was not so bad. Carloboy admired his father. He would regard Sonnaboy's massive frame, meaty forearms and biceps and the pantherish way he moved and then consider his own thin, white arms ruefully. But Daddy was always away, driving trains to places he had never seen or known. It wasn't that Beryl made life for her son unpleasant. It was just her way and the fact that being married reminded her that she was only twenty-two, had three children and was once again feeling that morning queasiness in this queasy year and was haunted by images of babies by the dozen, clotheslines full of diapers, cupboards full of gripe mixture and Dr Rutnam's latest wisecrack: 'Better if reserve a bed for you in the maternity home.' But between her bouts of temper and shaking Poddi by her hair and screaming at her son and daughter and nursing the baby, there were those softer periods when she sang, and sewed, and sang, and brushed Diana's hair and sang . . .

Carloboy liked to hear her sing, to listen to those old love songs of the times, and quickly picked up the words and hummed the tunes even in class where stout Mrs Bartholomeusz with a pair of rabbit teeth biting into her lower lip, stuffed her standard two pupils with such gems as:

What does little baby say
In her bed at peep of day?

and

I love little kitty
Her coat is so warm . . .

After Beryl's soft and sweet 'Ramona' and 'Pagan Love Song' and 'There's a lamp burning bright in the window' and her jollier 'When I'm cleaning windows' and 'Polly wolly doodle all the day', Carloboy paid little heed to Mrs Bartholomeusz who used to titter and say that he must have left his tongue at home.

Standard Two had a lot of Burgher children. There was Norman Dekker who always came in a white shirt with frills and a runny nose; Sheilah Mortimer who came with an ayah and kept darting out of class to ascertain that the ayah sat, waiting, under the tamarind tree and had not gone about some business of her own. Sheilah would toss her ringlets and say: 'Mama tole her to stay till skoolover. When skoolover she mus' take me home.'

Carloboy liked Therese Wendt who sat next to him and had shiny black hair and big black eyes. She brought her teddy bear to class. The stitches had given way in spots and bits of yellow stuffing showed through. It was quite disreputable both in looks and attitude but Therese would scream her head off if parted from it. She called her teddy Small Kum.

Mrs Bartholomeusz looked with favour on her Burgher pupils. So did old Mrs Poulier and the severe-faced Miss Poulier and Miss Rulach and Mrs Davidson. This was, virtually, a Burgher school with its fair sprinkling of Sinhalese, Tamil, Malay and Muslim children. There was a Sinhalese master who took the older boys in Geography and English and told them to read *Cedric the Saxon* and regaled them with stories of London and how he had seen shabby people who wore one suit of woollens everyday and lived on poor allowances of twenty shillings a week. The boys liked old Veegee, as they called him, because he was V.G. Fernando, and because he had a soft, near musical voice and never ranted at them. The most he would say, with a cocker-spaniel expression, was, 'Oh, you *are* a duffer!'

The children also liked the heavy-spectacled Sunny Herft who, although a Burgher, was darker-complexioned than Veegee and raised eyebrows each time he claimed Dutch blood. Mrs Bartholomeusz cold-shouldered the poor man and wanted no truck with such an oddity. She would tell Mrs Martenstyn who lived next door and had the largest pair of calves in Wellawatte, threaded with knotty blue varicose veins, that Sunny Herft was not to be acknowledged. 'Real shame to even say he is a Burgher. God knows what's been going on in that family,' she would sniff and glance at her own face in the hatstand mirror and consider her pink-powdered cheeks the very essence of Burgherness.

St Lawrence's was an accepted launch pad. Children were dragged in, howling and kicking, were taught to read, write, draw aeroplanes and bowls of flowers, long divide and recite their twelve times tables. Some dawdled on till Standard Five and were then crammed into convents and colleges where they were taught L.C.M.s and how twenty hundred weights made a ton and that dividers and compasses were not meant to dig holes in the desks with. When Carloboy was deemed to be too, too precocious for the general good of the Lower School, Mrs Poulier suggested that Beryl put him into a college where the priests wielded canes with zest.

'Such a bright child,' Mrs Poulier gushed, 'but he needs a firm hand.'

Beryl stared. She sensed the old lady's disapproval of her. Mrs Poulier also stared. How dare this girl—yes, a mere girl—have a six-year-old son who said 'damn' and 'bloody' and knew how to spell 'perspiration'. And to invite that boy . . . yes, that de Run boy . . . to come to his home to see his sister pass water. Mrs Poulier had trembled. Such goings on. Mrs Bartholomeusz had been quite agitated. She didn't want that von Bloss child in her class. Not ever!

'Lucky I was near and heard them talking. I was shocked. Telling that Bunny to come home and can see his sister doing number one.'

Mrs Poulier couldn't understand a word of this and quickly told her Bella to bring tea. Bella, the office dogsbody, was loth to leave. It had been a most innocent conversation, actually, although it did betray Carloboy's unseemly preoccupation with the passing of urine and the organs employed in such pursuit. It couldn't be helped, one supposes, considering how he was warmly unctioned by Diana every night and had realized, all of a sudden, that 'big people' had very big penises and that his own birdie, when artfully fondled gave him strange but satisfactory sensations.

Little Bunny de Run has 'left the class' twice that morning and just before the interval had raised his hand again. 'Please, miss, leave the class?' Mrs Bartholomeusz had been too engrossed with coloured chalk to even look up. She just said yes and Bunny trotted off to the loo. Carloboy was impressed. 'My gosh, how many times you went today,' he remarked, and this time Mrs Bartholomeusz was listening.

'You must see my sister, men, whole time she's doing. In the night how many times I don't know. All over me also. Damn wretch she is, my mummy is always saying. And Daddy says put her in the bloody bathroom to sleep. You come home and see if you like. I think if just tell to pippie she will do.'

Mrs Bartholomeusz gave a sharp yelp and rushed to the principal.

Mrs Poulier decided that Carloboy was a confusing boy— and she disliked confusions, conundrums, complications and corns, which she suffered from terribly. No wonder the child was such a trial. This girl seemed to be totally unqualified to be a mother. Too young to be anything, really, and Mrs Poulier couldn't remember ever being young.

Beryl ignored the disapproval. She considered herself a dyed-in-the-wool mother any road, having birthed three and knowing that number four was not far behind. 'I thought to keep him here till the fifth standard,' she said.

Mrs Poulier blanched. 'Now St Peter's College has a junior school. They admit boys from Standard Two.'

'Why?'

'Why?'

'Yes, that's what I'm asking. Why he can't learn here? You just now said he was bright, no? And see the other children who are in Standard Five and all. I know, no, how bright he is. When come home must see the way he's reading and writing big words and spelling also. That Mrs Bartholomeusz is telling how he is saying dirty words in class. But that's not his fault, no? Sometimes railway people coming home and he's listening the way they are talking and must have picked up.'

Mrs Poulier nodded. 'Ah, yes, children pick up very quickly. We know the sort of homes they come from by the way they behave here.'

Beryl's eyes flashed. 'What do you mean? You're trying to tell that our home is bad or something?'

Mrs Poulier said that the thought had never crossed her mind.

'Because he's saying damn and bloody?' Beryl gritted. 'So if you're the damn principal take the cane and give him a bloody whack, will you!'

'Mrs von Bloss, I'm shocked!'

'What to shocked. What do you know? You think your bloody school is too good for my son? If I go and tell my husband you know what he'll do? Come here and burn your bloody school down. You don't know my husband. No damn nonsense with him!'

Carloboy, quite oblivious of the drama in the principal's room, was helping Therese Wendt to change the sex of her teddy bear. Therese had suddenly decided that Small Kum was a strange name for her faithful toy and wished to call it Clementine. 'Then I can sing to it Oh my darling, Oh my darling like in the song,' she announced solemnly and fluttered her eyelids.

'We can make it a girl. Wait, I'll show you.'

The operation was successful. A hole was punched between the teddy leg's and Carloboy regarded his crude handiwork with proud satisfaction.

'You tore it,' the girl wailed, 'see the hole you made.'

'So now it's a girl, no? All girls have like that. As if you don't know. Just go and see. I can see at home my sister also have. And the baby.'

Therese Wendt saw reason. She regarded her Clementine and touched the hole and squirmed a finger into it and who could tell what went on in that little-girl head? She kept regarding her teddy all the time and several times that morning she put her hand under the desk, under her short dress, to pull apart her frilly knickers and touch her own little hole. Yes, her teddy was a girl now, just like her, and she loved it more than ever.

It was a jolt to be told that he was to be taken to St Peter's. 'Uniforms for you,' Beryl blared, 'white shirt, blue trousers, white socks, black shoes and tennis shoes for games. Now come with a filthy shirt every day if you can. Best thing is khaki for these buggers.'

Sonnaboy was disappointed. 'Never mind if going to the actual college,' he said, 'have to go to the seminary because the Army is in the college.'

'And haven't any girls there?' asked Carloboy.

'Why? You want to learn with girls? No more girls! Only boys—and not like that Poulier nonsense. You behave yourself and talk properly. Damn and bloody full in the mouth! I heard yesterday you talking to that Potger boy. Hullo you bugger . . . that a way to talk?'

'So never mind all that,' Sonnaboy interrupted Beryl's tirade, 'what did Father Paris say?' (Father Paris was principal of St Peter's).

'Said can take. You think these Catholic schools won't take? Pay the fees—that's all they want. Entrance fees also, and from fifth standard library fees and if playing games must give grounds fees or something. Wait and see. Every father's feast day also will ask for money.'

St Peter's College had been turned into an Army camp and barracks. The British had commandeered the school because of its excellent in-city suburban location, because it skirted the old Dutch canal south, empty acres of brown-green fields east, and the main Galle Road and sea west. Northwards, the main road offered direct link with the Royal Air Force camp at Kollupitiya and that most essential institution, the British Club, while a mile or so on was the Royal Navy Headquarters, H.M.S. Highflyer, the Governor's mansion and the port of Colombo.

St Peter's, fat calved sergeant-majors imagined, was a local Sandhurst. The mess served bitter beer and the orderlies had knobbly faces and raw beef complexions and bad teeth.

The British in Ceylon were, well . . . not the best of the litter. They had such a superior way of swanking around. They would never have admitted that many of them had simply copped out of the muddle that was England—that they were just a bunch of colonial opportunists who, disenchanted with being nobodies among the forty-six million-odd in their own splintered isles, had decided to inflict themselves on the 'heathens' of the tropics.

Africa had some ripe ideas: they boiled a few missionaries for breakfast. Ceylon, however, was balm to the British soul.

Here, they could think, even fondly, of the chaos of London, and the suet puddings and the unending roar of traffic on the Great North Road and the lines outside the Labour Exchange, and tell these dim black buggers with their knotted hair and splayed feet of the wonder that was England and how Nelson had to tell them what was expected of them.

The British had this monstrous idea that they were actually doing the natives a favour. *Behold! We have descended from our cloud realm to show you how to eat peas. Go! Bring out your daughters!* That was the general idea. It was easy to see how the people of Ceylon quickly became not only a subject race but also quite an abject race. They even considered it an honour to be addressed. 'Bo-oy!' even if such 'boy' was an old man who shuffled up with the gin and Roses and had his hair bunched in a grey knot at the nape. These white masters were a bunch of hamfaced layabouts . . . yet, they thumped tables and wore monocles and bibs at the dinner table and perpetuated an image of indomitable courage, heroism, chivalry, romance and sportsmanship. All others were dismissed as lesser beings, cast in cracked moulds. The Spanish? Oh, such cruelty to animals! Italians? An excitable people. Can't achieve unless they make a deafening noise. The Chinese? A bunch of gamblers, and slitty-eyed too. The Germans? Ah, the biggest cut-throats in Europe, and we, the Brits, are going to pulp Hitler anyway. (King George I of England was a German and didn't know a word of English but that was not for native consumption).

Thus did the British hold centre stage in Ceylon and the islanders aped them and simply adored England and Dick Whittington and riding a-cock horse to Banbury Cross and King Arthur and Saint George who couldn't abide dragons. A certain permanency of attitude remains, evidenced by the queues of visa seekers at the British embassy in Colombo to this day!

Thus was Carloboy, and boys and girls in their thousands, immersed into this essentially British cauldron and wrestled with a spelling system that defied analysis and a quite unintelligible hotch-potch of weights and measures while teachers constantly kept saying how lucky they were to be introduced to Chaucer whose English was so full of 'ffe's and 'lde's that in later years Carloboy remarked that it sounded like a Frenchman with boils on his tongue.

To Carloboy, St Lawrence's School was quite a honeypot. Besides subjecting Small Kum to a sex change, and earning the admiration of little Therese Wendt for his clinical and surgical expertise, he enjoyed his classroom mornings even though Mrs Bartholomeusz sang atrociously and always clapped out of time when the children were marched round the room, exultant in the fact that 'London Bridge is falling down'.

For small boys, school hours, however pleasant (or otherwise) are quickly shelved no sooner they come home, wolf down their food and hasten their shirts into the bathroom tub before mothers shriek at the stains from collar to tail. Carloboy had no such luck. Beryl would come for him and inspect him narrowly. 'What have you gone and done to your shirt?' She would insist on knowing: 'What is that red mark on the pocket, and see the socks! And you're kicking stones again? Look at the state. Bloody brute! Never listen to what you're told, no? Come go! You think I have nothing else to do, coming in the sun everyday.'

But they don't take the bus home. Beryl has things to do in Wellawatte. She trips ahead, Carloboy trailing, vainly pushing in the tail of his shirt. He meets other children also being hauled home and grins or stares as the case may be. They manoeuvre the Manning Place junction and, at the Elephant House outlet, swing into a little alley. Carloboy perks up. They would visit Aunty Lillian who lived in the last house. Lillian Nora was Beryl's elder sister, a thin, shapeless woman who wore dresses that were uninspiring tubes of unattractive cloth, had bony shoulders and deep lines around her mouth. Lillian was married to 'Bunny' Toussaint and had a boy, Maxwell, who was seven and who was taken to St Peter's College by his elder brother Dodwell who was twelve. Lillian had just had her third son, Wavell, and relations kept popping in and out to fuss over the new baby.

Lillian beams. 'So how? What, taking him home? Come, come, come and sit a little. Some job, no, coming in the sun like this.'

Beryl is still rankling. 'That even never mind. Just see the state of this devil. Every day have to find clean shirt and trousers. Have been tearing the socks today. Don't know what they're doing in the class.'

Carloboy stares blankly. He is not inclined to throw light on this issue of stained shirt and torn socks. He is hungry and school is already several light years away. He eats Aunty Lillian's ginger biscuits and drinks two glasses of water, drips water down his shirt front and then goes to the bedroom to gaze at baby Wavell who waves clenched fists at him and blows little bubbles of spit. He then perches on the veranda wall to watch a man chopping wood in the next garden.

Carloboy likes the return home. Beryl uses the outing to do all manner of things. She may go to the Elephant House shop to buy sausages or dehydrated meat. Fat Mrs Ebert behind the counter always unscrews the lid of a tall sweets jar and give him a chocolate toffee. The boy would push the toffee into a side of his cheek and put the coloured wrapper in his pocket to give to Diana. It always raised a howl from his sister who protested that all she got was the wrapper.

Beryl may also enter the grimy, slushy, pungent world of the Municipal Market where vegetable sellers are shouting their wares and there is always the ring of knife on steel as the Muslim butchers hacked away at thin, blood-daubed haunches of cattle, and goat heads were piled outside the mutton stalls—brown, white, black, grey, curly-furred heads with parchment ears and opalescent eyes—and crows filched any and everything and stray dogs with large, raw patches of mange, lapped at the blood in the drains and flies clouded the dustbins. The floor was treacherous with blackened salad leaves, banana peel, rotting eggplant and maggoty tomatoes. Urchins in ragged trousers dragged trolleys with reeking piles of dripping leaves. Old women picked soft onions, squishy beetroot, soggy potatoes. Pitifully true, to this day in this same market. One man's garbage was a poor coolie-woman's banquet! There was always a queue for meat. It wasn't so a year ago, but it was wartime now and Wellawatte's butchers sold meat on rotation. Only two stalls would function each day instead of the usual eight.

Best of all, Beryl would never fail to stop at Danny's, the little bookshop opposite the Police Station. The block held a sleazy eating house, an indistinguishable store, Danny's, a bicycle repair shop and a tumble-down oilman's store. Carloboy loved Danny's. Old Daniel used to be a door-to-door 'bookman'.[1] Beryl would seek the latest copies of *Girls Own* and *Girls Crystal*. Daniel's fastest line were the two and four-penny weeklies that regularly came in in unbelievable variety. There were hundreds of these badly printed papers with lurid covers in two or three colours. And the comics!

Beryl knew she would have to buy Carloboy a comic— a Radio Fun or a Film Fun or a Hotspur. She had her own favourites. There was the popular *Titbits*, of course, but she leafed through the story papers first: *Oracle, Secrets, Peg's Paper* . . . hmmm, not bad, the stories. She needs number 54 of *Peg's* to continue the serial by Emma Brooke. She picks up the latest copy of *True Confessions* ('I went to bed with my sister's husband') and a copy of *Magnet* because she likes to read about Billy Bunter. She regards Carloboy with some softness. Look at him, clutching a copy of Beano and Film Fun and a Captain Marvel comic . . . and a Wizard also, and practically sparkling at the pictures on the covers of the Sexton Blakes and Nelson Lees and those new American Fight Stories and Action Stories.

Beryl was drawn to these more expensive 'Yank Mags'

---

1. Daniel is introduced in *The Jam Fruit Tree* (Penguin, 1993) p. 126.

but felt a certain self-consciousness in even riffling through them. She had picked up a copy one day. One advertisement claimed to know how a flat-chested woman could improve her social lot by developing her bust. Another announced 'Naughty stickers'. She squinted at them. Nothing naughty about them, surely. Big bosomed, yes. Too curvaceous, yes. But the wide mouthed girls with hands on hips and legs invitingly apart were all quite tolerably clad. She slipped the magazine with the others she had selected and tried to look offhand. Daniel made a cursory check, squiggled on a pad and said, 'Four rupees, lady, and then baby also taking two-fifty.'

Beryl said, 'Give here to see . . . you're mad or what? Just taking like this. Here, put this back. No! This one. See the price, will you? I told, no, only one comic.'

Carloboy surrenders the Captain Marvel and pulls a face. Sulkily he stands at the door to watch Jamis, the bicycle repair man, wrest the pink inner tube from a tyre.

Jamis is a black-skinned Sinhalese with high, bushy hair, an Indian film-star moustache, grease on his hands and he wears his sarong tucked over his knees. He winks slowly and puts the tip of his tongue out at Carloboy. He squats beside a bicycle, a few oily spanners beside him. Jamis has inflated the damaged inner tube and immerses it, section by section into a tin basin of water to check where the leak is. Carloboy edges closer to watch. Jamis winks again and pushes his tongue into his cheek to make a bulge. Then, glancing quickly around, he slyly raises the bottom of his sarong and exposes a large brown penis with its knob of black-mauve-pink and a bramble of dark hair. Carloboy stares, fascinated, as the penis throbs, rising in little bobbing jerks as if it were a live thing. Just as swiftly Jamis rearranges his sarong and bends over the basin as pedestrians approach and Beryl emerges to lead her son away. The boy clutches his satchel, his comics and follows his mother and looks back at Jamis' wise smile. The man gestures with his fingers over the spot where that big cock lay and Carloboy frowns and feels quite restless and strangely excited. Such a size.

And the colour. He had seen a grown man's sex. No, a big man had actually shown him!

They crossed the Galle Road to the bus stand and took a red South Western bus to Bambalapitiya. At home, Beryl reads the small print on the pages of 'naughty stickers'. Why, she needed a tumbler of water. She was instructed to fill a glass with water, then affix a sticker on the outside of the glass and look at the back of the sticker through the water. She smiled hugely. Viewed as so instructed, the girl's clothes disappeared. She was big breasted, voluptuously big-hipped, narrow-waisted, altogether gorgeous, and completely nude. My, the things these Americans think of!

Carloboy had serious things to think of too. He ran to the lavatory and raised the leg of his trousers to regard his own male equipment. So small, and sheathed with a foreskin that made a squiggly bit at the end. He fondled it and thought of that big brown cock and the way it kept rearing up and he found his own penis grow stiff and stick upwards. He tried to pull back the sheath but it parted to ride a little way over his glans and wouldn't go any farther. He kept stroking, pushing at the foreskin, back and forth, then dropped the leg of his trouser to watch the little bulge slowly disappear. The tenseness, the inexplicable feeling that he was on a tightrope of his own nerves also subsided.

He tried again. He squeezed his penis. Nothing happened. But he let his mind go back to the bicycle man, the sly flick of that sarong, and suddenly he was hard again. So hard that when he tried to urinate, he couldn't. And he felt the strangeness rather nice. Exciting. As though he had made a most pleasurable discovery.

'What are you doing so long in the lavatory?' Beryl shouted, and he emerged, looking down anxiously. No bulge. But there was a flush on his face because a nagging thought warned him that there were some secret things in a boy's life which parents would never condone.

Poddi called: 'Baby, come and eat,' and he sat at the

little table in the rear veranda and Poddi said, 'Have murunga[1] and beef and rice have. All must eat, right?'

---

1. The long green pods of the horse-radish tree, eaten as a vegetable. The pods are commonly called drumsticks.

CHAPTER FOUR

The boys of St Peter's, deprived of their school, were pushed into two temporary locations—one, a row of made-over cowsheds, hurriedly readied in the grounds of the seminary of the Oblates of Mary Immaculate in Bambalapitiya, and the other a large rectangle of palm-thatch buildings behind St Mary's Church, Dehiwela. Carloboy saw little sense in this switch in schools. 'Funny thing,' he said, 'when we are here, going to Wellawatte school. Now when we are going to there will have to come here to school.'

Beryl didn't think so. 'You shut up,' she countered, 'coming to poke the mouth.' She had made up her mind. Diana must go to the Holy Family Convent next year. Sonnaboy wanted to know why.

'So my school, no? And Mother Gonzaga will be happy when I go to tell. And now Millie also teaching there so can keep an eye.'

Millicent June, another of Beryl's elder sisters (she had several) had 'not been a small one'—which in the Burgher argot meant that there was more to her than one would imagine. Millicent had had her fling—cigarettes in long holders and dancing the box step at the Sailors and Soldiers Institute and going to matinees at the Regal Cinema with her bosom friend Zoe Charlotte Prinsz who was known, naturally, as Charlotte the harlot. The two women were inseparable.

They went for walks on the beach together, ate together, chattered to each other like house sparrows and decided that they should marry on the same day. They never reckoned on the zigs and zags of life. Millie, with an earnest young buck ready to swoon at her feet, would look at his Adam's apple and say no. Very crisply, too.

Elva Columbine, her younger sister, would wish to know why. 'What? You told that Rulach boy not to come to see you again? Only las' week you saying how nice he is.'

Millie would glower. 'None of your business. If I don't want I don't want. Getting entangled like that, and then what about Zoe?'

'So what about Zoe?'

'See, will you, no boy for her, no? If I say yes and that Aldo Rulach and I get engaged and all, and if he says come go somewhere, Zoe will be all alone, no?'

'So?'

'So what will she feel? Sin, no?'

Elva, born with no compunction whatsoever, couldn't understand. 'What to sin, men. Just let her be. Funny thing, I think. If you get married you'll take Zoe also and go for the honeymoon?'

'You shut up! What I do not for you to talk. Too much you're getting for your age.'

So Millie whiled away her youth and eventually decided that she would teach. An easy decision, for Zoe and she both answered the call for teachers and the Holy Family Convent accepted them. They seemed to have made a pact to tread the long, dreary road of spinsterhood together.

Millie or no Millie, Sonnaboy grunted objections. He didn't like to be reminded of Mother Gonzaga and had stayed clear of that forbidding nun ever since his first encounter with her.[1]

Beryl had apparently thought the matter through. 'We will be shifting to Wellawatte, right? And have to send this bugger to Bambalapitiya . . . and Diana also have to send to

---

1. See *The Jam Fruit Tree* (Penguin, 1993) pp. 103-109.

Bambalapitiya convent . . . so we get a rickshaw to take both.'

'Rickshaw? My God, everyday to go? Two rupees a day for sure.'

Beryl sniffed. 'When drinking six rupees, six rupees arrack everyday good. Can put both in the rickshaw and send. Rickshawman put him at St Peter's and take Diana to the convent. Then he wait there.'

'Huh! He's just going to wait. If get a hire he will go. Or if go to Kollupitiya and drink toddy at the tavern and get drunk will take the child and go somewhere else!'

Beryl grew cross. 'That time in the morning how to get drunk, men. You thought he's like that driver Ferreira? And only have to wait till 'leven thirty, no?'

Sonnaboy was thinking about Ferreira. 'Still can't get over the way that bugger is drinking. I told you how I went to his house in Fussels Lane?'

'Yes, yes, you told. Now the rickshaw—'

'Eight o'clock in the morning. Pouring arrack in the teacup and drinking!'

'I know, I know. How many times you told I don't know. So rickshawman take Diana, come to seminary and put this devil inside also and come home.'

Sonnaboy looked gloomy. 'All easy to say but you think it's easy? Take and go, bring and come. In class never mind. Can go and piss. Now will piss in the rickshaw also. and you think she'll go alone after dropping this bugger? Howl all the way.'

'This bugger' is not pleased with the exchange. 'I can't go to school with her,' he says.

'Shut up! What do you mean you can't? Slipper you if try your nonsense.'

Carloboy sulked and edged away. 'One day she will pippie and pippie and I'll get drowned for sure,' he muttered.

Sonnaboy scowled. 'The way you're shouting at him. What men, he's the one who has to go, no. If piss in the rickshaw will wet his clothes also.'

'So what to do? She also must start school, no?'

As a lot of parents grumbled, going to the seminary was

all well and good, but why the seminary cowsheds for God's sake? The seminarians were quite special. They would one day be ordained and wear white cassocks with black sashes and a crucifix and grow saintly beards. These boys had their teachers—stooped priests with dusty robes and ink-stained fingers who mumbled in class and at Mass. One exception was Father 'Jive Boy' who was the music master, choir master, played organ, piano, violin and cello and moved around as though he was keeping time with some be-bop chorus of rebel angles. He swung and swayed through Mass and every turn at the altar seemed like a slow Spanish fandango. Even his fingers seemed to dance when he bestowed the last blessing and sang out 'lte, missa est' ('Go, the Mass is ended').

The classrooms built for the Peterites were, in truth, the seminary's cowsheds. The oblates had their pinta day until wartime privations overtook the country. The cows disappeared. So did the knock-kneed men who humped the bales of fodder. The cowsheds were cleaned out, whitewashed, roof rethatched, and made ready for the grim business of stuffing knowledge into young heads.

Until the family moved, in a procession of bullock carts, to Wellawatte, Carloboy was propelled across the Galle Road every morning and shoved through the seminary gates. There, he was greeted by a white, marble statue of Our Lady of the Immaculate Conception, a grove of coconut palms, badly pruned lines of box hedge and an imposing tombstone. To his right, the cowshed classrooms. The seminary nestled deeper in this sprawling land tract which swept down to a white-stave fence beside the railway and the sea. A belt of Indian almond trees and hardy allamanda shrubs hid the seminary. It was a squat, yet airy building with pillared verandas and innumerable doors. It was, in short, a priest factory, and operated on the lines of a sacerdotal sausage plant—push in a boy, grind him into submission, stuff him with Latin and Church history, marinade him with the Apologia, toss in a rigmarole of ceremonial and an awareness of the 'pecking order' and then roll him out in a uniform that is supposed to desex him, to spend the rest of his life telling the rest of the gullible world that he can forgive sin and can touch the body of Christ and advise daughters on how to comport themselves in their marriage beds. They emerged, too, as sleek as prime sausages. After all, priests live not by bread alone.

Carloboy was a dreamer of the worst sort. And, like all small boys, was all ears. He liked to listen to his father and the railway cronies when they came home to sit around a couple of bottles of arrack. Conversation, as the spirit level dropped in each bottle, was extremely colourful. And he would be always pressed into service. Sonnaboy would call: 'Here, come here, son, go and bring five Peacocks,' and Carloboy would take the twenty-five cent bit and race to the kiosk at the top of the lane where old Kadayman, 'market man', sold cigarettes, Sunlight soap, packets of tooth powder, round crackly bread rusks, cigarettes, coconut oil, envelopes, notepaper. Kadayman also had lots of boiled sweets in dirty jars and rows of garishly coloured aerated waters.

Sonnaboy smoked Peacocks, which everybody said were the strongest cigarettes. They were dubbed 'coffin nails'. Carloboy would sometimes put a cigarette to his lips and taste the tobacco. The Peacocks were not tipped. Sometimes a little thread of blackish tobacco would remain on his tongue and he would turn it in his mouth, then spit it out. It tasted terrible.

'Colon uncle'[1] smoked Sportsmans, which cost two cents more and were very mild. On paydays, Sonnaboy would buy his Peacocks in tins of fifty. The tins had sharp rims and were excellent for cutting pastry circles when Beryl made patties. Sonnaboy used to smoke Elephant cigarettes, just one cent each, but switched to Peacocks after the Elephant company puffed itself out of business.

Uncle Totoboy[2] preferred Diving Girls. There were so many brands in the market, including the Capstan Navy Cut (which the natives called Naicut) and Players, that Carloboy

---

1. Richard Dionysius Colontota, Sonnaboy's sister Anna's husband.

2. Sonnaboy's elder brother.

began to collect empty packets. Uncle George,[1] who worked in the port, could always be relied on to bring home something new—like Craven As and Markovitch and Wild Woodbine, which he pinched or cadged from sundry seafarers.

When Daddy was home, Carloboy became a 'gopher'. 'Go and bring a bottle of ginger ale', 'Go and get five eggs, and don't drop on the road. Carry and bring carefully'. Beryl, too, used the boy to bring this, that and the other. He ran for bread, for two limes, for ten cents worth kotthamalli, (coriander) for a packet of pappadams, an exercise book, a *chundu* (a local measure, usually a quantity slightly less than what could be held in a cigarette tin) of salt.

All over, boys became both street-wise and market-wise. Merril Cockburn would say: 'Don't go to that Thambi[2] market when nobody else is there buying anything. Dirty fellow, he is.'

'Why?'

'You don't know, men. Yesterday I went to buy a soother. Mummy said have there plastic ones.'

'What for soother?'

'I don't know, men. Can't find the baby's soother. Dog must have taken I think but scolding me. One thing, anything get lost at home everyone saying I'm the one.'

'So what happened?'

'I went and nobody else there. Only I. So I said want one soother. He pulling me to go inside to the back. I said what for, there have soothers in the front, blue colour ones—only Mummy said to buy pink if have—'

'Never mind that, what happened?'

'I got 'fraid, men. Nobody else also. Putting hand round and pushing me to go inside. Telling will give lot of sweets if I come. I pushed and ran. Had to go to Light Stores to buy the soother.'

Yes, whether six or sixteen, Burgher boys were the runners, the fetchers, the bringers. They quickly found

---

1. Sonnaboy's sister Leah's husband, George de Mello.
2. A local Moor.

shortcuts through private gardens, scaled walls, crept through barbed wire fences, raided fruit trees, dallied to take in anything that appealed to them, stopped to gaze at padda boats[1] on the canals, threw stones at dogs bonded after a horny public performance, stole flowers, mangoes, guavas, kicked over dustbins and even rolled bicycle rim hoops as they ran.

Moving to 34th Lane, Wellawatte, Carloboy could do his market runs in either direction—race down to Hampden Lane and the little tea kiosk and stores by the canal, or run, kicking clouds of red dust to the Galle Road where shops stretched in either direction. It was a busy life for a small boy who got very used to haring about, barefooted, burnt berry brown and with a marketing bag that was sorry to behold.

The garden in front of the 34th Lane house was 'private'. There was a rusting metal sign which read, NO ADMITICEN, and which everybody ignored. The garden was a jungle of briars and lantana and led to the bottom of St Lawrence's Road where the church stood to left and Carloboy's cousins, Marlene and Ivor[2] lived below the bend to the right. The new home was all very well . . . but now he had to share a rickshaw with Diana and voiced protest.

The rickshawman was a wizened little Tamil who may have been anything from forty to sixty. He had a white cloth around his head and big feet and a shirt that was all patches. He wore baggy trousers that hung, frayed, below his knees and salaamed furiously. These human beasts of burden were a familiar city sight in the Forties. Millie had a rickshaw wallah who bowled her jauntily to the convent, and so did George de Mello who hated travelling by bus. The rickety men, hauling their rickety contraptions, ran all over the city roads. Reverend Mothers went sedately in their 'convent

---

1. Long, flat bottomed scows, poled along the waterways, used by the Dutch to transport salt, areca nuts, cinnamon, etc. on the canal system. The boats subsequently became the floating homes of a type of river people and are used to this day to transport river sand.

2. Children of George de Mello and Leah.

rickshaws' and a rickshaw would be usually sent to fetch a doctor. Fat merchants transported their goods in them if the load did not warrant the employment of a cart, while the rickshaw was deemed the ideal conveyance for taking drunks home from the various bars in Hospital Street, Chatham Street and Bristol Street. This was always an event. There in the gathering night raced a rickshaw with old Pukface Adolphus, soused to the sacroilliac, conducting an invisible orchestra and bellowing:

> Arssoles arr cheap today
> Cheeper dan yeshterday

to the tune of 'Santa Lucia.'

Indeed, the Colombo Municipality created Rickshaw Stands where the conveyances would park and the men wait for custom.

Carloboy would sit and dig an elbow into Diana, who would pull down her lower lip and prepare to screech her indignation. Every morning the rickshawman would stop at the top of Station Road, put down the shafts and skip into the Municipal Lavatory. Diana would remark, 'Again he's going there.'

Carloboy reads the yellowing sign. The air around this public convenience is positively foetid but the thought would strike him that the man must be having a penis as big as the one Jamis had exhibited. 'That's the road lavatory,' he said. 'If go in can see him pissing.'

'Chee! Wait, I'll tell Mummy what you're telling.'

'You tell to see. I'll take the scissors and cut your hair when you're sleeping.'

'As if you can.'

'As if I can't. You wait will you one day.'

'I'm going to tell Mummy.'

'So tell.'

When they reach the seminary gates, Carloboy whoops away and Diana is dragged six blocks farther to the convent. Beryl's formula seemed to be working . . . until Carloboy raced across the Galle Road to talk to a classmate, and was run down by a car. He was struck, fell, and the wheels passed on either side of him with a whine of torment. The boy saw them sizzle by and as they whipped past, he reached up, felt his fingers close on metal and hung on.

He was dragged for forty fiery seconds and the burning of his bruised flesh made him gasp, let go, and lie still.

The roar of people, traffic pounded on him. A sea of faces seem to wash over him and sounds of fierce argument broke out. He was picked up and struggled to be put down. His shirt was tattered and the flesh of his chest smarted and he had lost a shoe. Somebody picked up his books and Father Cyril rushed up and Mrs Ekanayake, who taught English, danced on the pavement and croaked that a boy had been killed. 'Cars, cars, cars,' she grated, 'only know to knock down children. Catch the driver! Take to the police!'

When Diana arrived, her brother had already been taken to the Bambalapitiya Police Station where Inspector Leembruggen summoned the police doctor to put salve on the boy's bruises and press him here, there, and ask, 'Paining here? Not here? Where does it hurt? Lucky no bones broken.'

'Just running like that,' the driver of the car said hollowly, 'What can anybody do? Suddenly in front. Blood went cold when I saw. And how to stop? Not that I was going fast or anything. If going fast and knocked would have got thrown, no? See will you. Only bruised and blue mark on the hip. And catching the back bumper. Just got dragged for nothing.'

Leembruggen looked severe. 'Running all over the road. You're mad or what? If it was a bus? Would have got killed. Now come go home . . . you know where your house is? And tell to take for a check-up. You're hungry?'

Carloboy shook his head.

'Don't you go to do silly thing like this again, did you hear? And catching the back of the car.'

A sergeant, grinning, said, 'Mussbe tried to catch and bring here.'

So, while Diana and the rickshawman each had their own brand of hysterics and were told to go to the police station and the general hospital and also 'go quickly home and tell your mummy' and Mrs Ekanayake expressed her conviction that 'poor child must be dead by now', Carloboy rode home in a police car and caused, as expected, quite a rumpus.

Sonnaboy said, 'Told, no, this will happen. Just putting and sending with nobody to keep an eye.'

Beryl was annoyed. She dosed Carloboy with Venivalgata,[1] fomented his hip, and took him to Doctor Raeffel who looked him over, shone a light in his eyes, hummed and hawed at the bruises and said: 'Take him home and give him a slap.'

Beryl glowered at father and son. 'So you want me to take and go I suppose?'

The upshot was that Poddi sat Diana on her lap and the three did the school safari, which pleased Poddi no end, and Carloboy was told, 'You get out of the gate after school to see. Skin you alive, that's what I'll do!'

And life rolled on. Abridged versions of *Mill on the Floss* . . . 'No! sundries are not what ladies wear under their dresses . . . ?' 'Why didn't you do your homework? You want me to send a letter to your father?' 'No! You cannot leave the class?' 'Bring that catapult here!'

Rowdy games in the seminary garden were frowned on and Father Theodore, who did most of the frowning, was never in the best of moods. He had enjoyed being in the real St Peter's where the tennis court beckoned. Now, the army marched all over it and it irked him . . . and when he was irked he developed a fierce dislike for small boys. He also disliked Carloboy with growing passion.

'Come here, you little liar!'

Carloboy would jerk his head nervously and shuffle up.

'What is this famous story of yours, then? You like to tell stories, eh?'

---

1. The stems and bark of the Calumba wood shrub—a spiky medicinal plant which makes a strong antiseptic infusion. It is drunk in Sri Lanka to ward off tetanus and is a preventive and protective decoction after deep cuts, wounds, poisonous thorn pricks, animal bites, insect stings, etc.

Carloboy stares vacantly at the dark priest's face. He has this trick of fixing his eyes at some point past a person's head, gazing through bone and brain to see something only his mind could create. It unnerves his teachers and annoys Beryl. Mrs Ekanayake felt that she was always expected to squirm. The boy would look at her, then the look would fix and pass through her. Focus disappeared as the big eyes burrowed through her, making her unseen, unacknowledged. There was not a hint of thought or emotion in that look. Just a boy and his eyes, looking into a world no one else could enter.

At staff meetings, his looks aroused much comment. 'Lord know what's going on in his head. Suddenly he goes blank.'

Father Benedict would harrumph: 'Boy's a dreamer. No use for dreamers. Dreamers are bad news. Trouble makers. Take him by the ear. That's the thing to do.'

It was Father Theodore's turn to growl. 'Don't look like that!'

'Yes, Father.'

'Well?'

'Father?'

'What's this story about someone lying on the railway line and an engine going over him?'

'Yes, Father.'

'What do you mean yes Father? Do you know how dangerous it is to tell lies like this?'

'Father . . .'

'What?'

'My daddy told me, Father.'

The boy had lapped up the story—and it was absolutely true. Sonnaboy had come home, showered and gone to the General Hospital. It seemed that he also had to pay driver Armstrong twenty-five rupees. So did several other drivers, guards and sundry railway officials.

Armstrong, who was a wiry little daredevil who roared the rails, making streamers of black smoke and battling railway authority at the drop of a hat, had decided that he could make a packet. He had strutted into the Way and

Works Office and said that he could lie between the tracks and an engine—any engine—could be driven over him . . . so there! 'Like to bet?' he asked.

It was opined that Armstrong had to be mad, it being too early in the day to be drunk. The man was neither. He just needed to liven up, as he later muttered in his hospital bed, the generally grimy outlook most railwaymen affect when it is the middle of the month, money is at low ebb and it is another thirteen days to pay day.

'What's the bet,' he crowed, 'I'll sleep on the track. Send an engine over me.'

In the railway yard all manner of railway engines were doing all manner of things. They shoved wagons and freight cars around, hauled stock cars to sidings, introduced some to others, and chugged here and there with black intent. Driver van der Wert set the process in motion. 'Twenty-five rupees,' he said, 'twenty-five rupees if you'll do it.'

'I'll do it, don't worry. Fifty bucks.'

'Nothing doing. You'll die or something and how will I get my money then?'

'All right, all right, twenty-five. Anybody else?'

Sonnaboy had grinned and bet twenty-five. Guard de Vos entered the lists and others followed. 'Let's go to the coal sidings,' Armstrong invited.

Armstrong had done his homework. He had found that the lines humped inordinately at a spot where engines were diverted to the coal shed. It was a much travelled track, thick with the grime of the bucket trolleys which were hauled to the tipping point. Armstrong pointed. 'Here. I'll lie down here. Engine is sure to come soon.'

The engine did come, hooting querulously because the driver couldn't understand why so many people stood around and energetically waved to him to come, men, come! Also, there was someone lying in his path, face down, unmoving. The driver, named Schumacher, was nonplussed. He stopped, and hung on the whistle cord.

Sonnaboy ran up. 'It's all right. You just go.'

'Go? How to go? Who is that bugger? He's dead or what?'

'Just lying, men. Never mind him, you go, will you.'

'What? Run over him! How if he dies or something?'

'Tchach! Good thing you said. Wait a little, I'll tell the other fellows and come.'

Schumacher shrugged. He examined his fingers, shrugged again and began to pluck hairs from his nostrils. Sonnaboy had an issue to raise. 'How to get our money if the bugger dies?' he asked. 'You think the wife will give?'

Assistant Electrical Engineer Algy Ferreira scratched his head. 'What nonsense. Might even say we put him and told the engine to go. Women are like that. I know, no? *Ado!*[1] Armstrong!'

Armstrong raised his head. 'What, men, send the bloody engine, will you. How long you want me to lie here in the sun?'

Meanwhile, half the population of the yard had streamed up to gibber and jabber and take side bets while a cheer party stood around the engine and jollied Schumacher.

'You put the money down now,' Sonnaboy insisted.

'What for?'

'If you die, who's going to pay?'

'Who says I'll die? Anyway, I haven't any money now.'

'Ho! You're going to die like a bloody pauper?'

'Shut up and send the bloody engine!'

'*Ado*! Schumacher!'

Schumacher, poised on the footrail had taken note of the humped rails and felt a lot easier. 'What?'

'Drive, men, drive. Come slowly. If cowcatcher touches him you stop, you heard!'

So Schumacher sent his engine over Armstrong. The humping track ensured that the cowcatcher passed a comfortable inch over the latter's head. The rest was easy. And then a nugget of fiery coal fell onto Armstrong's thigh. The coal smouldered through his khaki boiler suit and bit angrily into his flesh. He kicked out in agony. A wedge of

---

1. A rude, rough and ready way of gaining somebody's attention. Could be framed insultingly, venemously, angrily or, as in this particular instance, in a spirit of camaraderie.

moving metal caught his foot, pushed at it, twisted it as one would screw a wad of crêpe, and the scream seemed to come from every direction. Armstrong passed out, Schumacher passed on, applied vacuum and peered out. Men were picking up Armstrong and a leg dangled grotesquely. Schumacher asked: 'Is he OK?'

Sonnaboy said yes. 'Leg broken. That's all.'

Schumacher eased the regulator. Never a dull moment, he thought. He had come for coal. Coal he would collect.

This was the story which Sonnaboy brought home, and all Beryl did was sniff and say, 'Twenty-five rupees! You're also mad. Should have said five rupees, no?'

Father Theodore was also inclined to sniff. 'Rubbish, boy! This is all your make-up. You're a born liar, do you hear?'

'But, Father—'

'No games in the lunch interval. After you eat, you sit in the class. I'll see that Mr John gives you some work. And don't let me hear any more lies from you, did you hear!'

Carloboy gulped. 'Yes, Father.'

'Now get along!'

The boy went; and he was angry and couldn't understand why one part of the grown-up world did things which, when described by a child, are dismissed as pure piffle by other grown-ups. He was miserable too. It was a new feeling—the hurt of being misunderstood and cruelly labelled.

Last year, before the army had moved in, his parents had taken him to St Peter's College hall. Neighbour Vernon Coteling had given Sonnaboy two tickets to a recital which was to be held in the hall. St Peter's was noted for its many cultural concerts, plays, recitals and soirées. A great many Tamil events were staged there because the college was ideally located between Wellawatte (which had a large Tamil population) and the thriving Tamil community which lived around the Kathiresan Kovil (Hindu temple dedicated to Kathiresan, also known as the deity Murugan) in Bambalapitiya.

Carloboy had been taken because Sonnaboy had

remarked: 'He's under ten, no? Under ten children free. Have here written on the ticket.'

A young Malabari named Madhavan had launched his Bharathakalalayam Ballet[1] to open a season of cultural events at St Peter's.

Carloboy had sat through the recital entranced. Here was music and colour he had never experienced before. It bewildered him, stormed his senses, and he sneakingly ran a hand on his thin arm to feel the tingle of goose pimples as he watched each graceful gesture, each sharp, darting movement, the vitality that seemed to stream in crimson ribbons from the lithe, vivacious dancer who seemed to hold a heartbeat in every step he took. Carloboy pestered his father with questions and Sonnaboy had no answers. 'Just sit and look and don't worry, men,' Sonnaboy had growled.

Then a kindly lady with fat cheeks and a double chin who sat beside the boy told him that this was no ordinary dancer, but someone who was quite the best in the world.

'What is this dancing called, Aunty?' he asked.

'This is Kathakali, child. You know what that is?'

The boy shook his head. 'Not like the way we dance, no?'

'Oh no. Definitely not. In the Kathakali every dance tells a story. Stories of gods and heroes and kings and queens.'

Eyes glued on the stage. 'I also know . . . about King Alfred and Hercules and all.'

The lady smiled. 'This is Indian,' she said. 'India had great kings and the most beautiful stories in the world.'

Beryl, listening, looked across and smiled. She had thought Carloboy would fidget and be a nuisance but he seemed to be quite taken up with the show. Strange little devil, she thought.

'See,' the lady said. 'This is a dance about Parvathi. Parvathi is a goddess,' and later, 'this is the peacock dance.'

---

1. A Bharatha dance festival performed by a troupe. The Bharatha dance form is unique in that it was originally created to be a devotional dance, to pay obeisance to the gods. It is a temple dance ritual, assuming the several attitudes of devotion and is performed with great mastery.

'But where . . . there's no peacock.'

'He is the peacock. Have you seen a peacock?'

Carloboy nodded. 'In the zoo, I saw.'

'Ah, then you think about that peacock. And look at him dancing. Can you imagine a peacock now?'

Carloboy stared and his gaze went beyond the red velvet backdrop and suddenly there was Madhavan the peacock, full in the glory of an opal-studded plumage and the colours that swirled out of his mind hurt his eyes and he blinked and nodded his head, acknowledging some fertile power that seemed to stream out of his head like a sequinned river.

And so the enchantment went on and his foot tapped to the beat of the *Samhara Thandavam*[1] and the *Kamadhahanam*[2] wrapped him in the embrace of the god of love and he rose, too, as an ecstatic audience gave the young dancer a standing ovation.

Madhavan, let it be recorded, was lionized wherever he performed. The Governor of Ceylon, Sir Andrew Caldecott and Lady Caldecott honoured him. Sir Andrew garlanded him and referred to his performance as 'nothing finer in the world of Indian dance'.

It would be appropriate to record what the *Times of Ceylon* and its Sunday edition the *Sunday Illustrated* said of the great Madhavan:

> *The Times of Ceylon*—23.9.40: Madhavan, the great Indian dancer, gave conclusive vindication of the encomiums paid to him as the outstanding exponent of the Kathakali . . . It was a bewildered audience that left the hall, bewildered at the mastery of the art displayed by this young Malabari. This was the first wholly Kathakali recital ever seen in Colombo. Madhavan's remarkable music control, quick, sharp and darting movements, all lend flavour to the minutest action in his performance . . .

---

1. A Shiva dance performed in a spirit of anger.
2. Literally, 'the fires of lust'.

The Times of Ceylon—Sunday Illustrated 22.9.40:
Madhavan made the Western world sit up and
take notice of the national dance of his country,
the Kathakali, which he was the first to take to
Europe and America . . . the young Malabar
dancer soon became the sweetheart of the ballet
world of Europe and America. Madhavan created
a revolution in the ballet by carrying out a
re-orientation of the Kathakali. He succeeded. The
West applauded him. This man was described by
art critics as a magnificent human . . .

Sonnaboy took his son by the hand and steered him
through the crowds. They walked home and Sonnaboy
wondered why the boy was so quiet. Beryl, eminently
practical, said, 'Now will want to dance like that, I suppose.'

'Like that?' Sonnaboy could be practical too: 'Who can
dance like that?'

And on that 21st day of September 1940, he never said
a truer word.[1]

Seated in class, kicking at the leg of his desk, Carloboy
made a furrow of his forehead and thought darkly and
fiercely of how he had seen a man dance as a peacock. Or
was this, according to the epistle of Father Theodore, another
lie? What are lies to a boy who has a whole world to
understand? A spirit of rebellion seized him. Mr Johns stalked
in, glowering. 'Do these sums!' he barked, tossing an open
arithmetic text before the boy, 'and stop kicking that desk! If
these are not finished by the time interval is over you'll get
it from me.'

The twenty L.C.M.s were no big deal but Carloboy was
in a bad mood. He glared.

'What are you staring at?'

---

1. Author's note: Faction is stranger than fiction. I write these words in
   Sharjah, United Arab Emirates, where I work. One of my colleagues here
   is P. Ravichandran of Palghat, India, and guess what . . . he is the son
   of Madhavan, the man who danced his way into the wonder world of
   Carloboy's imagination over fifty years ago!

'Sir, I won't, sir.'

'What?'

'Sir, this is my interval, sir.'

'Interval? You're punished! Do those sums!'

But the iron seemed to have entered Carloboy's soul. He just stared. He was rapped on the head and kept staring. Johns twisted his ear. He winced and the tears came. He jerked away, pushed back his chair and fled into the coconut grove. Johns' roar had no effect whatsoever. All he wanted to do was hide, hide until the rickshaw came. He would scale the wall and get into the rickshaw and go home. He chose a huge knot of ground palm and skulked behind it. And what of his bag of books? How can a seven-year-old have so many problems?

Sonnaboy was furious. He cycled to the seminary and came back with a tropical storm on his face. 'Going to tell everyone what's said in the house in the school,' he fumed, 'why can't you just keep your mouth shut and learn? Any more nonsense from you and I'll keep you at home and make you the servant-boy, did you hear?'

Carloboy stared dumbly. But later he heard his father tell his mother, 'I gave that bloody priest tight. Punishing for nothing, no? Said he's telling lot of lies in the class. Only went to tell what Armstrong did, no?'

'So what for he's going to repeat all that?' Beryl demanded. 'Listening to everything we're talking, that's what. Other children go and come and no trouble.'

Sonnaboy thought different. 'What other children? Like that Bryce next door? Can't look at him hard he runs.'

Bryce was Victor Ratnayake's son, a long-faced little brat who would come back from school with his shirt still clean and his stocking hose in place and who would sit in the veranda and memorize his multiplication tables until he was blue in the face. Bryce blubbered a lot.

The blubbering had begun early in life because his father, a bald man who had been a headmaster in his heyday and later became something quite nondescript in the Department of Education, liked to use a cane. It was a hangover from his headmastering days, and the cane he kept at home was most impressive. One could, if impelled, write a sonnet on it. Victor Ratnayake did not believe in sparing it either. When the beatings began, many households in the immediate vicinity listened with a sort of outraged silence. All Bryce got were 'six of the best' but Victor made the six last.

Bryce would be dragged to the bedroom and made to lie across the bed, legs on the floor. Victor would then take the thick rattan from the top of the wardrobe and, fondling it lovingly, begin to talk to his son. 'You know, no? You are the only boy. Our only son. Can you think about that? You know what it means? It means . . . you're listening? It means in this family you're like someone special, no?' Bryce, who has started to blubber thinks he sees Hope smiling benignly.

'But every day you're getting bigger,' Victor intones, 'and now you must know how to behave, no? And then you want to be like a baby. Have you seen me any day pouring the whole bottle of ink on the cat?'

'N-n-no Daddy . . . Daddy don't beat me . . .'

'Beat me? Who said I'm going to beat? Beating is one thing. Punishing is another thing. See me. I have to go to work and bring the salary and come to give everybody here to eat and pay the fees and buy the clothes and the ink for the pen also, no? And now what? Now I must buy another bottle of ink. Why?'

Bryce declares open the waterworks. Victor stands behind him and Bryce turns his head anxiously. The boy's long face is drawn longer and his mouth curves downwards. He looks ghastly. More so his nose begins to drip.

'Turn your face to the bed,' Victor raps, 'who said for you to move. Did I say? Do you know the way the cat ran and rubbed ink on the kitchen wall? And paw marks with ink all over the hall. So why? Can you tell one reason why you went and poured ink all over it? One reason?'

Bryce shudders. Boys don't need reasons. There's the cat . . . there's the bottle of ink. How can one explain impulse as reason? It was such a novel idea at the time. A blue cat. Everybody said it was a blue Persian but there wasn't a bit of blue on it. All he wanted to do was make it truly blue. Also the cat had scratched him but that was not credited.

'An' another thing,' Victor went on, 'that is an expensive cat, no? Bought it because your mummy said to buy. And now how to get the ink from all the fur? You think we can bathe and scrub like for a dog?' And all the while the cane makes little swishes in the air and Bryce, who is too young to have a heart attack, presses his face into the sheets and prepares for the holocaust.

The single stroke across his buttocks comes suddenly— a searing, cutting, vitriolic stroke that brings with it all the native charm of a branding iron. The boy's shriek splits the air.

Just six cuts. A six-second administration of parental ire if done at a tolerable rate. The six cuts on Bryce's blistered bum take all of thirty minutes. Victor would wait. A patiently vicious man; a man who never admitted to the fear and loathing that crowded him during his headmastering days when he took savage delight in walloping pupils willy nilly. Oh, there were stories. It was even noised around that he left St John's College under a very sour-faced cloud, but he stoutly maintained that he was a dedicated disciplinarian. It is the stamp of the good headmaster, he said. Uncaned is untamed!

Carloboy would listen to the howling next door and shudder. He hated this 'Uncle Victor'. Diana would blanch and run to the loo and Poddi would say, quite sepulchrally, 'There you heard? Again to that Bryce baby beating.'

Carloboy always wondered what went on during those pauses. Swipe! Scream! A strange sort of gibber and silence. Quite a long silence too. Bryce has just ceased to suffer when the cane sings again. Another howl, another huddled silence . . . and thus were many half hours of Bryce's young life accounted for, while Sonnaboy would threaten to go there and put a stop to it and Beryl would say no, because: 'Nobody can interfere, no? He can punish the son.'

'Punish? That is punish? That is torturing!'

'So that's not our business. If can't torture let do anything.'

Sonnaboy would scowl at his son. 'You can hear? That's the way must give you also. Next time push you next door and tell to whack you also.'

CHAPTER FIVE

Life seemed to be full of 'moments', moments that came and went, filled with magic, drama, disaster, unease, revelry, joy, desolation. The chronicler passes lightly, even with timidity, over the events of the year. Even Carloboy dismissed it as nothing but 'war, war, war' and immersed himself in war stories and comics and listened avidly to the adults who gathered to regale each other with what they would do if they were Montgomery or Wavell or King George the Sixth.

This took on a keener note at family parties where the ladies would discuss prices and other people's vices and the men would sit around the dining table on which cut glass decanters glowed and twinkled with the amber of arrack and the conversation, like the devilled beef and pawkies and stuffed peppers, was spicy, racy and as brash and breezy as a sailor in the Jacuzzi.

'So what do you think that Rommel will do, men?' old 'Amba' Geddes would quaver. 'Fine thing, no? If can't advance two miles in two days. What men, this is an army or what?'

'Pooh, what do you know, men?' Totoboy would say, 'all strategy. That's what—here, pass the bottle men—had in the *Observer* also about this strategy.'

'What the devil is all this strategy business,' Sonnaboy

declared, 'if waiting for all this nonsense will have tragedy, not strategy.'

'My, child, the nonsense these men are talking,' Leah remarks.

'War, war, war,' Elsie says, 'if have war, enough for them.'

'Not enough the war when coming home every day,' Iris complains, 'drunk and singing and won't even go to the lavatory, men. Standing near the gate and doing all over the pillar.'

'No!'

'Yes, men, and people on the road also going, no?'

'*Anney*, I don't know how you're managing with him.'

'. . . and how what Hitler said once? Said all the Germans were only walking in the sleep. But how now? One thing, whatever anybody says that Hitler is a pukka bugger.'

'Sleeping and walking? Huh, if all are sleeping and walking how did they capture Poland and all?'

'. . . you must see the dance at home, men. Fighting to read the paper. Children also going mad about this war. Should have seen the nonsense yesterday. Next door house Mortier's boys taking brooms and marching.'

'. . . actually I think these bloody English can't fight. Only big talk. They don't know what to do with their army. Only polishing boots and shouting in the sun!'

The children would let their imaginations climb the walls. Carloboy, who read avidly and translated all he read into real-terms action, usually held centre stage. His listeners—assorted neighbourhood boys—would listen, openmouthed. Oh, lots of tall stories, artfully spun, twisted out of penny dreadfuls into first-person exploits and made to seem extra real, extra dramatic, and Bryce Ratnayake and Merril Phoebus and Michael de Joodt and Maurice Foenander would listen and shrug and try to air vestiges of their own outrageous imaginations to match or exceed what was tossed at them.

It was all a game, actually, but there was danger too, for seven-year-old Carloboy tended to believe in all he trotted out. He had his own Walter Mitty world. Suddenly he was a daring Nazi spy hunter. And surely he had only to say

'Shazam!' and become a caped hero. He had actually worn a pair of blue socks on his hands one day, knotted a towel around his neck and hurled himself over the wall, a manoeuvre that made Phoebus' hens in dire need of a psychiatrist. The hens became alien invaders. Carloboy, the towelled tormentor from Planet X was saving the Earth. Or he was a secret agent for the British Intelligence with plans to be delivered to the Chatham Street office of the Captain of the Navy. And what about the day he saw a man, very furtive, slouching along outside the Wellawatte police station?

'I knew the moment I saw him he was up to something.'

'How did you know?' asks Johnny Bulner.

'The way he was, men. Not like other people on the road. Very sus-sus-suspicious.'

'My gawsh, if you see the people in our lane,' said Sammy Redlich.

'Why? What about them?'

'All like what you said. Suspi-suspi something. Just going upan' down, looking at windows. Not going to anybody's house even. Just walking.'

The boys nodded gravely. The pedestrian art was henceforth to be looked upon with the gravest concern.

'So never mind your lane, listen, will you. This fellow near the police station. Suddenly he went to top of Hamers Avenue and stood near the lamp-post. Just stood.'

'Gawsh. Muss'ave been waiting for his gang, mussbe,' Sammy Redlich hissed.

'Gang?' Carloboy frowned. 'No gang anywhere to be seen. Anyway I also went quietly to the market there and waited.'

'Gawsh.'

'Shut up, men. You and your gawsh,' Michael de Joodt told Sammy.

Bryce Ratnayake gave a small shiver of excitement. 'So you saw his face and all?'

'Had a hat,' Carloboy decorated his mystery man, 'just like hats they wear in that serial picture *Shadow*. Also in 'Merican detective stories. Covering whole top of the face . . . an' a beard also.'

'Beard?' Bryce squeaked.

'Yes, black beard. Real crook he looked. An' a bicycle also.'

'But you said he was walking about, no?' Merril Phoebus objected.

'Yes, men, so listen, will you. Have been keeping the bicycle near the lamp-post.'

The boys are enthralled. Carloboy thought fast. He was actually seeing himself, the 'Shadow', stalking a man who held the fate of Ceylon's coastal defences in his hands. A German spy. 'I knew at once he was a German.'

'G'wan! As if have any Germans here. My daddy said all are fighting now in Italy.'

Bulner sniffed. 'You buggers don't know anything. I saw the papers, men. That is only some Germans helping that Mussolini fellow. Now Germans are everywhere. France an' going to Russia also. If can go to Russia why they can't come here?'

Carloboy also sniffed. 'So don't listen then if anybody don't believe. As if I care.'

'Never mind them, men,' Bulner said, 'so what happened?'

Carloboy was a good storyteller. 'I waited near the kaday and then again he went near the police station.'

'What for?'

'How do I know? Can I go an' ask for what he's walking near there?'

'Foo, I would have gone quietly behind an' when he was near the gate given him a bloody push to go flying inside and shouted German, German!'

Carloboy frowned. 'I thought to do that,' he said quickly, 'but how if he shouted and said I pushed? Will say he was just walking and I came and pushed. *Thoppi*[1] for me then.'

---

1. Thoppi—hat. This Sinhala expression indicates 'trouble'. To put a hat on something is to cause trouble. This was Anglicized to the extent that boys would also say: 'Hell of a hat' meaning a sticky situation or big trouble.

Phoebus rose to a point of order. 'So even if he shouted who can unnerstan' what he's saying? You said he's German, no?'

'So you think German people don' know English?'

'Dass true,' said Foenander, 'see in the comics how all the German soldiers saying Achtung! Achtung! and funny things like that but still they're talking English also.'

Carloboy welcomed the crosstalk. It gave him time to embroider his story, build it up to a big scene. 'Lucky I had some money. Not like for you, my daddy always gives me money.'

'My daddy also gives when he is in a good mood. Yesterday when I bought cigarettes from the market he said where the balance. Had thirty cents an' first he took it, then he called an' said to take and keep it.'

'You're giving balance?' Bulner asked incredulously. 'Be like me, will you. I just feel in the pocket and then say must have dropped on the road.'

'*Ammo*,[1] if I go to say like that I'll get a *kanay*.'[2]

'So that even never mind. Have the money, no?'

'Anyway,' Carloboy said, 'I quickly went to the market and bought some toothpaste.'

'What for?'

'Hee, hee, to brush the German's teeth?'

'You laugh. Only know to laugh. Slowly I went to the bicycle and put the Swastika mark on the seat with the toothpaste.'

'No!'

'Yes.'

'My God. What for?'

Carloboy was enjoying himself. 'Listen, will you!' Suddenly he had his climax. He was a hero. He was about to unmask a spy and earn the gratitude of the army and generals and admirals and everyone else he could drum up.

---

1. *Ammo*—Oh, mother!
2. *Kanay*—a clout on the ear. Kana is Sinhala for ear.

'He came back and whole time looking back at the police station. Then two police *kossas*[1] came out . . .'

And so the fevered dreams were spun out and Carloboy became in turn, adventurer, explorer, the king of the cowboys, a comic book hero. Small wonder his teachers found him tiresome and everybody regarded him as a 'bloody little liar' and never knew what to expect of him.

A great contributing factor were the Saturday afternoon 'serials'—those popular cliff-hanger films which were screened at the Capitol Cinema and the National Talkies. Second grade cinemas with wooden seats which housed colonies of bugs but places of weekly pilgrimage for hundreds of small boys who would scrimp and scrounge and beg and, yes, even steal, to follow the exploits of such swashbucklers as the Green Arrow, Zorro and Sir Galahad, or tingle in excitement as Larry 'Buster' Crabbe flicked through the curtains of space as Flash Gordon on a trip to Mars.

Pure escapism. All these serials came out of Republic studios, or Universal or Columbia and they held their young viewers enthralled. And they were 'serialized', hence the name. Carloboy would join a gang of boys who had the good fortune to own an adult who was a passionate serial fan. Uncle Aloy, as they called him, lived in 34th Lane and being a bachelor and well liked by all and sundry, was trusted by the neighbourhood to 'take the little buggers to the pictures'.

Of course, going to one serial, which only lasted thirty minutes of real film time and gave young viewers thirty bug bites per minute, was of no real use whatsoever. The only real guarantee was that a few enterprising bugs could be carried home. The charm of the serial was that there were fourteen 'chapters' seen, week after week. The 'talkies' did a roaring business even if the children were on half tickets (just fifty cents) while Uncle Aloy paid a rupee and they would commandeer a row as close to the screen as possible and impatiently count the bells.

---

1. *Kossa*—Sinhala derogative for constable. Actually the Sinhalese took the word 'constable' and made it 'Kostapol'. This was shortened to 'Kossa'.

Three bells in all, the first fifteen minutes before curtain just to tell the audience that the management was pretty peeved about the number of vacant seats in the two and four rupees rows, the second to say that the management was in a better frame of mind and since the public had not broken faith, the film would commence in five minutes and would those in the toilets kindly leave off whatever they were doing and return to their seats.

With the third bell came the eclipse. A sudden darkening of the hall and a serried creaking of seats as couples in the four rupee rows learned towards each other and fumbled.

Below the rupee seats was the 'gallery' (popularly referred to as the 'gallows') where, at twenty-five cents per head, hordes of street urchins and ruffians in hitched-up sarongs and dirty T-shirts, hissed, hooted, whistled and brayed as they wallowed in the action. Marvellous fist fights. Congo Bill or Tarzan killed panthers, each in his peculiar way; Congo Bill would use a wicked double bore while Tarzan would thump his chest, yodel and leap on the animal's back.

Another favourite character, Jungle Jim would dangle over a hiccoughing volcano while a villainous bushman would saw at the rope with a spear and everyone in the 'gallows' would get quite hysterical.

Carloboy loved every minute of it. The end of each serial was always the most nerve-racking, the most nail-biting. Holt of the Secret Service would be drugged, tied to a railtrack and left to say hello to an oncoming train. The music would grow very bassy and drums would tattoo and there was the train, rushing, rushing, and Carloboy would grip his knees and poise on the hard edge of his seat, and there would be an explosion of white stars and the serial ended.

And so, week after week, the serial was the most potent, most galvanic, most magnetic event for Burgher boys of all ages and Uncle Aloy the most adored of adults in a galaxy where most adults were usually regarded as too heavy handed and too fond of wielding slippers, belts, razor strops, sticks and anything handy. Sometimes Uncle Aloy treated them to Kit Kat chocolates or Mars bars and bottles of orange barley water. What more could Carloboy wish for? He had Buck Rogers on a spaceship to Venus, Don Winslow taking his battle cruiser into Gibraltar, the Black Hawks zooming out to meet a squadron of German fighter planes, Dick Tracy on the trail of counterfeiters, the Shadow stalking a homicidal maniac, the Spy Smasher on the heels of a bunch of Chinese who wanted to do something nasty to Hong Kong, Red Ryder plunging into an ocean of stampeding longhorns and the Lone Ranger with his silver bullets and secret silver mine. There was also the Ghost Who Walks in his Skull Cave and with a skull ring which left the mark of the Skull on every lowlife he clouted.

Biff! Bam! Pow! Wham! Wow! became a part of every small boy's vocabulary. Carloboy lapped it all up, gorged on every fantasy, became part of this never-never world. Could he slip into a telephone booth or a broom closet, strip off his shirt and plunge out as Superman? Or just say some abracadabra, wait for a bolt of lightning and be transformed into Captain Marvel? Dell Comics of America furthered the legend. They produced a boy who had only to shout 'Captain Marvel!' and lo, a burst of atmospherics and he became Captain Marvel Junior. Later, a girl joined the family— Mary Marvel—and Carloboy wished and wished that he could be in America. These superheroes were so delightfully devastating. Yes, he was in the wrong country. Batman was in America. So was Superman and the Marvel family. And what about Torch and Toro . . . and the Submariner . . . and Captain America . . . and why weren't there cowboys in Ceylon? No Gene Autry, no Roy Rogers, no gunfighters, no Kit Carson . . . Ceylon was a drag. Sometimes he wondered why his father couldn't wear a cape and tight plants. Daddy would be a marvellous Superman. Daddy had bigger muscles too!

But there was no Daddy and certainly no Superman on the day Carloboy ran to ask Uncle Aloy if he would take the boys to the Gamini Theatre to see the 'Full Serial' the cinema advertisements were screaming about.

Uncle Aloy twinkled. 'Full serial? My goodness, that is three hours, no?'

Once every while a Full Serial would come along and the queues would be tremendous. This was when one could sit through the entire story, episode by episode. There would be two ten minute and one twenty minute intermission.

'If you ask Daddy is sure to allow.'

Aloy hummed and looked at the boy. 'Your mummy knows you came here?'

Carloboy shook his head breathlessly. 'I jumped over the wall and came. Uncle, you'll come and ask? I'll tell Johnny and Sammy also. Bryce I don' know. Uncle Victor sure to say can't go for Bryce.'

'Mmm, but three-hour show. Come, come inside. You standing there if your mummy comes out and sees . . . come inside. You want some Necto?'

It was the first time Carloboy had been inside Uncle Aloy's home. He was led to the bedroom where, on a small bedside table, was a bottle of fizzy wine-dark Necto and an upturned tumbler. Aloy poured the boy a drink, sat on the bed and gently, most casually, took the boy by the waist and drew him backwards to stand between his outspread knees. His hand moved caressingly from the boy's hip, down and around to rest lightly across the pit of the stomach. All the while he talked, smoothly. 'Full serial no half tickets, no? Have to pay one rupee and another ten cents for entertainment tax also. Even for you. How's the Necto? You want a little more? Just keep the glass then. Ah . . . will your mummy give one rupee? Other times she only gives fifty cents and twenty cents for the bus, no? How if she says no? And three hours also . . .' The hand moved down, pressing, thumb and forefinger probing into the trousers to touch the small penis . . . 'and may even say you have homework to do and bad to sit and see for so long . . .' The other hand stroked the boy's thigh, pushing upwards, under the trouser leg. Fingers worked on the trouser strap . . . 'and then what to do?'

Carloboy hardly noticed that his trousers had been undone and were slipping off his hips. He was wrestling with the problem of persuading his mother for money, time, permission for this film of films. 'I can go and ask my

granny in Lawrence Road. If I ask she will give me—
Uncle Aloy!'

'Shhh, don't worry. Just wait like that a little.' The man
was stroking his penis, making it hard. He was breathing
hard and Carloboy stood stock still, confused, watching the
big fingers moving. Then his trousers fell and Uncle Aloy
was pushing them down to his ankles. 'What? You're afraid?
Don't be afraid. Turn round, I'll show you. You want to see?
And never mind asking anyone for the money. I'll buy your
ticket and I'll come and tell your mummy to send you,
right?'

Carloboy nodded. He was turned around, kicking off his
trousers and Uncle Aloy was unbuttoning his own trousers
and holding him close, drew him to the bed. 'Don't worry.
Nobody know, no, and don't tell anybody, you heard?'

Carloboy nodded.

'You don't worry about anything. You come here
everyday and we will do this and all the pictures I will take
you and I will pay for you, right? Here, catch it. What's the
matter? You're shy? Nobody did like this to you? See, it's
big, no. Catch it nicely. Now shake it like this, ah, that's the
way . . .'

Carloboy felt a stickiness in his hand and Uncle Aloy
shook his own little cock, forcing back the tight foreskin
until he felt a short sharp pain. He cried out briefly, struggled,
and the man grasped him, wrapped a big leg around him
and pushed his organ between his thighs. The bottle of
Necto seemed to teeter and the table rocked and Aloy spent
himself and rose to hurriedly dab at the boy's penis with a
dirty towel.

'It's paining?' he asked.

Carloboy shook his head. He simply stared at the blood
that welled up from beneath the foreskin. 'Uncle Aloy, why
it is bleeding?'

'Don't worry. Here hold the towel until it stops. It is all
right. Nothing to worry, men.'

But Carloboy was horrified. He sat silent, holding the
soiled orange towel, watching the blobs of blood spread on
the cloth. Aloy poured him the last of the Necto. It took a

long time for the bleeding to stop. Only a long time later did the boy understand what had happened. Aloy had pulled back his foreskin so forcibly that the little flesh thread that held it at the end of his prepuce had snapped. So now he could pull back his foreskin all the way. It was yet another discovery.

'Now it's all right, no? See, no more bleeding. Here, put your trousers, and come again, right? You'll come?'

Carloboy nodded.

'Good boy. And don't tell anyone. I'll come and tell about the picture. I'll come in the evening. You want some water?'

'No, Uncle.'

'Come tomorrow if you like. You can come?'

Carloboy nodded.

'Good boy. Then you go now. If you come tomorrow about this time is good. I'll be at home.'

It was a most definite end of innocence.

*

The world becomes a different place to a child who has been abused by an adult. To Carloboy it was a welter of emotional ladles, whirling, swirling in a sort of sexual mulligatawny. At six, he had thought Uncle Dunnyboy quite funny. Uncle Dunnyboy, his father's eldest brother was considered extremely strange by all and sundry and was regarded most cautiously by Beryl von Bloss.

'Poddi,' she would shout, 'see who door is knocking.'

'*Nona*, Dunny master have come.'

Beryl would groan, then say: ''Nother damn curse. Not enough the work in the morning, have to watch him now.'

Dunnyboy had a strange alto-husky voice. Slightly whining.

'What for you came?' Beryl would demand.

'Where Sonnaboy?'

'Gone to work. You go an' come some other time.'

'Walked and came, no? Tired also.'

That was another thing about Dunnyboy. He walked.

Buses, rickshaws never held any charms. Nor did trains. He was, say, in Maradana. It seemed a good idea to go to Wellawatte six miles away. He walked.

Beryl shrugged. 'So sit a little. You want some tea?'

'Eh?'

'Tea! Tea! You want?' Dunnyboy was deaf too.

'Can make some tea?' he asks hopefully.

'That's what I asked, no?'

'Eh?'

'Oh, you old bugger. I'll bring some tea!'

'Little water also never mind.'

And the man would range around the house and go to the kitchen and the bathroom and ask for more water from the earthenware goblet and pick his nose and leer at Poddi and stare at the chintz curtain at the bedroom door.

Carloboy was greatly taken up with this oddball uncle who looked quite old, shrunken even, and quite harmless, and who was quite deaf and made queer, clipped remarks and had no conversation whatsoever. A shabby uncle, who never had any clothes of his own. He wore Sonnaboy's shirts and Totoboy's trousers and an old coat Viva had given him and a lot of junk which Terry had dumped on him. Anna, too, would give him Colontota's old shirts and vests and Elsie let down the hems of Eric's old trousers for him.

Elsie was most annoyed, which was not surprising. She lived in a state of permanent annoyance. She would snarl: 'What men, every Christmas giving new shirt for him. Where all the shirts? God alone knows. And the ties and socks he has. Damn shame for me, no, going about and asking other people's clothes. What is new won't wear. Locking in the almirah and keeping. Keeping for what? For rats to take and eat? And won't stay in the house. Suddenly telling I'm going out and going. Going to where I'm asking but won't tell. Just putting on some old torn thing and somebody's big trousers and going.'

Anna would give a gusty sigh. 'Coming home sometimes. When see the state I feel sorry, men. Las' time I gave three old shirts of Mister Colon's and two rupees. Told to go by bus.'

'Bus? Don't give, men. Walking everywhere. And just coming and putting in the almirah. Madness, no?'

Anna would sigh again, Dunnyboy *was* a trial. Beryl would snort. Her husband had regaled her with some pretty weird things about Dunnyboy. Carloboy found this uncle quite intriguing . . . until the day Dunnyboy had slyly reached for him and squeezed his penis. 'Let see,' he had said, and raised the boy's trouser leg.

It was a most fleeting encounter. Beryl had stormed in, slapped her son and dragged him into the kitchen where, having administered another slap, had gritted: 'Don't you go near him again, you heard! Nex' time he comes you go to the garden and play. Damn cad, he is! If I see you going near him again you'll get with the firewood stick!'

And yet, Dunnyboy went through the family with a kind of insane doggedness. He had carnal knowledge of his younger brothers and sisters when they were children together. He had opportunity to also abuse his nephews and nieces. Before he died, mercifully enough, he had demonstrated to an ever-widening family circle that he had some sort of avuncular right to meddle with their private parts, put his cock between their legs, masturbate the boys and push a big finger into the girls' vaginas until they cried and struggled against him. It was the unspoken, unsung family sin. Everyone knew, but no one dared acknowledge it to the other. Parents strove to keep their children away from the old man, yet they accepted him in their homes. As Beryl said, 'Need five pairs of eyes when that Dunnyboy comes.'

The old man was sly. He would loll around, pretend to doze, let his lower lip sag, and although as deaf as the psalmist's adder, would stir in a most predatory manner when Poddi minced in to dust the furniture.

Carloboy worried himself to a frazzle about his sore foreskin, but it healed quickly enough and he was soon quite taken up by his ability to push it back and expose his glans. The skin would roll back to stay around the rim of his glans, curling thinly. The pink tip would suffuse redly as he grew hard and in his child mind he would feel some panic too. What if it became as big and as thick as Uncle Aloy's? How would he wear his short trousers? All manner of small-boy fears assailed him and yet, he discovered that arousal came with the seeing, the showing, the hasty flick of Jamis' sarong, the raising of Poddi's jacket . . .

That evening he ran across the garden to St Lawrence's Road and, scaling a wall, shinned up an adolescent mango tree which grew in Mr Bakelman's garden. Straddling a low branch which overshot the wall, he saw Mrs Joachim's servant walking a toddler. The woman was in her twenties, swathed in a flowered cloth and with a tight jacket that accentuated her pointed breasts. Carloboy adjusted the end of his short trousers, allowing his penis to show, and pretended to be totally oblivious of the young woman now strolling slowly below.

He knew that she had stopped. Even as he sensed that she was staring up at him, seeing his nakedness, he felt his organ swell. Casually he pushed back his foreskin.

'Eessssssch.'

It was the woman. She made a sucking hiss, trying to draw his attention. His eyes flicked towards her, saw her tight smile, and he looked hastily away.

'Esssssh!'

He looked down. 'What?' he asked.

The woman smiled archly. 'Baby from the tree can come?'

'What for?'

The woman nodded to him to climb down. She pressed the toddler's hand into her crotch. 'Baby come, will you. Our house no one at home. For a little while come.'

Carloboy clambered down. 'Joachim house, no?' he said.

The woman nodded. 'Wait, I first will go. I inside after going and calling, baby come.'

'What for?'

'Baby come, will you. One rupee I'll give,' and the woman walked away.

Carloboy stood, uncertain. 'Uncle' Joachim did not like him. Not since the day of the mangoes and the milkman.

The Joachims had a very tempting mango tree. Grafted

mangoes, old Joachim would boast. In season, the tree would be laden with fruit and, being grafted, each mango was a luscious globe of purple-red and honey yellow. Old Joachim's pride and joy, irresistible to the boys of the neighbourhood.

One long afternoon, when all Wellawatte seemed in a stupor, Carloboy had crept in to raid the tree. He had reached a branch, fifteen feet up, and perching there, began to devour as many mangoes as he could. No use taking any home. The distinctive fruit were unmistakably Joachim's and Joachim's only. He would be branded for the pillage.

It was a pity that the Joachims preferred cows' milk in their tea. The milkman would come at dawn. He had a canvas carrier strapped to his bicycle bar, and in this he carried his bottles of milk for delivery. It was pity, also, that the milkman returned at two p.m. each day for the empty bottles.

Carloboy with his mouth full of the forbidden fruit, was unnerved when the milkman suddenly bicycled into the garden, dismounted and leaned his machine against the mango tree. What was more, the milkman also coveted those mangoes. He gazed longingly up at the bunches of colourful fruit which hung in such tempting profusion, and saw a large-eyed boy, mouth smeared with orange pulp.

'Ho! Mango *hora!*[1] Here, mangoes breaking!' he bawled.

Carloboy froze. His first urge was to shin down, leap the bicycle and flee, but the man stood threateningly at the foot of the tree and was in second wind. 'Here! Tree on top! Mangoes all eating!'

There was no help for it. The man had to be silenced, better yet driven away from where he stood. Also he was rousing the neighbourhood. Ammunition, too, was freely available. A hard, unripe mango shafted down to take the man on the head. Then another, and another. Carloboy began to enjoy himself. Also, he had a good throwing arm and the big man with his big mouth was an easy target.

The man yelped as several mangoes made contact. He roared: 'Here! Mango fruit to me hitting! Mango *hora!* All

---

1. *Hora*—Sinhalese 'rogue'.

breaking and throwing!' But he rushed away to thump on the door and Carloboy streaked down, upset the bicycle in his desperation to get away, fell, rose and bolted to more anguished howls of: 'There going! my bottles broke and running!'

Mrs Joachim, emerging with a headful of curlers, gaped. But she caught a glimpse of the fleeing boy and fumed. 'That little devil! You wait,' she screeched, 'you wait, I'll come and tell your father!'

That evening, for Carloboy, had been most painful. Sonnaboy did not like old 'Monkey' Joachim. He particularly resented entertaining complaints from the man. He took a leather slipper and went after his son, who had paled and fled to the kitchen when Joachim stood at the door.

And now here he was, hesitant at the gate with its peeling yellow pillars, as the nanny, carrying the toddler, went around the house. She was soon at the hall window, crooking a hand, urging him to come. He went.

Inside the small living room, the toddler sat on a mat. Some stuffed toys had been tossed down. The infant sucked happily on a teddy bear's head. Carloboy looked around nervously. The woman took his hand. 'He will stay,' she said of the infant, and led him into the maw of the house. He wanted to break free and run, but he also looked interestedly at the frayed curtains that hid beat-up beds, striped pillow slips, the piles of clothes slung across the tops of doors and the long kitchen table with its red-checked plastic. She led him to a bedroom with a hideous dressing table on which talcum had been liberally spilt. His knuckles felt warm and he jerked his head when he realized that his hand was pressed against a furry vagina, pushed through the folds of her cloth. Slowly, she rubbed the back of his hand against her crotch. Carloboy stood stock still. He watched her drop her cloth and his penis stiffened. She pulled him to her. 'Baby trouser take out,' she breathed. Her fingers slipped the buttons. With a hiss, she raised the tail of his shirt, hitching it in a crude knot around the bottom of his chest, arched herself and bent to rub her vagina against him.

Carloboy dumbly sank to the bed with her. 'Baby on top come,' and she gripped him to her and her fat brown legs cradled him and he breathe the garlicy smell of her breasts as her fingers held his penis, rubbing, rubbing, in a stickiness that daubed over his small testicles and across the pit of his stomach. She was breathing heavily, jerkily, and her mouth was open and a near-whistling sound came from her throat, 'Hard, hard, you hold me,' she croaked and Carloboy buried his face in her cleavage, felt the impress of a safety pin on his cheek and her hips plunged and he was suddenly bouncing, riding her and felt as though something was bursting inside him. And then she lay still, gasping as a hand fell away from his buttocks and the other slowly unclasped his cock which was steeped in her tumescence.

Carloboy was sweating. What had happened, he thought wildly. He thought he was going to die or something. And that marvellous, awful delirium that had flooded him. His penis was a little, shrivelled thing now, but an instant before it had been rock hard and something had caused a starburst within him. He had squirmed, wriggled, his knees trembling. It was a feeling he had never known before—something like pain and ecstasy, like holding an ice cube to a flame.

The woman told him to get up. He did so, looking at her outspread thighs, her cleft with its dark hair. She giggled. 'Baby like?'

He nodded.

She reached out and he came close to her. Gently she stroked him and told him to sit. 'Finger you put inside,' she said, placing his hand on the inside of her thighs.

Carloboy spoke for the first time. 'Where?'

'Here. I'll show.'

He felt her wetness. His forefinger disappeared into this wetness.

'Other finger also put. Baby's hand small, no? Put all to see.' Holding together his thumb and fingers she pushed in his hand up to his knuckles. 'Now well put inside. Slowly, slowly.' The knuckles disappeared. Carloboy gazed, fascinated, as his fingers slipped snugly in. He pushed hesitantly. The woman gasped. 'Now a little take out and again push. Like that do. Quickly do!' The boy eased his elbow and began to pump his fingers into the orifice. The woman's raised knees began to tremble and she clutched at the boy's hip. She flung her other hand to the head of her vagina, fingers kneading her clitoris until, with a sharp cry, she locked her thighs, gripping his fingers inside her, pulling Carloboy against her, pressing her mouth to his hip and she squirmed with the paroxysm.

She gave him a kitchen rag to wipe himself and went to a store room where she took a one rupee note. Treasure indeed for Carloboy who took it eagerly.

'Again come you must, right? Another rupee I'll give.'
'How?'
'Baby mango tree near wait. I'll come and tell.'
'All right.'
'Baby like, no?'

Carloboy nodded. He sniffed at his hand. It smelled funny. Like egg in the fridge. He seemed to smell it all over him. 'I'll wash a little?'

She said no. 'Home run and wash. Now *nona* come. Quickly go.'

He went.

The chronicler would like to stick his oar in at this juncture to make what he considers a pertinent observation. It was a peculiarity that in those times, sexual assaults on children left them besmirched more in mind than in body. One cannot say which is worse, of course, but one had little doubt that thousands of today's upright citizens could say— if they have a mind to, that is—that childhood sexual encounters were, at the worst, rather messy, quite shameful at the moment, but never physically hurtful. Mental degradation, oh yes, but physically unharmful. It has been gleaned from many latter-day admissions of young adults that the sexual assaults they were subject to were mostly extraneous. Mutual acts of masturbation and the satisfaction of genital friction at the most. This, although most deplorable, carried little in aftermath. Sodomy was, somehow, abhorrent.

Virginity was rarely violated. The natural resilience of childhood helped too. The only fear was in being discovered and there remained, too, an initial sense of shame that prompted children to avoid further contact with any person who had inveigled them into a sex act, used their bodies briefly and rewarded them with coin or sweets. Of course, some found it a source of revenue and thought little of allowing this uncle or that to meddle with them as often as it pleased him. There was danger in this, of course. Beryl's brother, Charles Whitechapel da Brea, who married Hazel Marjorie Peterson, sired four children. The eldest, a girl, was Pamilla, the second, also a girl, was Eliza, the third, a boy—and the only boy was Geordie—and he was followed by yet another girl, Rosabelle. In the rumbustious history of that family (where Pamilla married Chootyboy Brooks and Eliza was screwed in the rear seat of a car in Saranankara Road and had a beautiful bastard boy, and Rosabelle thought nothing of groping for Carloboy's cock at every family get-together) Geordie became darling of a long procession of men up and down the lane, of prefects and masters in schools, more prefects and masters in an upcountry school where he was boarded and finally came to regard himself as a sexual plaything for any and every male who wished to use him. Geordie also had a huge cock and was incredibly effeminate. He liked to be kissed by the men he openly courted and when he found that his eight-inch organ was an impediment to short trousers, would artfully tuck his member between his legs and walk tight-thighed like a girl, thus making him more attractive to all and sundry.

But more of this later. It is necessary, the chronicler maintains, to place Carloboy and his ilk in raw perspective. This is not a social study in any sense of the word, but too often Society tends to keep a lid on what should be dragged out, debated. As would be imagined, and as Father Grero of St Lawrence's Church would have decidedly said, the cohorts of Hell were working overtime on the innocents of the parish. It was all part of that ever-popular triumvirate: the devil, the world, and the flesh—and it made those tender years in many homes quite a circus!

And there was the war, of course. The war, and sadly, an unholy preoccupation with the war. Fathers discussed Rommel. They were proud to know the German Field Marshal by his full name, Erwin Rommel, but would never know or care to know of the name of the man who was giving Pattiboy ten cents to shake him until he ejaculated.

Sonnaboy thought highly of Rommel. 'How the story? That bugger Rommel went to the prison camp and gave tea to the British prisoners.'

'Yes, men,' old Phoebus would say, 'one thing, not like the other bastards, no? Killing civilians and putting massacres and all.'

'Had a big article in the papers last week. Imagine, men, his father was a schoolmaster. And must be quite old now, no? Was in First World War also. I remember about twenty-five–thirty years ago how he fought in the mountains. Won some pukka battles.'

'I think he's the one who took Czechoslovakia and Poland and France.'

'Then what? Who else? And how the way he went to Paris? Our bloody engines taking four hours to go to Galle. Rommel took his Panzers to Paris in eight days and not fast those tanks, no?'

'Anyway, our Montgomery also not a small one.'

'Dass true. If anybody licks Rommel, it will be Montgomery, you wait and see.'

'Why just say Rommel the British are scared, men.'

'His son also putting in the army.'

'Who? Rommel's?'

'Yes, men, and Hitler gave the Iron Cross also.'

'To who? The son?'

'No, men. To Rommel.'

'Ah!'

So what could be more important? Oh, plenty, when one considers the giddy-go-round events of the time, and especially when the cowshed school was adamant that Carloboy should go to the Dehiwela branch of the same school because Father Theo couldn't abide the boy. Sonnaboy, too, moved over the rear wall of his 34th Lane house into a house in Mahadangahawatte Lane where Carloboy found a common wall which allowed him to still sneak over to Uncle Aloy's whenever the serial bug bit and which gave Uncle Aloy much satisfaction.

It all began with Father Theo who found a slate-eyed Sonnaboy most distasteful on the subject of railway high jinks. Also, Sonnaboy's visit to the school had unnerved the priest whom everybody called 'Glamourboy' because he fancied himself, pomaded his hair heavily, and spent as much time at his mirror as he did in the chapel.

'It is not what happened or did not happen,' he had said primly, 'these are not the sort of things that must be aired in a classroom. Boys are young and young boys are impressionable.

'What?'

'Supposing a child in our charge thinks that he could lie on the rail track and allow a train to go over him?'

Sonnaboy raised an eyebrow—the equivalent of a Victorian 'pshaw!'

They parted with many things unsaid, naturally.

When the letter came Beryl was not in the sunniest. 'See, men, telling that after taking distance into account, he must go to Dehiwela St Peter's.'

'What? Who is saying?'

'Here the letter. From the school. All students living past Manning Place to go to Dehiwela.'

It was pleaded that the cowsheds were crammed to distraction. Pupils home in from as far away as Slave Island, from Kollupitiya, Havelock Town, Timbirigasyaya, Wellawatte, etc., etc. It was impressed that the coconut thatch complex in Dehiwela was also St Peter's under the benevolent eye of St Mary's Church and hence extremely Catholic in character with every priestly effort to keep it that way. Henceforth, it was patiently explained, distance would be the selective force. Geography *had* to be taken into account, proximity pandered to. Carloboy, it was deemed, was approximately 500 yards closer to the Dehiwela establishment than he was to Bambalapitiya.

'Any bugger came near the gate with a measuring tape?'

Sonnaboy wished to know. 'Bloody priests. Now have to send this bugger to Dehiwela. Let Diana go alone and send him by bus.'

Sonnaboy had other fish to fry so he allowed this school change to go unchallenged. Since Germany was now in a sort of reverse gear and Japan was occupied in the Pacific and since the worst of it seemed to be over, and the Easter Sunday air raid had come and gone[1] and North Africa and Italy were where the mopping up operations by the Allies had begun, many nervous Ceylonese who had headed for the hills returned to their Colombo haunts. House rents rose sharply as demand grew, and Sonnaboy's landlord remarked that thirty rupees was no self-respecting rent. He demanded sixty-five and got instead such a slap that he raced to the police station and found that it hurt him too much to make a vocal complaint. But Sonnaboy found the house behind his backyard vacant and, on inspection, was satisfied that it was bigger, had a servants' lavatory and a very nice strip of garden. Also, Beryl said, she loved the purple bougainvillaea which rioted spectacularly in a corner of the garden, and the road beyond the gate was tarred and not a red dust road which raised clouds of dust with each passing vehicle.

Rental, too, was 'reasonable' and there was a closed-in veranda and a hall, and Sonnaboy's friend Georgie Ferreira, who was an auctioneer and always wore his wife's frilly nightgowns to bed, lived opposite.

'Not bad, no,' Sonnaboy told his family, 'and have a back veranda and big kitchen also. Over the wall, Ratnayake's house and over that wall Phoebus. Only next door have some Tamil fellows but only men there. Nothing for you to go an' talk.' This to Beryl who sniffed and said, 'So when we are going?'

---

1. For a detail of the Japanese bombing of Colombo, the reader is exhorted to see *The Jam Fruit Tree* pp. 196-206 (Penguin, India 1993). The author cannot abide repetition, this book being big enough as it is!

CHAPTER SIX

Carloboy found St Peter's, Dehiwela a strange place and the pupils too decidedly rougher, even quite eccentric. There was Feddo Holmes who carried his sandwiches in his Atlas and Maxie Ribeiro who made shocking whistles with two fingers stuck into the sides of his mouth and Lanny Gogerly who wrote letters to his classmates inviting them to suck his cock. A kindly soul, he would remind them to bring their handkerchiefs to wipe his cock after they had regaled themselves.

A border of long thatched classrooms enclosed a large, sandy quadrangle and boys of many sizes, and colours were marched in column to St Mary's each morning where prayers were said and then marched back again. The only trouble, as the boys agreed, was 'Pottaya', a weedy master who had one squint eye and the other which looked suspiciously false and, as anyone will tell you, a pottaya is a cock-eyed coot, a blind person or one who, due to some conjunctival defect, has to look in the general direction of Barcelona if he wishes to focus on the legs of the girls next door. 'Pottaya', like all every-day Sinhalese words, is not a nice one. It is used in scorn, with derision, contempt and particularly to draw universal attention to one's drawbacks. There are many such words that make up the interesting vocabularies of schoolboys all over the island. A man is 'bada' is he's got a stomach that is a close contender to the Sugar Loaf mountain. A 'thattaya' is someone who has more hair on his bum than on his head; a 'pakaya' was reserved for a very nasty type of human being who was widely accepted to be full of low, organic desires and if there was an identified homosexual named Perera or Silva or whatever, would usually be titled 'Puk' Perera or 'Puk' Silva as the case may be. Any person with an offensive body odour was invariably a 'gandaya', while 'lapaya' was reserved for any antagonist who had a facial blemish, a mole, an ugly scar, birthmark, and so on. Indeed the chronicler feels that this is as good a place as any to recall a distant day when a British covenanted engine driver,[1] who was heartily detested by Sonnaboy, decided to bridge the gap between his surly Sinhalese fireman and himself by speaking Sinhala. The driver, a florid fellow named Keating, had listened to assorted types like porters and other lowly railway life who liked to speak rough and in a universally accepted argot. Porter Sarnelis would yell to porter Joronis:

'*Adai*! Joro! Here come, *yako*!'[2]

'What, *yako*?'

'This is *yakagey* (a devil of a) job. Come some help give!'

'Just go, *yako*, to me other work have.'

Keating, who prided himself on a good ear for language, was overjoyed. Clearly, *yako* was an accepted form of address. He met his fireman and decided to go ape. 'Good morning, *yako*,' he sang.

Fireman Jayamanne stopped his shovel in mid-swing and earnestly studied this *sudda*[3] driver. No, the man was revoltingly normal. Clearly the man also was in that weird stage of trying to pander to the natives. He sighed. There was no help to it. 'Morning, sur,' he said.

Keating rubbed his hands. His first Sinhalese word. He'd

---

1. Engine drivers brought in from England. Readers could fill in on these characters in *Yakada Yakā*.

2. *Yako*—Sinhalese 'devil' or 'demon'. Never used in any fearsome manner, but simply in a spirit of relating to one another in conversation.

3. *Sudda*—whiteskin.

soon have these fellows eating out of these same hands. 'Open steam cocks, *yako*,' he said.

At the end of the day Jayamanne was feeling pretty overwhelmed. He met Sonnaboy and his voice quivered. 'Morning from time to me *yako* saying,' he groaned, 'here come *yako*, some more coal put *yako*, hullo *yako*, cheerio *yako*—he's mad? Colombo to Galle *yako yako* saying and going!'

Sonnaboy went to Keating. 'What is this, men, you're saying *yako yako* to the fireman?'

Keating beamed.

'You're crazy.'

The beam switched off.

'You know what *yako* is? Devil! My God, men, you calling your fireman devil, devil. Galle and back!'

Keating gasped. 'Why,' he squeaked, 'I never knew . . . Oh rhubarb, is he annoyed?'

'Annoyed? Push you off the bloody engine—that's what I'll do! Nex' time you say *pako*[1] right. What, men, must know the right word to say, no? This Sinhalese not so easy.'

Keating was grateful. It's the way these awful people spoke, he told himself. One can't rely on one's ears especially when these natives talk with their mouths full of betel leaf and salivate redly. He had obviously misheard a 'p' for a 'y'. Well, dash it, he would effect rectification.

'I say, thank you, von Bloss, thankee, thankee. I'll set things right, don't you worry,' and the next afternoon he stood on the platform, twinkled at Jayamanne who, as the Fates would have it, was holding the shovel, and carolled, 'Hullo, *pako*!' A long twelve seconds later he was being carried away by a knot of Running Shed workers while Jayamanne, most unrepentant, shouted to all who would listen that even if the Governor-General castrated him he didn't care. 'Yesterday all the day to me *yako* saying! I just keeping quiet! Now see will you. Now coming to *pako* say! Sudda even like this dirty words to me can tell?'

The flat of the shovel had taken Keating across the diaphragm and he purged blood in the hospital and couldn't

---

1. This is a diminutive of that awful word 'pakaya', dealt with earlier.

sit up in bed for a week. Jayamanne was subjected to a lot of departmental torture and covenanted drivers were also advised to leave the Sinhala language to those who understood it and thus maintain the dignity of the white sahib.

Oh, and by the way, Jayamanne was known as Pako Jayamanne thereafter which made the man a most bad-tempered individual.

Pottaya was Veyappapillai—a Tamil master who always wore a coat three sizes too big for him and a permanent leer. In class, he would turn an eye on Holmes, impale Ribeiro with his glass eye and say, 'Gogerly, I can see what you're up to!' No one could, try as they would, know where he was looking and what he was actually looking at. Most disconcerting. Mrs' Harridge, who taught Art, was never sure. 'Where he's looking I don't know,' she would tell Mrs Lappen, another teacher who had galloping adenoids and a voice that was like a box guitar without an A and D string.

'Hngh! Ownly gno to detain aevery wun. Gnot wun day without gniving detenshung, gno?'

Mrs Harris nodded. 'The way he's looking, mus' be punishing the wrong boys also, I think.'

Pottaya was, to say the least, peculiar. He relished, revelled in detention. 'You, you, you, you!' he would squeal, 'yes, you also! All stay after school!'

Dreams of barefoot cricket in the sand lot are shattered. Bittharay[1] Gomes, who was a particularly repulsive boy with large, unwashed ears, would be among the detained. Within the first ten minutes, Pottaya would look fifteen points over his head and say, 'You, Gomes, you can go.'

Ten minutes later he would tell Holsinger, 'You also can go. Others read your *Latin for Today* Chapter Three.' The

---

1. Sinhalese for egg. Gomes was so labelled because he had to shave his head after a prolonged attack of scabies. His life was never the same in school thereafter.

others would make small sounds of exasperation. A quarter of an hour later: 'You, Matthys, you can go.' This left Carloboy and Maxie Perera, and outside all the buzz of a day's school had evaporated and the evening was yellowing and the sand lot was empty and the evening wind was taking a break and had stopped its cello recital in the tamarind tree. Five o'clock. 'How long is this bugger going to keep us here,' Carloboy thought.

'Perera! You can go.'

That's bad news. The boys knew that Pottaya had this cane on his desk and he always caned the last boy in his detention class. Carloboy scowled at his Latin text. Pottaya rose and came around the rostrum to lean against his desk. Maxie made a face. '*Thoppi* for you,' he hissed, and went.

As in most classrooms, the master's desk sat, like a birthday cake, on the rostrum, and the master sat, thus elevated, to glare down at his class and wonder what he had done in a previous incarnation to deserve it. This was all well and good, said Mrs Harridge, but was greatly put out when a story rocketed through the school that on a particular day in the week she had worn pale blue knickers. She had, of course, but how could every boy in the school know? The titters and hisses and stage whispers in chapel made her a near basket case. The bigger boys, privy to more things in heaven and on earth than the smaller fry, embroidered the story, adding that there was a distinct brown stain on those knickers. It was then noted how boys in the front row, seated under her very nose, mind, kept bending to pick up pencils, erasers, books, and spending much time at floor level, where they undoubtedly found a worm's-eye view of Mrs Harridge's lower section most entertaining. They bent down, groped around, gazing through the portals of her desk, studying her legs, waiting for that delicious moment when teacher would spread her knees and give them a peep show of fat white thighs and her underwear.

It took Mrs Harridge a week to work this out and then, with an outraged howl that made the school watchman's hair stand on end, she demanded that the gap in her desk be boarded up. Also, she vowed, every boy who ever bent down to pick anything in her class would be immediately marched to the Principal for a flogging.

When Pottaya stood against the outer edge of his desk there was barely room for another to stand on the rostrum, facing him. 'You, von Bloss, come here! Here! Stand here in front of me. Not down there! Come up here!'

Carloboy stood on the edge of the rostrum. 'Sir, haven't room, Sir, I'll fall.'

'Nonsense. Stand still. If you think you'll fall come closer,' and Pottaya took up the cane. 'You know why you were detained? Talking in class. How many times am I telling not to talk in class?' He seized the boy, pulled him close, clasped him around the shoulders, held him trapped against his body and struck him across the buttocks with the cane. 'It's paining?' he asked.

Carloboy did not speak. His face was pressed into the man's chest.

'Put your hands out and hold the desk!'

This was worse. Pressed against the man, arms thrust out around Pottaya's waist, hands holding the edge of the desk.

'Ah, that's good.' The grip around his shoulders and back tightened and the cane sang again. 'Now paining?'

'Y-yes, sir.'

'Good, good.' The man was thrusting out with his hips, pushing himself into the boy, gripping him fiercely. Another stroke, very light, and then another which the boy scarcely felt. But something hard and alive was boring into the pit of his stomach and suddenly Pottaya dropped the cane, embraced the boy and heaved against him, once, twice, and stood still, lips quivering. 'Right,' he said at length, 'you can go now. Next time you'll get six cuts and have to stay till six o'clock. No more nonsense in class, do you hear?'

Carloboy gulped, gingerly stepped down. Was he wrong or was there a patch, a wet patch on Pottaya's trousers? He collected his books and crept out, and Maxie stuck a cautious

---

1. Schoolboy term for a homosexual act. A cupper is a homo, to be cupped is to suffer a homosexual attack. A cup boy is a boy who welcomes homosexual advances.

head out from the next class and whispered, 'Hssss! I saw, men. How the way he caned and what he tried to do. Tried to cup[1] you, no?'

'Tried, I think,' Carloboy said, 'but didn't try to take out my trousers or anything.'

'Yes, but I saw, no? The way he holding and all. If I were you I'll go an' tell my daddy what he did.'

'You're mad? You don't know my daddy. First he'll catch and hammer me.'

But things got out of hand. Maxie bristled with the news the next day and boys, always blessed with lurid imaginations, spun the tale through the school. Knots of the nastier types would waylay him. 'That Pottaya cupped you, no? Hoo! You're Pottaya's cup boy! Hoo!' This led to scuffles, torn shirts, bruised knuckles and the attention of priests and lay staff who deplored any sort of unrest in the ranks. Carloboy, hounded by those he used to call friend, grew increasingly belligerent. The tussles were unbelievable. Boys who had suffered the same treatment by Pottaya and had never been witnessed did not sympathize. Rather, they became Carloboy's worst tormentors. It was on the day that he traded punches with Trevor Wise and dislodged Trevor's front tooth that things became increasingly unreal. Mrs Wise stormed in and Carloboy was caned and Mrs Wise nearly stunned him with a mean swing of her handbag. Letters were dispatched, and Sonnaboy dragged his son into the hall and wondered whether he should first stripe Carloboy with his army web belt or kick Mrs Wise up and down Hill Street, Dehiwela.

And then the dam broke. Carloboy related, haltingly, all that had happened. Sonnaboy listened, 'Did you tell all this to the principal?'

The boy gulped. 'Yes.'

'So?'

'He-he said I'm a-a liar.'

'Stay at home tomorrow.'

Carloboy sniffed and stared at the floor.

'You heard? No school for you tomorrow. I'll go and see

what all this is about. But if I find that what you said is not true I'll take your bloody top skin off! Did you hear?'

What happened the next day was quite ordinary as far as Sonnaboy was concerned. He cycled through the gates, got stuck in the sand lot, swore, and wheeled his machine to the office hut. He strode to the outer rim of the quadrangle, peering into each classroom until Pottaya was sighted.

Schoolboys pray earnestly for diversions of any kind. This time there were transports of hysterical joy. Never in their wildest had such a diversion been thrown their way. St Peter's, Dehiwela, they all agreed, was the victim of a wholly natural disaster!

CHAPTER SEVEN

War is a funny thing. It tends to push lots of other little dramas out of focus, making it hard, sometimes, for a chronicler to get things spot on. Take 1943 for instance. The Burghers of Ceylon liked it very much. Oh they were just as bitter as everyone else about shortages and the rationing and having to settle for dehydrated meat which Sonnaboy declared was horseflesh, hooves and all, but this war was certainly the goods!

In gabbing about the days, fifty years ago, one is amazed at how well the war is remembered. They, the Burghers, will still tell you about how Goebbels was the guy who developed the Hitler cult. 'He was Hitler's arse-licker,' a small, bad-tempered Burgher tells the chronicler. (And he said, of course, that Lord Haw Haw was Goebbel's acolyte!)

Now isn't that marvellous? We actually remember that there was a Nazi propagandist who went gobble, gobble, gobble! But the times they were a-hectic, so to say, with the Americans in, the Japanese in, and late 1943 saw war swirling to both east and west of the island, making everybody very excited. The Yanks got into the Sicilian campaign and marched into Messina with amphibious attacks by the Third American Division. Colontota would tell Anna: 'Now going to have a conference.'

'What for?'

'To discuss how to invade, men.'

Anna tinkles her rosary. 'Anyway, now nothing will happen here. Gave, no, whole of Ceylon to the Virgin Mary. Building a basilica also. Have in las' Sunday's *Messenger*.'

'How, Roosevelt also going for the conference.'

'So let go anywhere. Why, appa, they can't finish this? Father Grero also telling we must pray for peace.'

Totoboy meets Eric de Mello at Bambalapitiya. 'How, how, what, men you're looking like Good Friday. Elsie gave you a kanay? How the Eight Army? Going like hell, no?'

Eric gives a nervous cackle. 'Mus' go, men. Told to buy some candles.'

Totoboy ignores this. 'Whole bottom of Italy now Fifth Army took. Germans running. Come go to that boutique for a little. Told the man to get a pint for me. You like to put a small shot?'

Eric shudders. 'No, men. I'll go, getting late also.'

'What, about five, no? What late? Sha, must be pukka, no? All bayonet fighting ipseems. Germans running from the trench. Americans and British chasing and landing with the bayonet. Chakass! right through the back!'

Eric flees.

Sonnaboy goes to Florrie da Brea. The old lady beams. Sonnaboy says: 'Hullo, Ma . . .' He always calls his mother-in-law 'ma'.

'Come, come. Riding in the sun like this. Who, child, is this Clark general chasing Germans in Italy?' (General Mark Clark was commander of the Fifth Army).

Sonnaboy smiles. 'Yes, he's giving that Kesselring fellow guts. But that's not the thing; you heard? Again have lot of Japanese ships coming round here.'

The old lady is still sorting out things. 'Clark, Clark. Had some Clarks in Vaverset Lane, no? Nice girl; comes to church; Colleen Clark, I think.'

Sonnaboy snorts. Spinster daughter Millicent June

chuckles. 'What, you're trying to talk about the war with Ma? Everything she's mixing up. Real fighting going on, no? Russians are giving the Germans properly also.'

'Yes, men. But you saw the papers? *Daily News* said Lord Mountbatten going to tell the Asia Command to attack Burma. Japanese also getting ready for big fight in Malaya and Java and all. And now again lot of Japanese ships roundabout here. Naturally, no, when put East Indies fleet here and Mountbatten also. Might come and bomb again,' and Sonnaboy rides away well satisfied that he has raised a scare and that 'Ma' will soon be telling the McLeods and the Paulusz's that Colleen Clark was a general who was going to Italy to bomb Burma!

It was, truly, a fierce turnabout. The Russians were fighting, driving back the Germans with great violence. October 1943 was a bloody month. Japanese planes had been spotted over Brussels, and Eisenhower's armies put paid to German resistance in Voltuno and Capua. Allied bombers knocked the stuffing out of Yugoslavia and suddenly a smashing Russian tank drive deep into German lines captured everybody's imagination. The destruction of over a thousand Panzers and tractor-mounted guns near the river Dneiper swung everyone's attention to the Russian war machine. Montgomery's capture of Capri was all well and good. The Fifth Army's advance on Naples was quite exciting even if Leah de Mello was wont to say, 'Where, child, this, Naples? An' who is this *massina*[1] they're bombing?'

'Not massina, men, Messina,' George would grunt, 'you women don' know anything!'

Two thousand sorties a day to pound German tanks to a pulp was nice to know of, but Sonnaboy, who bought a squat Ferranti radio and spent a lot of time between wavelengths, raising whines and squawks of protest, found the near-crazed determination of a vicious Russian onslaught as beautiful as a sonata. When Stalin issued a battle order which was printed in the *Daily News*, he clipped out the item and waved it proudly under Georgie Ferreira's nose. 'See

---

1. *Massina* is colloquial Sinhalese for brother-in-law!

what Stalin sent to Rokoss-Rokoss-bloody jawbreakers, these Russian names. Yes, Rokossovsky. And how? Named the battalion with the name of the town they captured.'

Georgie Ferriera would raise an eyebrow. Together they would read and reread the news item while Mrs Ferriera would titter and tell Beryl. 'If have any battle here or there or anywhere enough for them.'

> Our forces on the Central Front today, after two days of stiff fighting captured the town and important railway junction of Nezhin—a most important centre of the enemy's resistance on the road to Kiev.

> In honour of the victory won, the units which distinguished themselves in the liberation of Nezhin will in future bear the name of the town.

'See, I told you. And read the rest—'

> Tonight, Moscow, in the name of the motherland, will salute our victorious troops by twelve salvoes from 124 guns.

> I thank the forces under their command for their courage and devotion to duty, which resulted in the liberation of Nezhin.

> Everlasting glory to the heroes fallen in battle! Death to the German invaders!

'My God, men, 124 guns twelve shots each. For the noise alone Germans will run summore.'

Beryl says: 'Can you hear? That's all they want. If fire like that whole of Russia will get a headache!'

Every day, in thousands of homes, cheers were raised. Every action of a war that was thousands of miles away in any direction was a ready excuse to sit around a bottle, clink glasses and hold forth. Greek soldiers have entered Samos and chasing the Germans up and down the beach . . . cheers! Russia's General Vatutin is routing the Krauts down the river Dneiper . . . cheers! Have another drink! What? German stukas are pounding the British in Greece? What's wrong with these British, men? Can't send some buggers to blow up the German bombers in Rhodes? Here, fill your glass, men. Don't worry, can get some more arrack. Anyway, Bomber Command is not so bad, no?'

'That's the ticket,' a three-parts-inebriated Totoboy tells Carlo Wouterz in the Brown's Bar in the Fort. This is a favourite 'watering hole' and there was a Union Jack draped behind the bar and, depending on the degree of being sozzled, one could hear such robust renderings such as

Bless 'em all,
Bless 'em all,
The lean and the short an' th' tall,
You'll get no promotion
This side of the ocean
So come on my lads, bless them all!

Sometimes, Royal Marines and off-watch sailors from the H.M.S. Highflyer shore station in Galle Buck would also drift in and get crying drunk and sing brokenly of home and how London's children were being evacuated and how they missed their wives and sweethearts and their mummies. A great favourite was a sentimental song by Vera Lynn who was a forces favourite.

When you hear Big Ben
You're home again,
Home is where you belong,
Though you're far away,
Each night and day,
You'll sigh when you hear this song.
He stands by the river that leads to the sea,
His hands are together, like ours used to be

When you hear Big Ben you're home again
Home in my arms, sweetheart.

and everybody would become most maudlin and sing it again until Aubrey van der Bona, who doesn't like music, throws a chair and the resultant uproar has all patrons of Brown's Bar staggering out quite red, white, black and blue.

The scene also had this unnerving quality of shifting mercurially. December 1943 saw the bombing of Formosa, the American invasion of Bougainville and the battles of Empress Augusta Bay. And suddenly everybody went quite British and revelled in the way English pilots were carrying their bombs to Berlin. Carloboy and gangs of small fry knew all about the Mosquitoes and the Luftwaffe and how German Commander von Manstein was considering how to run. In churches, too, Catholic priests urged prayers for the safety of the Pope and bells were rung when the allies began their drive for Rome. Discussions at home became quite exciting. Sonnaboy would point to the dining table. 'Here the Moro river,' then to the dinner wagon, 'this is the Foro river. No place to go. Only forward between the rivers. In front German tanks, guns and here Montgomery coming. How the fight?'

The children grow just as excited.

'And they whacked the Germans. Christmas and all. Took almost six thousand prisoners also. Canada soldiers also came to help.'

With all this, one could forgive the population of Sri Lanka for not chalking up the famous battle of St Peter's, Dehiwela, although it did make Father Paul very hysterical and the entire student population cheering and shouting 'mad parent! mad parent!' in high glee.

Pottaya was seized by the top of his oversized coat and the seat of his trousers, shaken until his eyeballs corrected themselves, and then hurled out with an accompanying roar that blew holes in the cadjan (coconut leaf thatch). The man, trying to rise, was grabbed, smacked and pushed, mouth open, into the sand lot, raised half-choking and smacked again because Sonnaboy did remember that a choking man required a thump to get various internal tubes in working order. Trying to run he received the Order of the Boot, which propelled him to the gate and to this he hung, terrible to behold.

'My godfather,' squeaked Mrs Harridge, 'who is that?'

'Von Bloss boy's father. Killing Pillai, no? Why the watchman even won't run and tell to the police!'

Why not? Pillai was obviously dying. He drooled horribly and looked like an abominable sandman. 'Bloody bastard!' Sonnaboy was roaring while sundry priests and masters hung on to him and the parish priest scuttled in, puffing and waving his hands. Sonnaboy turned on Father Dominic. 'Taking my son to the police!' he growled. 'When he told about this bastard what you did? Said liar and caned him, no? One boy said he saw what he did. Did you ask? What about this bugger? Because your master anything to the boys he can do?'

Boys knotted round, agape. This was a spectacle. This was more. It was justice for all who had been Pottaya's victims. It started suddenly. Someone flung a handful of sand at the bleeding man. Hundreds followed. It was a struggle to dislodge Pottaya from the gate, drag him through a crowd of murderous children and into the office where the door was shut and hundreds of boy milled around, chanting very vile slogans. The parish priest clung to Sonnaboy in a long process of pacification. Father Dominic was summoned, Maxie Perera was dragged in. Other boys said their piece. Several little devils who had never passed the time of day or shared a rostrum with Pottaya also volunteered the most amazing information, no doubt culled from homosexual encounters at other times, other places. Mrs Harridge too ventured that one can never trust a man who is 'Colombo looking Galle going' and there was something 'funny' about the man. Clearly he was a monster of depravity.

Carloboy was told by a father who returned home in a most sunny mood: 'Tomorrow you go to school. Anyone try anymore nonsense you come straight and tell, you hear!' Carloboy heard.

He also heard that, whatever scratch solutions had been reached, his father had taken a grave dislike to St Peter's.

Also, there were school fees to be paid and although the boy had been given a hero's welcome and Pottaya had disappeared, the Royal College in Colombo was a very good school, very big, was also a government school and levied no fees whatsoever. Problem was that there was a very strict, public entrance examination. Sonnaboy determined that Carloboy should have a shot at it. 'You study well and pass the exam and go to Royal and I'll buy you a bicycle,' he said. It was all the incentive that an eight-year-old boy needed. A quiet time descended. So quiet, in fact, that even Victor Ratnayake told his son, 'See that Carloboy. Learning nicely and not up to any nonsense anymore. Going to put in Royal also next year. What are you doing? Only know to pour ink on the cat!'

It was not really so. Carloboy was one of those Burgher children who had this uncanny knack of contributing to adult discomfort. The less strait-laced Burgher way of life abetted enormously. Naturally one would always hear a mother say: 'Very quiet the children. Don' know what devilish thing they're up to.' But one could also hear—and more often, too—'Why you are so quiet today? You're feeling sick or something?' A quiet Burgher child was a source of worry, both up and down the scale. Parents, teachers, Sunday School teachers, all adults in whatever position of authority, lived with the knowledge that these Burghers may be ever so seemingly angelic, ever so seemingly attentive, ever so seemingly amenable or tractable, but nothing, absolutely nothing, could be assured. In each, a demon of chaos resided, popping out at the most disadvantageous times.

This was the age of the cricket picture craze, collecting fish craze, playing marbles, catching guppies in the Wellawatte canal, fighting, cheering hoarsely at school matches, bullying and being bullied, being always hungry and running the shower behind a closed bathroom door to show that a bath was in progress. This was also the age of a new flowering in the field of art, and suddenly the new rage became the topic in many Burgher living rooms. Burgher artists were commanding the attention of society.

Everyone knew of Aubrey Collette, of course. He was a

genius, surely. His newspaper cartoons were turned to, chuckled at and his barbed wit hailed by the highest in the land. 1943 saw a decided renaissance. There was Lionel Wendt, stout, round-faced, a close fit in an upholstered chair and with hair combed back despite his slowly receding hairline. Geoff Beling was quite headmasterish, tending to look over his spectacles. George Keyt was lost in a world of his own while George Claessen was young, energetic with a determined set of jaw. Collete, like his contemporaries Harry Pieris, Richard Gabriel, Ivan Peries and Justin Daraniyagala, was lean, whippy, full of raw energy. Together (and not forgetting the Buddhist monk Manjusri Thero[1]) they formed the famous 43 Group—the most revolutionary milestone in the history of Ceylon, and later, Sri Lankan art.

Carloboy liked to draw. With effort he was pretty good, too, and Sonnaboy couldn't understand where it all came from. 'Don' know like who he is,' he would sometimes tell Beryl. 'Can see how he's picking up the piano? Nobody to show even. Just putting the hands and playing. And asking for Bristol board and big box of Reeves. Drawing on all the exercise books also.'

'Give, men,' Beryl would say. 'If like to do must encourage, no?'

It was a thrill, then, to go in clean white shirt, bow tie, sharkskin trousers, hosed and shoed, to Darley Road where the 43 Group held their first exhibition.

Carloboy was both shy and bemused. He found the show a sense-dazzling, mindstorming one. He was seeing daubs on canvas for the first time. He was seeing the haunting splendour of George Keyt, the bold intensity of Daraniyagala, the simplistic washes of Claessen with shades of El Greco and the delightful near stylistic, delineated works of Beling. So a naked woman was art! He had never drawn a naked woman. Not really naked. She was holding a cloth near her crotch. But it made the boy self-conscious to stare

---

1. Thero—the title given to a monk. In the art world of the times (and since he was a true artist and not averse to painting female torsos) he preferred to be accepted as L.T.P. Manjusri.

at the grainy picture. Richard Gabriel drew women with their clothes on. All with big breasts and black hair and some with *kondays*[1] also. Browns and chromes screamed at flaring reds, mottled backgrounds, grey-visaged powerful faces, slumbering flesh tones and oh, the geometric juxtapositions of a typical Keyt—ribbons of colour meeting shards of clear tints. He thought of sunsets and cracked mirrors, tram lines and ruffled feathers, a maelstrom of imaginings that raced through his head like paint-daubed brushes streaking to the sun.

'You like?' Sonnaboy asked. 'Came because of you. See how real paintings are. Not just to scribble on your exercise books and then tear the page and throw.'

Carloboy nodded. He had no comment. He just went, zombie like, and he wondered why someone was screaming inside his head.

There was, as expected, press reaction to this first showing of the 43 Group. One reporter, adopting the 'popular' approach (and thinking himself very smart, of course) wrote:

> To begin with, there were the surrealistic surroundings amid which one discovered that hidden hall in Darley Road. Then there was the crowd of artists and their 'arty' friends. Hardly a Philistine in sight: but many a proud papa and fond mama basking in the reflected glory of their offspring's genius.

> Models were also apt to come to life disturbingly. You admired the portrait of a despondent chess player in khaki, and suddenly the identical slim lieutenant stood beside you in the flesh. One or two pianists obstructed your view of their painted conversation piece.

> Dominating the scene was an artist who explained his pictures, or the correct attitude towards art with almost ferocious intensity.

---

1. *Konday*—the bun of hair, twisted and knotted at the nape.

Some people were more thrilled by the titles of
the pictures than the pictures themselves . . .'

It seems revolting, almost, that the sarcasm should have
dripped while little was said about the paintings. It was a
report on the event, not its substance. They should have
asked Carloboy!

And so Carloboy painted and studied and when
St Peter's came together again there was a tremendous to-do
and the cowshed boys and coconut thatch boys were one.
That was in 1944 when the Germans were falling back to
Montgomery's onslaught and the French rallied and kissed
each other and went around taking German prisoners and
the Russians reached Latvia and the Americans kept giving
the Japanese beans.

CHAPTER EIGHT

Boys everywhere (and that includes their fathers, uncles, grandfathers too) were in their element on D-day. The beaches of Normandy were so real that Aldo Markwick on a borrowed bicycle and Trevor La Brooy on his own battered machine, raced down Hampden Lane, down the weathered steps which led to the canal and plunged in, roaring lustily and upright in their saddles as they hit the water and swallowed more primordial brew than this world was made of! They were, they said, tank commanders.

Aldo rode a Churchill, Trevor a Sherman. They were going to give the German Panthers what-for!

Arguments were fierce. 'Huh! Can see what the Germans are calling the Shermans? Tommy cookers! Why can't put big guns on the tanks like the Germans have?'

'But still our tanks are fast, men.' (All allied tanks were 'our' tanks).

'Fast, yes, but see, will you, how the Germans just waiting and shooting. Our tanks have to go close to shoot. By the time Germans are shooting from far.'[1]

---

1. Amazing the way the children ingested every scrap of the war. Truly, Allied tank units were shocked to find how easily the Shermans burst into flames. The German Panthers and Tigers were heavily armoured and, with their long guns, could stand off and fire without actually engaging the enemy.

Discussions grew quite fierce among the adults.

'How the story? Ipseems all lies telling, men, about how American tanks going in waves and Germans are turning and running.'

'Don't talk rot, men. Saw in the Majestic cinema last night the news. Showing pictures of German tanks burning. Our fellows are giving them hell.'

'Lissen, will you. I was putting a drink at Lord Nelson. Then one bugger came an' sat. Asking for gin. Then some other buggers also came. English chaps and all sitting next table. And who is playing the piano? Blind John—'

'So never mind Blind John. Everyday he's playing there.'

'Anyway these fellows drinking gin an' talking. Ipseems Monty is very angry that fellows in France are saying that Allied tanks are hopeless not like the Germans. Then one fellow said Guards Armoured Division mustn't complain. Do or die dear boy he's saying and putting another gin. Blind John playing "Just before the battle mother" also.'

'Let him be, men, what else they were saying?'

'Couldn't hear much, men. Said that five Shermans not enough to knock one Panther and our tanks burning all over. One shot from Germans enough.'

'Gwan! All bloody rubbish. If burning like that how everyday they are advancing. Going to Rome also.'

'How do I know? Only telling what I heard, no? And when they saw me looking, bent the heads and muttering so couldn't hear what they said after that.'

'Just go, men. The way you're drinking must have heard all wrong. You think people will talk like that in the open?'

'But I heard. And only had two arracks. You think I'm just talking. Pictures will say one thing. Papers will say one thing. But what is really happening who knows.'

'*Anney* just keep quiet men. You think we are going to lose? What? You want the Germans to win?'

'Oh go to hell, men. Don't understand anything I'm telling.'

'You go to hell! What you're coming to tell me to go to hell? Coming here to side the Germans? Bloody bastard!'

(And World War Three begins . . . almost!)

Years later it was grudgingly confirmed that the Allies actually named their tanks Ronsons, after the popular cigarette lighter which was guaranteed to 'light the first time'. American General Omar Bradley, who registered the decimation of the Shermans, wrote: 'The willingness to expend Shermans offered little comfort to the crews who were forced to expend themselves as well.'

Field Marshal Montgomery raged about the complaints. On receiving a complaining report, he had written: 'I have had to stamp very heavily on reports being circulated about the inadequate quality of our tanks. When equipment at our disposal is used properly and the tactics are good, we have no difficulty in defeating the Germans.'

This drew comment from a British tank driver: 'It was all right for Monty and his officers in their best uniforms going to church at headquarters on a Sunday when boys were being slaughtered on the frontline a few miles away. I suppose that's the military for you.'

Nobody knew, really, what it was all about. It was just the typical reaction of thousands of people who never acknowledged that a little learning was a dangerous thing. None knew of the real metallic clash of giant war machines. Montgomery's brother-in-law actually designed tanks which were immediately labelled 'Hobart's Funnies'. He, Major General Percy Hobart, actually came up with his 'swimming tanks'—the Crab and the Crocodile. The Crocodile was, in reality, a mechanized flame-thrower with a capacity to jet a stream of fire thirty metres. A dirty machine which was born with blue murder in mind. Who cared to ponder on the God-awful business that war actually was? The Crocodile wrought terrible devastation when it was used to spray napalm. Burghers of 1944 didn't want to know what napalm was. All they did was chalk up the victories, exaggerate the kill and cheer loudly over their glasses of arrack. God, they were confident, was very good in saving the king. Hadn't the Allies landed at Normandy? And hadn't Rommel been defeated earlier at El Alamein. And what about that intriguing incident of the *Daily Telegraph* crossword?

Two ordinary words they were, in answer to the

crossword clues—Overlord and Mulberry—but they had been identified as a code connected with the Normandy landings. The story fired young imaginations. Coded messages became a hotly applied school pursuit. Carloboy was pressed into service by his school fellows who agreed unanimously: 'Your English is best, men. Get a code for all the dirty words first. Then anything we write an' pass, even if teacher sees an' takes, won't be able to understand what we are saying.'

It was an exciting year. All the best and worst of the two St Peter's were now together. Old friends, old enemies, the Bambalapitiya boys quick to scorn those from Dehiwela, and punch-ups galore. It was a proud event for the Catholic Church. The College flag was hoisted, the College anthem sung.

> Lend a heart and lend a hand
> And keep the flag on high
> Let its glorious colours ring
> A greeting to the sky,
> Golden gleam and silver sheen,
> And blue that rounds the world,
> Keep the flag a-flying, boys,
> Keep the flag unfurled!

Quite a rousing number, too, although the boys of St Joseph's, who were St Peter's rivals and clashed with frantic regularity on every Big Match day (when the schools met at an annual cricket encounter) made up their own vile version and would march to the Peterite tent, and sing:

> 'Lend your ass and bend, don't stand . . .'

and then do the bunk to the safety of their tent.

So, with the blue, white and gold flapping wearily under a hot Bambalapitiya sun, various priests gave speeches and education department officials kept nodding and a High Mass was sung in the college chapel and the Bishop, too, was in attendance. Masters and teachers were sweat-shiny in their best clothes. Boys fretted at the nerve-racking rigmarole and then, magically, it was all over and there were classrooms to march to and desk lids to bang and the usual scuffles for rear-row seats which kept masters at a goodly distance.

The end of the war, too, could be sensed, but even the bomb plot to kill Hitler wasn't as exciting as this sudden move to the school proper. There were the old regime— 'Glamour Boy', Father Paris, Father Anslem, 'Pathol' Croos, 'Pappa' de Ness, and a crowd of others. Above all there was a geography master who taught from his own book and had a red lower lip which he curled disdainfully at every boy he disliked. He rode an autocycle to work and for some time earned the nickname of 'Put-put' Baptiss, not because he had any inclination to put or put-put, but because that was exactly the sound of the infernal machine he rode—a sort of adolescent motorbike or, one may say, a bicycle that had graduated.

'Put-put' was a good man. A steady, studious man, and as many knew, a devoted family man too. He was quiet in manner, appreciated a good joke, was accepted warmly in many circles and, like all good men, made the butt of schoolboys who tormented him to distraction. Why this is, is hard to tell, let alone analyse. Boys are, if 'Put-put' was permitted to describe them before a Senate Committee, the lowest order of Creation. That was what the poor man must have felt. And yet, as the chronicler learned, no word of the many indignities he suffered in school were ever mentioned at home. He had the facility to drop the hours of school as he would discard an old shoe and become the fond father, the respected neighbour, the loving husband, and always, the scholar.

It never occurred to Carloboy or hundreds of Peterites that so diligent a man, whose book on geography was a standard text for many years, must be a person of both substance and stature. Boys are cruel. They bully, taunt, hiss and boo, are incredibly selfish. They make rotten judgements, and, as all parents will vouch at some time or another, are destructive, rash and unfeeling. Now, many of them shared the determination to make 'Put-put's' life as miserable as possible. Why, was hard to determine. Because he was serious-minded, a dedicated teacher, never gave his class a 'free period', or was a stickler for detail when calling for contour lines, mapping rivers and indicating the Humboldt current with little blue arrows? It's hard to tell, but he had one quality all boys detest. He had a tedious manner and somehow, a forty-five-minute Geography class always seemed to last two hours. When 'Put-put' Baptiss entered a classroom, Time seemed to go under an anaesthetic. And so, a major operation was planned.

An autocycle is the answer to many a middle-class man's prayers. When the Italian Vespas hit the market later they became the darlings of young and old. Agencies had this thought-provoking campaign where billboards carried lipsmacking pictures of local beauties with the shapeliest thighs in the tropics. They wore hot pants and sat astride their snazzy Vespas. Their Romeos sat behind, muzzling, and the blurb screamed: 'It's better on a Vespa.'

By rights then, 'Put-put' on his circumcized motorbike should have earned all plaudits. True, he hadn't a Vespa, and the rackertacker he rode looked like the offspring of a sewing-machine and a combine harvester, but the offensive machine carried the man most economically to wherever he wished. It didn't ask for much. A litre of gasoline in its slim tank, a little oil around its knobs and in its many orifices, a blob of grease on its chain, and it was content. Never in its wildest did it think that four schoolboys would surround it, seize it, stand it on its head, unscrew its petrol cap and grin vilely as all its lifeblood drained away. And what sort of transfusion came next? When 'Put-put' came for it that afternoon, it was in a state of post-operation shock.

Father Paris sat in his principal's office fondly admiring his rack of canes. A swarthy priest with a poll of grey-dusted hair and the makings of a middle-aged spread. The bell had rung (must do something about that bell, it has a vile, tinny sound) and the multitudinous clamour of a thousand boys whooping out of school had died down to a tolerable buzz. He expelled noisily and then caught his next breath sharply. There stood 'Put-put' and any priest could tell the man was distraught. Baptiss stood, wild-faced, slightly dishevelled, red around the neck and with beads of perspiration that hung from his forehead. His lower lip twitched. The man was grappling—yes, grappling, the priest thought—with a most emotional problem. They didn't notice the faces of boys who peered with extreme caution, at the window.

'Someone,' Baptiss grated, 'has put pol thel!'

Yes, the man was disturbed. Nary a doubt. He had even slipped into the vernacular in a rage he could scarcely contain. He hadn't said coconut oil. He had spat the words 'pol thel' instead in the same way any red-blooded man would say 'fucking bastard'.

'P-pol thel?' the priest stammered.

'Come and see!' Baptiss hooted. 'Black smoke coming, all ruined!'

Outside the window, the heads disappeared. 'Pol thel,' Gogerly chuckled. Dabare covered his mouth. Lappen hissed, 'Don't laugh, men. If hear, hat for us.' Cautiously the four villains crept away.

'Put-put' marched into school the next day to be greeted with long, low-key hoots that seemed to bounce at him from every corner.

'*Adoo*! Pol Thel!'

'Put-put' was henceforth re-christened. And generations of schoolboys will never, ever forget 'Pol Thel' who taught grimly on, at St Peter's and then at the Royal College (where the nickname followed him) and until he retired after long, dogged and meritorious service to remain 'Pol Thel' until he died, and the writer even now demands that God keep him close, for blessed indeed are they that suffer schoolboy persecution for the sake of righteousness!

Art master de Ness was a short, scowly no-damn-nonsense man who wore white suits, badly-knotted ties and carried his cane up his coat sleeve. He believed in a sort of carpet bombing. Suddenly, magically, the cane would appear—an act of prestidigitation much dreaded—and the man would storm down the rows of desks flailing right and left while everybody scrambled on top of each other and bunched along the walls with fearful eyes while de Ness marched blindly on, slaying bottles of ink, boxes of crayons, and wheeling to advance on any boy who had not cleared out fast enough.

This usually created such an uproar that the entire row of classrooms suffered. De Ness was always 'Pappa' because he was as irascible and bad-tempered as a 'pappa'—a tempestuous old grandfather who liked to throw things at people. And yet, a glorious artist who became soft-faced and charming as he sat in the clutter of his Dehiwela home, smeared in oil paints and filling canvases with unbelievable patience.

Carloboy found St Peter's proper a rollercoaster. For one thing, life was full of great uncertainty. He was being tutored at home for his entrance examination to the Royal College. He was going on ten and was competing fiercely with Bryce Ratnayake for the favours of the pretty Christine Phoebus. His father had decided that boarding-school might be the best thing after all and had suddenly decided to can the Royal College and pack him off to St Thomas' College in Gurutalawa. There was talk of transfers and Anuradhapura and what about the promised bicycle?

'Sure to get transfer,' Sonnaboy would say. 'If put this big devil in boarding better.'

'But see the fees at Gurutalawa,' Beryl would object. 'Can't keep with Anna or somebody to go to school here? Can always come and see, no, when working to Colombo?'

'Ye-es. But who will see what he's up to? You think Anna can manage?'

Then, Glamour Boy got a wastepaper basket on his head and Carloboy, with others of his class, was sacked. 'You have the option to remove him from school,' Father Paris said. 'Then it will not go on his school-leaving certificate that he has been dismissed.'

Sonnaboy, amazingly, neither fretted nor fumed. He just said stonily, 'All right, I'll take him out. Have to sign anything?' He did, and for the second time in his ten years Carloboy had no school to go to. Instead, he was taken to the Royal College Hall where for six days he sat the entrance examination. And he passed and there was cake at home that day and his father celebrated with the neighbours and two bottles of arrack and roast pork and a stringhopper[1] dinner.

Also, there was the bicycle. A Raleigh racer, mind, with cable brakes and sweeping handlebars and three-speed gears too! Carloboy never loved anything more than that bike. He took it down the front steps, through the gate, patted the narrow saddle and the white dazzle of each wheel rim blazed in the sun. Everything around him was wrapped in tinsel—the high rear wall of Phoebus' house, the dense green hedge over the Wickremasinghe's low front wall, the road that called to him, the road that met Hampden Lane. All he had to do was ride there, turn left, then left again and he would be in 34th Lane where his Christine would be sitting on her garden swing. She would be in her short, embroidered frock and her gold-brown legs would glisten and her long black hair send straying strands across her cheeks. Carloboy knew he loved Christine. One day he would marry her, he told himself, and take off her clothes and put his fingers inside her the way that Joachim's servant had shown him. He could put his cock inside also. Who ever thought girls had holes like that, going all the way inside them? But today the bicycle was all. Nothing could ever take its place. His own bicycle.

He looked past his gate—a new gate after Daddy had wrecked the old one in that big fight with Sita's boyfriend[2]—and then at his father who said, 'Go on, ride it. Get up and go,' and the warning, 'Don't go too far. Only in the lane.' So he went, and tried out the gears and raced up Hampden Lane, swerving past old Mrs Pollocks who gave a whoop of alarm, then cruising, flaming-faced past Christine's front gate, ringing his bell, stopping to meet Bryce and Merril, and Christine

---

1. Steamed circlets of flour. The flour after steaming is pressed through a mould to drop in wriggly strands on the little basket-weave trays which are then re-steamed in batches until done. A favourite anytime meal in Sri Lanka.

2. For details of this incident, see *Yakada Yakā* (Penguin 1994).

hung on her gate and admired his bike with long-lashed eyes and Carloboy knew that this was a beautiful, beautiful day.

The chronicler hastens. For one thing much of the story of the von Bloss migration to Anuradhapura is told in *Yakada Yakā*. Suffice to say, Sonnaboy took his son to this malarial station where, as a temporary measure, he pushed the boy into St Joseph's school because (a) a lot of other Railway town boys went there and (b) because the boy couldn't be allowed to run wild while he worked train to Kankesanturai and Talaimannar and came to grips with the north of the island. Also, it was a time-killing exercise. He had arranged to keep Carloboy and Diana with Anna from next year. Carloboy would go to Royal, Diana to St Clare's. Carloboy could go to school on his bicycle . . . .

'*Anney* can't, men,' Anna had promptly said.

'Why?'

'You're mad or what. I can't take responsibility. If go loafing all over or meet with accident or something you'll come and scold. And roundabout here also all boys, no? Will join and go. Diana even never mind. Will go and come and closeby the school. Can go through Mallika Lane shortcut. But everyday cycling to Royal? See the way buses going on Highlevel road, will you.'

Colontota agreed. 'And small fellow also. See the distance. You know how he got knocked by that lorry, no?'

'He knocked the lorry,' Sonnaboy corrected, smiling faintly at the incident. 'Now he's more careful.'

'Careful *thamai*,'[1] Anna snorted, 'can see how he comes on the bike here, no? Coming like the wind and then catching the brake and tyres going *barass* in the sand.'

'Knocking the lorry' had been another grim business, made grimmer by an irate Mr de Kauwe who said that Carloboy had borrowed his son's bicycle and wrecked it. It had been

---

1. *Thamai*—a Sinhalese stress word to emphasize 'only' or 'this is' or 'this is it.' Used sarcastically too. Thus Anna would say 'Careful only', which is laden with sarcasm.

an impulse of the moment. There was this big lorry and it was going Carloboy's way. The boy decided to hitch a ride. He sped up on the borrowed bike, manoeuvred to spitting distance of tailboard and gripped it. The lorry rolled on and thus anchored, Carloboy free-wheeled with it. All he had to do was keep his handlebars in check with his left hand and be ready to swerve out of danger at the drop of a hat. But the lorry had braked without warning and Carloboy had been propelled into it. His head struck the metal hingepin and the bicycle slammed in, front wheel twisted. Men carried the unconscious boy into the Canal View restaurant and retrieved the bicycle that closely resembled a monkey puzzle. When Carloboy was revived he had a bump as large as an egg on his temple and it had turned an interesting blue with a patch of red that blotched around his eye and travelled around the cheekbone. 'Baby mad?' a man asked, 'to lorry hanging and going. Again like that doing don't, you heard.'

Carloboy stared woozily. His head swam, his hip hurt and he had to wheel a mauled bicycle to Ralston de Kauwe whose mother had hysterics and rushed to tell Beryl that her son came: 'Like dying, men, come quickly and take to the hospital. Like this the bump and whole side blue and red patch all over. Limping limping and came. Must see the bicycle. God knows what Kevin will say.'

Kevin didn't say much. All he asked was that Sonnaboy get Ralston's bike repaired. 'If fork is damaged then you have to get 'nother bike. Can't go to weld fork and allow to ride.'

And so, Carloboy was beaten (after the doctor has passed him as fit to be beaten, that is) and warned never to hang on to lorries, buses or any other vehicles which included municipal ambulances, co-operative store's lorries, Black Marias and dog-catcher vans. Oh, the beatings were part of that tender time.

Beryl would scream: 'Next time you hit Diana, get the broomstick across your back!'

Indeed, the girls ganged up. Through each day there was the constant whine. 'Mummeeee, this Carloboy is hitting!' which was the girls' way of keeping an elder brother in order. Carloboy would be smacked and the sisters would giggle. It became, to them, a nasty little game. 'Mummee, pinching me, this Carloboy!' or 'Mummee, look at this Carloboy!'

'Now what!' Beryl would shout.

'Saying will burn my doll!'

'Leave the girls alone! Go and take you books!' Beryl screams.

'What did I do? For lies they're shouting!' Carloboy yells.

'Shut up! Do what you're told! Don't you come to shout at me!'

'Fine thing, no? I didn't do anything!'

'Don't come to talk back. Know what a saint you are!'

'Bloody bitch!' Carloboy would hiss. 'You wait!'

'Mummee, now saying filthy words to us!'

'Will you get out of there! Come here! What did you say?'

'Nothing.'

'All lies, said bloody bitch. Marie also heard.'

Beryl slaps the boy fiercely. 'Sit in the hall and study!' she yells. 'And don't get up until I tell you!'

Yes, the beatings, the taunts of the sisters, were a part of it all. And the taunts especially. 'Bigger you get the worse you're becoming!' was a favourite indictment.

There was always the exhortation: 'Nice way you're behaving, no? Eldest must set an example to the others!' and those reminders which didn't actually mean a thing: 'See that Pinder boy. How he's studying. Why can't you also apply yourself a little? Brainless you're not, no?' (But there was also the favourite, much-used dismissal: 'Get out of my sight, you bloody brainless idiot!')

Truly, a ten-year-old never knew. The ob-la-di and the ob-la-da could fluster a boy for keeps. It was the same on that fateful First Holy Communion day when Beryl dressed her son in spectral white and pleaded that she couldn't go to church because she had 'the cooking also to do'. Sonnaboy just mooched around the garden in a singlet and khaki shorts and said. 'You're going? Receive, receive and come.

Told Mummy to make nice breakfast. Come straight after church, right? Bought currant loaf from F.X. Perera's also.'

Carloboy was disappointed. There was Norman Dekker. His parents were there. Some parents had even brought Kodak box cameras along. Families packed St Lawrence's. Carloboy saw Mrs Holsingher bearing down on him, 'Where? Your daddy an' mummy didn't come?'

'No, Aunty.'

'Sin, men,' Mrs Holsingher told pasty-faced Mrs Gray. 'Sent alone to receive and go. One even should have come.' So Carloboy joined the Dekkers who took him to their home in Manning Place where he had a slap-up breakfast and played cowboys and came home at lunch-time with a broken communion candle and a rumpled shirt and every bit of starch worked energetically out of his once immaculate trousers. He was beaten, of course, and on that day Sonnaboy used a hard Indian sandal which left large bruises on his calves and thighs. Nothing, he later said, is as good as a First Holy Whacking!

Schooling in Anuradhapura took time, but the move to that north-central town was greeted with a great relief by the Wellawatte neighbourhood. Old Phoebus was vastly relieved. He had vibrated indignantly when he discovered that his nine-year-old daughter—nine years old, mind!—was actually accepting love letters from Carloboy. And she was replying too!

'Damn cheek of the bugger!' he told Ratnayake. 'Can you imagine, men, at this age if doing like this what he will be like later!'

Victor Ratnayake leaned forward to mumble. 'Never liked them, men. Because my Ivy saying Mrs von Bloss is cousin or something I also put up. Engine drivers—what can you expect. And engine driver's son, no? My God, the dirty words he knows.'

'From over their wall passing to my one. And she also taking and writing. Lucky the wife told to see how our servant-boy is going near the wall when their servant-girl is sweeping. Caught the bugger and put two slaps. But keeping an eye I was and how, caught in the act! I saw, no. Coming to the wall and waiting. Just waiting. I was looking from the bathroom fanlight. Then Christine came running to the garage and I saw him wave the hand and give a paper. Straight away I went. Come here at once, I said and started crying and saying he gave and I didn't want to take and the bugger ran inside. Took the paper and how? My darling Christine and I love you and all the rubbish. Mother gave a good slapping!'

Ratnayake, who was trying to sort out this rigmarole said, 'Lucky didn't try with my ones.'

'Must have been afraid. Too close, no? When went to next lane that started all this.'

'So what did you do?'

'Do? Went to the wall and put a shout. Told that Poddi to call the mother. Came with big smile. When I showed the letter she got a shock. "I thought only children, no, and playing," she's saying.

'What to children, I said, from so early got such ideas from who, I asked. Not a word. Told will tell the father. Asked to give the letter to show so I gave.'

'I heard a big row there. Must have given the bugger tight.'

'I don't know. Didn't come to talk to me anyway.'

There was no need to. Sonnaboy thrashed his son until even Beryl had to intervene, and then with the mercury dropping, sat to marvel at a love letter that was too good to be true. 'From where he's learning to write like this?' he demanded. 'Must be reading all your love story magazines also!'

It had been a painful day for Carloboy who cried himself to sleep and woke with a stiff leg, a throbbing head and fever. Beryl dosed him with Venivelgeta and two Aspros and his sisters sniggered. True, Diana had pissed in fright when her brother received that terrible whacking, but she was now ready to sneer and mock. Carloboy thought it had to be very, very wrong to be drawn to a girl. It had to be . . . and his mind moved, drawing up pictures. When cousins Ivor and Marlene came to stay, Ivor would sleep with him and Marlene with his sister. He would go to Aunty

Elsie's and he had to sleep with Ian. It was not good, it would seem, to be with, play with, fight with, sleep with girls. He remembered the day his daddy had said: 'What? No friends for you to go and play with? Playing here with the girls? Trying to become a damn sissy?'

The problem was that Carloboy, at ten, was looking at girls in a strange and excitingly new light. He had even begun to cycle daily to Aunty Leah's where he looked long at Marlene, at her expressive eyes and rich lips and knew he loved her madly—just as he loved the Redlich girl and Yvette Foenander and Diedrie Ohlmus and Caryll Raux and the rafts of girls who came to church and Sunday school and the many he met on his way to school. So many, he had mused, and Christine next door and he would squeeze shut his eyes and try to imagine how Yvette or Carmen or Therese would look in their nakedness just as Joachim's servant woman looked each time she lured him to her bed.

So many girls. So many of his own cousins, too. And it was all bad, bad, bad! The beating told him so. It was bad to go to Joachim's again. Bad to look at Marlene the way he did. Girls were a source of trouble. 'I hate them, hate all,' he said and it grew in him, scorched him and his head buzzed until Beryl, finding him very hot and restless, placed an icebag on his head.

'That a way to hit?' she told Sonnaboy. 'Now high fever also.'

But recovery was swift enough, and with it the wisdom to realize that a certain wiliness of mind and secretiveness of spirit was needed if one had to consort, however innocently, with girls. Poddi, too, was soon to go away, and it seemed so easy to stand behind her as she made the beds and squeeze her breasts. Poddi would jump, then look and say, 'Apoi, baby no? I thought someone else.'

It was some comfort to a mind awash with doubts and fears. Poddi squeezed him. 'Now big, no? Those days so big only,' showing her little finger, and Carloboy followed her to the tiny servants' lavatory where she dropped her cloth and pressed him close and nuzzled his cheek and said, 'Baby to the mat come in the night,' and Carloboy said how he watched her in the light of the signal lamp and she never knew.

Yes, Anuradhapura put paid to a lot of things. Elsie's daughter Caroline, too, remembered how Carloboy had beat her over the head with a cricket bat. Beryl agreed that the boy was vicious. He was developing a hatred for his sisters and now this Caroline business.

'Lucky with the flat part that hit,' she said. 'Small crack. Had to rush to the hospital.'

'Where's that bugger? Break his bloody bones!'

When he flung a scissors at Marie, slicing open her forehead, Sonnaboy beat him senseless. Even Beryl found this quite unreal. 'How much going to hammer like this? Must catch and talk and see why he's behaving like this, no? Just hammering, hammering. See now, devil won't even cry!' And Beryl would drag her son away and get him to remove his tattered shirt and dab flavine on the places where the belt had broken the skin and say, 'Told, no, to leave the girls alone. Just going to fight and say things to them.'

'So they're the ones who start mocking and all,' Carloboy would protest.

When the transfer orders came, and Poddi had gone back to her village, and Sonnaboy had, with much bluster, cancelled wedding anniversary celebrations, Beryl said: 'Till end of the year even take an' go to Anuradhapura, men. If have a school for a little while even send there. Enough the botheration I will have with the girls and the baby also. And staying at Ma's in Millicent's room. Will drive everyone mad, that's what he'll do.'

Sonnaboy agreed. Beryl, as usual, was in the latter stages of pregnancy. The Mahadanghawatte Lane house was to be given up. She would stay with her mother until the baby was born. For a while, father and son would live in the new station. The neighbourhood cheered. It had been a fierce year and it was ending peacefully enough. 'Must say a thanksgiving Mass,' Mrs Swan told her husband. 'You wait and see will you. That small devil will be worse than the father!'

Old Albert Swan nodded. 'That Beryl gave the twenty rupees she borrowed?'

'Yes, yes. Came yesterday and gave. Going to stay at her mother's until go and get the house ready it seems.'

'My God, then that Carloboy still going to be loafing this side?'

'No, no. Taking and going. Next year will bring and come to go to Royal. How he passed the exam God only knows!'

Swan, who was an old Peterite, bristled. 'If couldn't learn at St Peter's you think he will learn there? You mark my words. No good. He'll come to no good.'

(Capitalize those last four words, please. A lot of people in a lot of places, in a lot of homes in lanes and gardens, from Racecourse Avenue to Pamankada, from Kohuwela to Dehiwela and beyond shared this conviction. Carloboy Prins von Bloss would Come To No Good!)

CHAPTER NINE

This, readers will say, is simply not done. Why should we read *Yakada Yakā* (or whatever the outlandish title of that book is) to learn about Anuradhapura? It's not fair!

You're right, of course, and I do beg your pardon, but I don't wish to do better or worse than what has already been recorded. I abhor re-telling and, pardon again my temerity, if you haven't read *Yakada Yakā*, you really should. Why? Because I wrote it, of course, and don't you want to know what the blue blazes a *Yakada Yakā* is? Case dismissed!

Anuradhapura could best be described as a place where boys became men and railwaymen became boys. Carloboy's world was railway town, the big irrigation reservoirs characteristic of this arid region, the Malwatte River (Oya in Sinhalese), dry jungles full of snakes and hook thorn creepers, a bustling railway yard, ponies to ride, fish to catch, go catapulting, and later, air rifle hunting and rides on his father's engine to the northern peninsula where stationmasters sucked foul, black Jaffna cigars and made weird sounds with their whistles. He also raised rabbits.

The chronicler will pass lightly over the short, catch-breath time Carloboy spent at the local St Joseph's school. He was in and out before one could shout 'Fire!' which was what the scamps of railway town did shout (and danced like crazy Red Indians too) when a classroom went up in flames.

It had to be the work of a railway town boy. Stout cadjan classrooms burn easily, true, but there had to be a spark. By the time water was toted in insufficient buckets, the classroom was overdone. Benches were saved as well as the blackboard and easel and a few tables. The rest became smoking wood and floating cinders that sorely threatened the rest of the makeshift school. The magnifying glass was his father's, he said, and he had 'borrowed' it. But he had given it to Vanderputt to examine some kind of a bug that had lodged between the boy's toes. These bugs would, for nobody bothered to wear shoes to school.

Some came in slippers because their mothers insisted, but most trooped in barefooted. Lots of earnest village boys, trying hard to learn, and a smattering of railway town ruffians who were, like Carloboy, between schools and merely marking time.

'Go home,' the long-nosed principal told Carloboy, 'and don't come back. Not learning, only coming, fooling and going. And for what you're coming? Next year your father putting you in Colombo school. So go then. All you fellows only coming here two-three months and going. And what about the classroom? Who's going to pay? Going to write to all your parents to pay.'

Sonnaboy couldn't believe his eyes. 'What? Why I must pay? You burnt the bloody school?'

Carloboy shook his head.

'Then who?'

Carloboy stared, then shrugged dumbly.

Driver Alfie Ribeira came to the fence. 'Oy, von Bloss, you also got letter from that school. Telling our buggers burnt the classroom and asking forty rupees.'

'Yes, men, I also got. Telling not to send to school again, also.'

'Same thing for me also. Edna is damn wild. At least had some peace in the mornings. So what to do?'

'Pay and put, men. If go and tell the police or something . . .'

'But Anton didn't do anything. Your bugger brought a magnifying glass or something. Must have held to the sun and burnt the cadjan.'

'What! What magnifying glass? You took from my desk?' That called for a swat on the head, and Carloboy decided he had got out of that pickle very lightly indeed. Beryl, at her mother's, was startled. 'My God, see what have been going and doing . . . set fire to the school! Here Sonnaboy writing and saying.'

Florrie da Brea stopped knitting. 'How?'

'Who knows how. Now taking and going all over on the engine. Allowing to run wild.'

'That even never mind, child,' Florrie said piously. 'With the father, so can keep the eye on him.'

Beryl nodded. 'Good thing didn't keep here. Dance I'll have with big stomach and all.' And Florrie mentally said a fervent Amen.

And yet, the chronicler maintains, Anuradhapura injected a strong dose of responsibility into the boys who were growing hard-muscled, berry brown, jungle-wise and ready to meet whatever was tossed at them. There were, in many railway bungalows, ponies. These were bought, quite wild and unbroken from Mannar, transported by railway wagon. It was always a celebration of the highest order when a pony arrived. Driver Benny Fernando comes home whooping. 'There, Benno,' he carols, 'brought pony for you. Run to the station and see. Told to tie near the water tank and keep. Tell the S.M., I'll come to take right?'

Benno Fernando is ecstatic. This is an event to be shared. His own pony. The pony, as the stationmaster later tells Vanderputt, is 'scared shitless'. It is surrounded by whooping boys and escorted home. It bites Terence Edema and contrives to kick Anton Ribeira in the midriff. Benno clings on to the rope around its neck and the boys yell and stay clear of its hooves and urge Benno to 'get on top and ride, men,' which he tries to do and which the pony strongly objects to. One bleeding head, one puffy arm and many scratched and limping legs later the pony is in the Fernando's garden where it rolls its eyes and shows wicked teeth and tosses its head. A man from the railway line rooms is brought in to make the beast tractable, muzzle it, get a halter on and a bit. 'Now get up and go must,' he informs. 'Rope hold and go.'

Beryl gets another letter. 'My lord, can see what's happening now. Riding horses all over.'

'Who, child?'

'That small devil, who else?'

'From where getting horses?'

'Bringing for the children. Fell in the drain also and scraped all over.'

'Who? The horse?'

'That Carloboy. Who else?'

Florrie da Brea has one answer. 'You light a candle, child, and pray to St Anthony. Not good telling all this. Just getting upset.'

'Who's upset?' Beryl flames. 'Wait till I go there, will you. Skin him alive. Father and son. One is no better than the other!'

Florrie sighes.

High jinks aside, as the chronicler has said, it was also a slow process of realization for these candidates for maternal flaying. Those were, as any Irishman would say, the 'good owd days' with each railway town rascal a 'regular broth of a boy'. They rode rattletrap bicycles and their wild ponies, shaggy-maned and chins flecked with spittle. They carried Daisy airguns, point two-two's and catapults. The mornings were always diamond blue and white and butterflies romped, blowing kisses at the lantana bushes.

The railway bungalow Sonnaboy occupied was a stone's throw from the station. Opposite, to the right, was the office of the Railway Transportation Superintendent who was Trans to railway folk and whom Sonnaboy called Trance. The Trans would smile and wave. He never spotted the difference.

It was truly a boy's world. They fished and hunted and roamed the scrubs, the wild woodlands, all olive and jade, the tank country where the large man-made irrigation reservoirs (tanks) lay breathless in the sun, and the marsh country.

Let's consider one rather unusual (unusual for Carloboy, that is) morning, shall we? He lazed on the upstairs balcony gazing quite disinterestedly into the lacy tangle of the upper foliage of the weralu (*Eleocarpus serratus*) tree. Bright, bud-like leaves constantly slapping at each other like a million midgets playing pat-a-cake in the breeze. Birds favoured this tree, which housed a large pair of rat snakes at its roots, especially the barbet, the forest bul-bul, the leaf bird, the white-eye. They would enter, flash a painted breast or rump for a heartbeat, then disappear. Only when they rummaged around could Carloboy spot them—inquisitive eyes, Punch and Judy head-bobs. The camouflage of the weralu was really superb.

The boy wanted to stir himself, but there are some haunting mornings when the most energetic cannot get started. There was a mesmeric quality about the lazy clouds. He saw the Indian roller, all lavender and dusky blue, sitting motionless on a telegraph post. Over the northern tree line a hawk eagle was gliding in a slow, patient arc over twisted etamba (*Magnifera zeylanica*) and badulla (*Semcarpus obscura*) which masked the banks of the Malwatte river. The eagle did not seem to move in its long reconnoitre, his pre-noon sweep for food. Why then, thought Carloboy, should I?

But he went into the garden anyway. He would go to the river and sit under the kotamba (*Terminalia catappa*) and drowse and see the sun patterns jigsawing on the water. He stuffed his catapult into his pocket. No telling, but he could bag a thalagoya—the iguana—and Daddy liked thalagoya flesh.

And then he saw that little pest. Tony de Zilva. The diminutive fellow, scarcely eight, who would trail behind the rest of the boys, catapult in hand, pockets bulging with pebbles. Tony was a nuisance. He couldn't shoot. When they fished he would tangle the lines or splash around and yell exultantly each time his float registered a nibble. He refused to take aim, and seemed to enjoy shooting off his pebbles and was quite unabashed at the jibes.

'What's the matter? You came to chase the birds?' Edema would cackle.

Tony was a regular spoiler, too. He would be the first to cut his leg, or lose a slipper, or get a thorn in his foot or trip, fall and skin his knees. It became a game of sorts. 'Let's scoot before that small bugger comes,' Benno would say. But Tony would sniff around in search of the pack. An eager puppy of a boy, anxious to belong, never realizing how patiently or impatiently he was endured.

'Look at me,' he would call, 'I'm going to shoot that bird.'

The bird was a blur of green perched far in a tree—a bee-eater with its twin-wand tail and pirate patch eyes. The pebble left the rubbers to fall twenty feet short.

'Shoot? Can't shoot for toffee!' Benno would chortle. There would be the usual unkind laughter. 'What? Your mummy made that 'pult?' and Tony would blink quickly. He always blinked.

Then he stopped tagging along. He may have realized that he was odd man out or who knows, he could no longer blink away those tears. Carloboy was shocked. There he was in the opposite garden. The bungalow was untenanted, the garden weedy, full of four o'clock flowers and lantana. Tony was parked under a bushy everlasting tree laden with purple blossom that stood in mauve-pink candle clusters on an olive-grey birthday cake. On the empty veranda was a pile of pebbles, and, in a neat row were the stiffening coloured corpses of two azure flycatchers, a flowerpecker and a small, drab tailorbird.

Even as Carloboy strode to the gate, the catapult twanged. He saw a beautiful sunbird drop and there was a grin of triumph on the face of the executioner. The sunbird lay, its blue sheen like jewelled electricity, flaring down the side of its neck. Purple gems glistened on its jet rump. The little boy seized it, added it to the row of the dead—a row of setting colour, deep-sea blues, buttery yellows, scarlet-browns and fern greens.

Carloboy seized the scamp, swatted him across the head, tore the rubbers off the 'pult. 'Bloody small shit!' he shouted. 'Look what you're doing!'

Tony blubbered, tried to run but he was gripped by his collar.

'So this is what you're doing these days? Coming here and killing all the small birds! Easy, no? Just stand under and shoot!'

Oh yes, the boys had their code. Nobody considered the tiny white-eye or the tit any sort of prize. They hunted the unwieldy iguana and went after crane and bronze pigeon or ash doves. The day's bag, including the catfish they caught would feature in a backyard cook-out. They would enjoy the feast, Boy Scout fashion, while sympathetic servants provided the oil, salt, firewood and even prepared the iguana flesh in the kitchen to become an additional dinner dish.

'Two feet!' Carloboy gritted. 'Damn shit! Standing only two feet under and shooting. How to miss! And see the amount of birds coming here.' He shook the boy. 'An' what you're going to do? Just throw in the drain and go?'

'I wanted to bring and show,' the boy mumbled.

'Show? For what to show. To show you can shoot? You think this is hunting? Come go, I'll tell your mummy what you're doing.'

'Don't, *anney*. I won't again. I won't!'

'Not won't, don't! You come here again to see. Give that karu[1] here. Catch you with a catapult again I'll hammer you properly!'

Tony fled. And yes, Carloboy was growing up. Not growing up in the sense that he was approaching manhood, but there was an overall acceptance of being a boy and living this boyhood in the accepted boyish way—serious at times, devil-may-care at others. Anuradhapura seemed to wash away many of the indignities of mind and soul he had been a victim to. It was a serious business, being a boy. Serious enough to know the difference between the sport of the hunt and the vile slaughter he had just witnessed. Above all, Anuradhapura allowed him to get on with this business of being a boy. There were no servant-girls to inveigle him, no adults to abuse his body, no vulgarity, smut, sexual assaults. Nor did he dwell on any of what had happened in the not too distant past. All he wished for was to enjoy each

---

1. The forked stick of the catapult.

golden day to the full. Wisdom, too, came in on tiptoe at times, with a clatter of realization at others. He bred rabbits: brought home creatures to feed, delight in and study; knew the snakes to avoid, the reptiles he could handle and how to bait a hook that would drag in the biggest catfish from the wewas or tanks. He learnt to avoid the marsh grass at dusk because the vipers would be hunting but had the confidence to raise the sluggish Russel's viper with a bent stick at midday because, as everyone knew, the viper would lie in a daze of sleep when the sun was hottest.

He knew he had but a short time for the New Year would deprive him, term by term, of this magical place. So he roamed, questing, discovering, sometimes quite alone, full of the stuff of dreams and imaginings. Red clay roads, forest tracks, springy river banks, scrub and marsh fringed with copper reeds and lilac grass flowers. And one day he found the Tree. There was no other like it—this solitary Elephant Tree[1] as the natives called it.

Everything else grew in profusion: thorny woodapple, spreading margosa, mahogany, bombu,[2] ironwood and the Bo Tree[3]—but this Elephant Tree was a loner, single, unique, an exciting find. Carloboy would trot, almost a mile, just to sit beside it, wonder at it and ask villagers why it waved its roots in the air. It was a lot later that he learned that it was the baobab—the African *Adansonia digitata*, probably introduced to Ceylon by Arab traders many centuries ago.

'You mean they came and planted this tree here?' he asked driver Don, who laughed.

'That must have grown long time ago,' Don said.

'How long?'

'Who knows. Hundred years may be. Have some more towards Vavuniya and places. They are protected.'

'Why?'

'Because rare, son. Won't allow anyone to cut down.'

---

1. The Sinhalese call it Aliya gaha (Elephant Tree—the baobab).

2. *Symplocos cochin-chinensis*.

3. *Ficus religiosa*.

Carloboy's fascination for the baobab grew. For one thing it was a most curious tree. Such an immense trunk, and so tough-skinned the bark. 'Just like elephant skin,' Don said and Carloboy nodded.

'Don't know if that's why they are saying Elephant Tree. But, Uncle Don, not a leaf on it.'

Don had a lot of patience with ten-year-olds. Also, despite the general headshakings that Carloboy was, after all, his father's son ('and if father is playing the devil son will be ten times worse!') Don liked the earnest-eyed boy who could still make any adult uncomfortable with his curious stare. 'Come go and see this tree of yours,' he said, and they went and spoke to the villagers and learned that in the rainy time the baobab did put out dark green leaves in tufts, like the fingers of a hand. There are also dingy white flowers that hang on stalks and melon-sized fruits.

'Monkeys very much like,' a man said, 'in gangs they come and fruit all eat.'

Anuradhapura is hot and tortuously dry for nine months of the year. It waits for the north-east monsoon to replenish itself between November and January. Carloboy never saw his tree with its new life in the wet months. All he knew was that it was some strange, upside-down giant, squiggling at the sky with its naked, stubby fingers.

Don was amused at first, then grew just as excited. 'Here,' he called, 'that man that day said about monkeys coming and eating the fruit, no? Come and see in this book. Here the tree. Take and read. In West Africa calling it upside down tree. There the people used to say that God planted the tree the right way but the devil got angry and pulled it out and planted it upside down. And because monkeys like, some people saying it is Monkey Bread tree.'

Carloboy was happy. He went to Benno. 'How? What you're doing today. Can bring your pony and come?'

'Where to?'

Carloboy told him.

'You want to measure a tree?'

'Yes.'

'For why?'

118

'Because it's bigger than all the trees here. See and bring a measuring tape if have.'

Benno was always ready to fall in with any schemes, even if he considered them hare-brained and totally incomprehensible. He riffled his mother's sewing basket. They trotted off.

And even Benno was impressed. When they recorded its girth at sixty-one feet after many false starts, he gave a low whistle and admitted it was like nothing he had ever seen. 'How did you find this thing? Just came loafing?'

Carloboy was pleased. 'Can you climb?'

Benno looked doubtful. 'Hard, men, nowhere to put the leg and go up even. My God men, must be about thirty feet up, no?'

They heeled the pony for a hectic dash into town, taking the railway level crossing in grand style. Racing ponies always annoyed the sub postmaster who nipped out of his office to shake a fist at their flying backs. Don, too, was amused. 'You know, son, I don't think even the Forest Department knows about your tree. In the forestry office I asked some fellows. They're telling have some baobabs in Vavuniya side and Kantalai and some in the Wipattu Park[1] but nothing here.'

'But if they don't know then nobody to tell anyone it is protected,' the boy cried. 'Supposing some people cut it?'

Don raised an eyebrow. 'Hey, hey, what you're so upset about. Only an old tree, no?'

In Don's house was a genuine grandfather clock. He was so proud of it. A family heirloom, he would say, over 150 years old. It stood in the corner of his hall, polished wood gleaming, brass fittings always aglow and its pendulum would swing in a sort of dignified, majestic way. Worth thousands and thousands, Don would say and expect visitors to regard it with due awe and reverence.

Carloboy struggled for words to explain, then said, 'It's like your clock,' and Don ruffled the boy's hair and said,

---

1. A national reserve in the north-west of the island.

'You know, son, you're right. You go and read that book I gave you.'

Carlboy would sit against his tree through warm mornings and hot afternoons and in the evenings when the air was tempered with a breeze and the rain trees sighed in a lovesick way. 'One of the oldest living trees in the world,' the book said, 'Adanson found them, wrote about them and they were named after him. He said that the African baobabs are over 5000 years old. Alexander von Humboldt called them the oldest, organic monument of our planet. Age is equated with girth. A hundred feet in circumference would make such a tree 1400 years old.' Carlboy worked out the age of his tree unitarily and told Uncle Don his tree was 850 years old. Don told Sonnaboy and Beryl was startled to learn that her son was 'dancing with some elephant tree or something.'

'See what saying now,' she told her mother, 'that small devil went and found an elephant tree. Never heard such nonsense.'

'Tell to lock in the house even and keep, child. If elephants have on the tree mustn't go near, no?'

'Told, no, how many times, to keep an eye on that devil. Mus' be drinking with the other drivers and don't care what that one is up to!'

'That one' or 'that devil' as his mother always called him, had no time for maternal endearments or blandishments. Stranger things than a mother's cross moods fire a boy's imagination. His book said how long ago, French sailors off the coast of west Africa saw the baobab's dark green foliage and called that westerly headland Cape Verde. He would go to his tree, run his hands over the elephant-skin bark. Villagers came to sit with him, share his enthusiasm.

'Rain time we fruit breaking,' said an ancient fellow, 'for medicine making. For skin trouble, sores, stomach pain, when fever getting, very good. But elephant if come then trouble. Elephant tree eating. Very soft it is,' and with a curved knife the man hacked away the bark and plunged in his blade.

Carlboy was shocked. How could he know that his giant was so vulnerable? Such clay feet, so to say. Beneath the bark was a light, spongy wood.

The old man cackled. 'This tree anyhow dying won't.' He showed where, in patches, the inner bast had been hacked away to make rope to tether buffalo. 'From this rope very strong. Elephant even tying up can. Baby afraid don't get. This tree dying won't. Two-three years before elephants coming tree all ate. Even that dying did not.'

The conversation was like a challenge tossed to fate. Elephants did trundle through the very next day—and there stood their favourite dish. Carloboy stood aghast as villagers crowded around. He felt as though he had lost the bottom of his stomach. His tree . . . his tree had been almost completely gouged out. Its gnarled tentacles of stubby branchlets actually teetered in the breeze like some gigantic crow's nest ready to topple at the slightest provocation.

'Six elephant,' a woman jabbered, 'small two ones also. Came and rub and rub then with the heads banging and pushing pushing.' The cow elephants had scooped out the fine inner fibre to feed their calves. The tree lay, almost on its side. Its inner wood, attacked by some sort of fungus, was so brittle, so porous, that it was easy to scoop into. Such a big, bulky trunk. Carloboy's eyes smarted. It was so . . . so . . . grandfather clockish, he thought wildly, yet a child could tear it apart!

The boy felt pain. His giant had cheated. He went home, downcast and Sonnaboy said, 'There, Uncle Don gave a book for you. A present, he said. Bought at Caves bookshop in Colombo and brought.'

Carloboy looked at it without much interest. *Fantastic Trees* by Edwin A. Menninger. Don had scribbled, 'All you want to know about the baobab.' Carloboy put it away and withdrew into a shell of self-pity. 'All I want to know,' he muttered fiercely, 'as if I don't know.'

He spent his days with the gang, collecting a gunny sack of leaves each morning for his rabbits, fishing, riding into town where behind the huge cupola of the Ruvanweliseya[1] the boys trained their catapults on the crude nests of roosting

---

1. An ancient and one of the greatest Buddhist dagobas in the island. It was built by hero-king Dutugemunu.

cranes. Cranes were fishy if cooked, but made an excellent meal when roasted outdoors. Sometimes, as a bird crashed down, it would tumble a nest too and when some po-faced pilgrims suddenly received a clutch of pale-blue eggs on their heads and began to shriek 'Saadhu saadhu!'[1] in contralto, locals chased the gang away with threats that this was a sacred city and a Buddhist city and 'if coming to kill birds and throw eggs catch and put in the police station!'

This cheered the boys no end and Carloboy shed that queer sense of injustice that had cloaked him. And then he met that old villager again. The man was carrying a straw bag of red peppers on his head. 'Ah, baby,' he said toothlessly, 'now coming not. Now *aliya gaha* to see coming not?'

'Now dead must be.'

'Dead? How to die? I said, no, dying won't. Elephant to ground pushing even, dying not. Go and see, will you.'

That evening twelve railway town boys made pilgrimage. They stole pomegranates and somebody broke Mr Wickremasinghe's window and Benno snagged his shirt on a fence and ripped his sleeve—but at the end of the trail there squatted the tree. Yes, squatted, yet proud, strong, enduring. David Livingston wrote once that he had seen baobab trees fallen, lying on the ground, yet continuing to grow. This was their magic.

For the first time that evening Carloboy really read Menninger . . . and understood the true wonder of his tree, its amazing vitality, its refusal to die, the phoenix of the plant kingdom. The days were becoming all too short. His daddy would take him to Colombo for Christmas and it would be the usual rounds of visits and wishes and eating cake and people to jostle and the roar of traffic and the smoke-smelling gritty city dust. He hated it. And he had a baby brother too and Mummy and all else would go back to Anuradhapura while Diana and he would be cooped in Aunty Anna's tiny room with its black doors and brown-stained glass and look out of window bars to see

---

1. A call of praise and reverence just a 'Hosannah' or 'amen' would apply in Christianity.

Mr Colontota's cluster of ground orchids that straggled drunkenly and the high wall which hid the houses beyond.

He felt a shiver and clenched his fists. Royal College. A new place to go, learn, be caned, oh yes, be caned. Some things are too much for a free-spirited boy to absorb. He lay in bed and scowled. 'I hate it,' he muttered and lay for a long time that night, staring into the darkness.

CHAPTER TEN

Suddenly, the Burghers of Ceylon—and to a large measure, the people of Ceylon—took the Americans to their hearts. The British, who fretted and strutted the stage, were large in their claims that they were winning the war. Of course they were. But American derring-do held centre stage. The first all-American air raid on Germany—that audacious daylight attack on Wilhelmshaven—was, as everyone said, a dilly. It made Hitler 'piss his pants' as engine driver Bertie Arnolda said, and Sonnaboy von Bloss was quite overwhelmed by the fact that Germany had begun civil conscription of women. The Burghers didn't take to the Russians as cordially. The news that Leningrad had been liberated occasioned a few desultory 'ohs' and 'ahs'. 'Godless Russians' as Leah de Mello always called them, were beyond the pale. Wasn't Father Sebastian, the new priest at St Lawrence's, always pleading with his parishioners for the conversion of Russia?

The problem with the British, as George Orwell so succinctly put it[1] was that deep down, 'the mass of the people are without military knowledge or tradition and their attitude towards war is invariably defensive.' No one tried

---

1. 'England, your England' – George Orwell, *Selected Essays* (Penguin, 1957).

telling that to the bristly British who held the reins, but even those who lorded it in the plantations of tea and rubber would sit in their airy verandas and the wife would cast baby blue eyes on the tea-cushioned mountains and hubby would sniff appreciatively at his b. and s. and think that it was certainly a great pity about those poor perishers back home and, Victoria Cross or no, this was the life!

Even when the soldiers paraded out of St Peter's, band leading, it was said that they sang:

I don't want to join the bloody Army
I don't want to go to fucking war
I want no more to roam
I'd rather stay at home
Living on the earnings of a whore!

Frankly, the only enemy the 'Tommy' ever acknowledged openly was his own sergeant-major!

Carloboy, pushed into the huge red brick building which was the Royal College, found the school imposing, quite unnerving and he was simply borne in, as by a tide of scurrying, bumping, thumping boys of every shape and size. Old Fernando, the Registrar, collared him, eyed him narrowly and gave his famous 'silly grin'. 'Form One C,' he said, 'upstairs, turn right, go to the end,' and there sat fuzzy-haired Mr Naths with his fat cheeks and black face and a chalk-dusted coat who surveyed this new batch of boys with a look that was quite paternal.

Linton Jayasekera hissed, 'You can fight? I'm the strongest here. If you think you're big, challenge you to a fight after school!'

Carloboy stared, shook his head ever so slightly and opened his *New Everyday Classics*. Sonnaboy had groaned at the booklist. It necessitated a special trip to Wahids in Bambalapitiya where thousands, he was sure, of other parents had also come, waving their lists, demanding attention.

Royal had its share of masters, and in heaping quantities at that. 'Bada' Eddie was headmaster. He had two canes, wore grey suits, sweated, and waited for boys to be 'sent' for punishment. There was 'Cow-pox' Abey who liked to slap boys. He considered a slap a form of art. 'Keep your face at the correct angle!' he would say, and the victim would assume a love-bird head position and, satisfied with the stance, Abey would then parade the class expounding on the sins of the sufferer who developed a crick in his neck and the look of a long distance runner who suddenly finds the finish line receding before his eyes. Oh, the slap is duly administered, of course, but the boy is stiff-necked for a further ten minutes and wonders if a slap on the other side on his face would help.

'Connor' Rasana was just that. He was inducted as a temp . . . and stayed. He was the filler-in whenever the regulars absented themselves and the boys would relax and grin hugely and lead the poor man into all manner of outlandish subjects where extrication was a source of much belly-laughing and desk thumping.

'Sir,' said Carloboy, 'in the old days camels and leopards used to mate.'

'Hmm. In the old days had a lot of different animals.'

'Yes, sir. And they were called cameleopards. Sir, how did the camel and leopard mate?'

'That's not a thing for you to know,'

'But sir, the leopard is in our jungles, no? And the camel is in the desert.'

'Those days were different.'

'But how, sir?'

History was interesting too, especially when 'Connor' stood in and gazed vacantly at the textbook. He would clear his throat, look importantly through his gold-rimmed spectacles. 'Today we are going to talk about the Six Year War. This Six Year War went on for six long years . . . von Bloss!'

'Sir? Me, sir?'

'Yes, you. If the war went on for ten years what will they call it?'

'Who, sir?'

'Anybody. That's not my question.'

'Ten Year War, sir.'

The man beams. 'Very good, very good. Today you're very bright. Abdi! What are you doing with your head inside the desk?'

'Pocket Billiards' was Mr Rupa who always had his hands in his pockets in which he played, possibly, with his keys or small coin or whatever his pockets contained. This, naturally, caused the usual boyish interest. They immediately seized on the notion that the man was playing with his testicles, hence the name. 'Lapaya' was the master who taught Sinhalese and there was 'Penda' who had flabby cheeks, taught Latin and spent long minutes of every period stuffing his charges with the proper declining of Penda. '*Penda, Pendere, Peppendi, Pensum*' he would keep bleating until the name stuck. Cantle was scoutmaster, drill master, cadet master and games master. Stuck, as he was, with boys in gym shorts and swimming trunks and with a hail-fellow-well-met smile that was accompanied by much back-slapping and general bonhomie, the school accepted his geniality and thought it needed dissection. Boys had been taken in by such jolly types before. A man would be so nice, so positively avuncular, and then, having wheedled his way past lowered defences, cup his victim. Most uncharitably, they labelled him 'Cupper' and senior boys would tell wide-eyed first formers, 'You be careful. Catch and cup you, that's what he'll do.' The fact that Cantle was also the boarding master, strengthened the myth.

The school was too prestigious for words. A school for the élite, although 'free'. The richest, most influential and important of Colombo's society had their children firmly ensconced in Royal where the motto is *Disce aut Discede*[1] and the colours are blue, gold and blue and the honour boards in the hall commemorate the scholastic achievements and the laurels won, of some of Sri Lanka's greatest sons. Principal, J.C.A. Corea, ruled the roost; but the man who terrorized both big and small fry and had a bullet head and a thick, muscular neck and kept six canes on his rack and sat

---

1. Learn or Depart.

in state in a large room hemmed in by bookcases, a globe, important-looking files, several prize shields and cups and a lot of college paraphernalia was 'Jowl Kula who caned Carloboy whenever he got the opportunity—which, alas, was frequent.

The chronicler will not dwell overly on those early years. Nobody paid much attention to first formers except the more randy prefects who had their own room and were allowed a measure of disciplinary enforcement. Prefectship came with honours gained—a swimming blue or a good scholastic record or after gaining colours at cricket and the merit of donning the school blazer. Eleven-year- and ten-year-old first formers were sized up for their 'cabbage' quality and a cabbage was a boy who was eminently 'cuppable'.

Strange stories would circulate with increasing frequency. Gustavus Ranks, it was said, was taken by three prefects into their 'study' where his trousers were pulled down, after which he was treated to many close encounters and then had had the tip of his foreskin burnt with a lighted cigarette! And again, there was Jayaraj who was fair, limpid-eyed, delicately featured and shy. Those who declared that they had succeeded in drawing him behind the tuck shop and gaining much satisfaction in the events that immediately followed, were given the dubious title 'cup god' and Jayaraj was acknowledged as being a 'pukka cabbage bugger'.

Carloboy, too, fell into this category but he had a working knowledge of what to expect and how to avoid the aftermath of those peremptory bum-squeezes at assembly and the lewder advances of the bigger boys. Also, Anuradhapura had made him whip-strong and independent. It was better, he decided, to be a maniac of sorts, lead the ragging, boo the loudest and be a pain in the butt to all and sundry, thus earning universal notoriety as a hellion and best left to create those many disasters, in school and out, which only he could do best. Let's put it this way. When Sonnaboy wished to place his second son, David, in Royal, Principal Corea shuddered. 'One von Bloss is enough!' he said and refused to unbend—not for all the fair maids in Christendom!

'You can see,' Sonnaboy had said (and that was years later), 'masters are biting the nails when even talking about you!'

Yes, Carloboy made his own space, did his own thing, was fierce in body and spirit and, yes, *disced* well enough so that he couldn't be faulted enough to be *disceded!* Aunty Anna, of course, complained to Sonnaboy each time he worked train to Colombo and came to see how his children fared, that she was losing 'Pounds, men, pounds.'

'So good, no? Too fat you are. If unlock the piano even and keep he will play and be quiet.' Anna, let it be known, had bought Sonnaboy's piano and was very proud of her purchase. She would sit at it with fat fingers that buried themselves into the keys and found chords that, even in these raucous days, are still to be discovered. Carloboy, who had developed a lively knack of playing anything 'by ear' was furious to know that *his* piano had been sold and more furious when his aunt kept it locked. 'Not for you to just thump and spoil,' she had said, 'when go out of tune will have to call that Ephraums to repair and you think your father will pay?'

Carloboy told Diana, 'How? Our piano! All those days we played and nobody said thumping. Let lock and keep. Wait will you and see what I'll do!'

What he did was spectacular enough. He found, in the tiny backyard with its old crates and a woebegone mattress and old strips of wire netting, a nest of rats. Mother rat had made a cosy burrow in the old fibre mattress. It was so simple to raise the top of the Metzler and pop four baby rats in. They disappeared among the ranks of wood and felt with tinny squeaks and found their new home vastly interesting. And that, he said to himself later, was that.

He disliked Mr Colontota who only ate fish in whatever form it was produced and was the fussiest, stuffiest person he knew. He also disliked living in a room with Diana who still 'pippied' to many disapproving 'chuk-chucks' by Anna and had to be taken to St Clare's where she grew very surly and strange, surrounded, as she was, by Sinhalese girls who were more robust in manners and physique. She would come in, out of the bathroom, in a thin slip and sit on her bed. Then, cloth in hand, raise a leg to wipe her feet. This, Carloboy knew, was the only thing interesting about his sister. Diana, in all innocence would wipe one foot at a time, propping each on the bed, and the boy would stare at her vagina with its very protuberant, red clitoris and slip a hand into his pocket to restrain his own impatient penis.

Yet, he switched off quickly enough and strode out to eat the buttered hoppers[1] with a ladle of yesterday evening's gravy, pick up his books and go to school. It was a long while before Anna told Sonnaboy that she had reached the end of her tether.

'Next door going whole evening and dancing with that Gerard and Anton and whole clique of boys in the behind garden. Going to play, fighting, people coming to complain. Sent, men, to front house for Sinhalese tuition. Big girl said will teach. Don't know what he's doing there, but came to the wall to tell not to send anymore. Won't listen to anything. Mr Colon said will give with the cane and how the cheek? Saying you're not my father. *Anney* can't keep, men. Diana even never mind but I have to sit in the bathroom to wash the sheet and pippie clothes every day. See, will you, both have bad reports. Mr Colon also grumbling and saying why took . . .' Anna sighs, clutches her rosary in a kind of desperation, 'You can't put anywhere else, men?'

'After the holidays will see. Now Easter holidays also close, no?'

'So how Beryl and the small ones. Like the place?'

'They're all right. Baby had cold and cough but now all right. If ask Leah don't know if can take Carloboy, no?'

'Ask to see. There even Ivor also so have some company even. And lot of friends roundabout, no, near your old house.'

'I'll ask anyway. For this term only you keep, will you.'

Carloboy, who had his ears wrung and was preached an Epistle with more foul language that ever the Ephesians heard in their heyday, glared at Aunty Anna. 'Waiting till

---

1. A thin griddle cake made of flour and fermented coconut water.

Daddy comes to complain,' he glowered, 'why you said for us to come and stay here, then?'

'Don't come to talk to me like that!' Anna would quiver. 'Your father must know what you're up to!'

The boy had the last word. At his room door he said, 'Good thing after holidays won't come here,' then thought a while and loosed a cutting shaft, 'Good thing you haven't children. If had they will go and commit suicide or something!'

Anna, aghast, sank into the lounger where Colontota found her red-eyed and palpitating extraordinarily. Angered, he banged on the children's door. 'Come here at once!' he shouted. Carloboy refused the invitation. Diana began to cry.

'You shut up!' he hissed. 'Let bang. If break, his door, not ours!'

'No dinner for you if you don't come out!'

It did not turn the trick. Answer, as from the oysters of the poem, there was none . . .

The overall gut cancer of the piano was discovered long after Sonnaboy took his children to Anuradhapura. It was the slattern, Sumana, who inhabited Anna's kitchen who raised the alarm with a screech which had its own poetry: '*Aiyoo! meeyo!*[1]' When sweeping the hall she had seen a nasty piece of vermin ooze out from the slot where the floor pedals were, flung the broom upwards in alarm and given vent to this particular emotion. Stripped to its action, the piano was a sorry sight. Gerard and Anton were hauled in from next-door to evict the rats, which they did, merrily enough. Anna held a stupefied hand to a shocked cheek.

'Whole inside have been eating, men,' she told Leah in the hollowest of tones.

'If played every day for the noise even rats won't stay,' Leah said wisely. 'How much to repair?'

'God alone knows. Mr Colontota very angry. Scolding me, child. Just locking and keeping, he's saying. Once in a way playing but the stool is uncomfortable, men. When sit getting a back pain also.'

---

1. *Meeyo!* – Rats!

131

Leah clucked. 'Sonnaboy came an' asked if can keep that small devil. You know George, no? Straightaway said can't but what to do, men. And whole day in school, no? So said to come and keep. Have that small store room, can put a bed there. Only sometimes that Dunnyboy coming and we put there.'

'Then Diana what's happening?'

'Going to keep with Mrs da Brea up the lane. How? Now telling in vain took from the convent. Now could have gone with Millie in the rickshaw. Anyway Millie said will take and drop top of Chapel Lane so only for her to come in the afternoon. They will arrange something.'

None of this worried Carloboy a whit. He was bobbing excitedly in a second class compartment. 'Don't know if have my catapult. Can make another one anyway.'

The sanitizing had begun once again. He pushed Colombo out of his mind. He scarcely dwelt on the corruption of the city—how he and Sumantha of his class would compare each others cocks; how the tuck shop man's assistant offered him a free meal if he would come around the counter where no one could see and masturbate him; how he had harboured hot thoughts about creeping upon Diana at night as she lay, her nightdress rolled up to her hips; how the vileness manifested itself everywhere and how he had to become a riotous hellion of a boy in order to earn a reputation that he shouldn't be tangled with.

'Bada' would give new masters the owl's eye and say: 'Here we have three cliques . . . or gangs, if you like to call them so. One is Linton Jayasekera's gang. Like to move in a herd and get up to all manner of tricks. Then there is the Vishva gang. You know, his father is an eminent barrister. A well-to-do gang, up to a great deal of mischief. You should approach this problem warily. The Vishva boy likes to lead. Thus the gang, actually his friends. We have many important pupils here. You will find that the wealth and eminence colours these boys somewhat. They come with a lesser sense of values. All boys at heart but careless with money, used to the good things of life. A class here is quite complex. Upper class morality and middle class morality together. Limousines and bicycles, if you get my meaning. These boys, fortunately have a sense of their destiny. They're upper crust, if you get what I mean. The third gang is von Bloss. One boy and let me warn you, he's a gang in himself. A peculiar boy. Ordinary family. Father is a railwayman. But the boy passed the entrance exam and has plagued our lives ever since. Oh, we beat him. And he is bright. Bit of a madcap, I believe, but there is upbringing to be considered. Let me tell you, however, since there will be little time to dwell on niceties, you can tangle with the other gangs. They will swear in a quite superior way under their breaths, but they will buckle down. Try not to tangle with von Bloss. I mean to say, don't get personally involved. Whack him and leave him be. He's playing a different sort of fiddle here and it will take a lifetime to understand the music.'

And that summing up was what kept the only von Bloss of Royal going. He was the school's idiosyncrasy. He was loathed, caned, cheered, disregarded, analysed, wanted, unwanted, even gated on occasion. But in later years he would march up to collect his gift voucher for the Dornhorst Memorial Prize for English Literature or the Sir James Peiris Memorial Prize for English Essay and be reminded, quite unnecessarily that he was the most-caned boy in the college which, in itself, was a distinction of sorts!

It got so that Carloboy, rushing to the Racecourse end playground would check, get on hands and knees and crawl past 'Jowl's' window. The vice-principal couldn't abide the boy. If he saw Carloboy he would roar: 'You, von Bloss! Come here!' and give him four cuts with a middling-sized cane, and then say. 'I don't know what you have done today but that's for whatever you did!'

Once the train pulled out of Kekirawa station, Carloboy was a fast-unwinding bundle of impatience. 'Next Anuradhapura!' he yodelled to Diana who was as eager to see her new baby brother and show how important she was to sister Heather. It was happiness time once again and Anuradhapura welcomed the boy in a green and glorious embrace.

The chronicler, in keeping however spasmodically to the Burgher saga, will skip regretfully over much of the boy's exploits to focus on Jaffna, where since the days of the Dutch, a strong-blooded Burgher community thrived. A feature of the holidays was the excitement of riding the footplate with Sonnaboy. It was Beryl's idea.

'For God's sake take and go. I'm with the baby and all. Can't keep running behind to see what he's up to!'

So Sonnaboy tousled his son's head and said, 'Come go. Show you the bloody Jaffna peninsula.'

'And tell to go and bring leaves for the rabbits. Had to pay that Karuppan to pluck and bring all these days. And see the amount now? For what I don't know allowed. You heard what Mrs Edema said, no? Can get diphtheria also.'

Beryl, as would be expected, kept exploding. She was Carloboy's mother and had decided long ago that the pain of bringing forth the 'little devil' was duty done, mission fulfilled. Thereafter he had to pay her back for all that splitting pain he had caused her. There were times she regarded him with black hatred and the boy sensed it. But he was a creature of pure Nature. Quite stoic at times, imaginative to a fault, a dreamer, a boy of devastating intellect and, quite uncharacteristically, a loner. He wanted to stand out. He also wanted to hear an endearment, a good word from Mummy and gripped himself, bit his own lip, when it never came. He looked elsewhere for tenderness and suffered the embraces of Joachim's servant and the sly caresses of Uncle Aloy and those close minutes on Poddi's mat. He learned like a sponge. He couldn't abide his sisters either and was thrashed terribly by Beryl on the day he yelled at Diana: 'You wait will you. All of you! Catch and fuck all of you. And if Mummy comes to talk I'll fuck her also!'

Sonnaboy and his railway engine were balm to the boy's soul. This was a flaring world of crimsom-tongued firebox, serpent steam, the rush of wind and the great force of big drive wheels as the black behemoth swallowed the dreary miles northwards. His first visit to Jaffna. He couldn't know, but perhaps his forefathers lived in this placid, largely Tamilian place. To this day, Kruys Kerk stands in the Jaffna Fort. Built in 1706, it is the oldest Dutch church in Sri Lanka.

CHAPTER ELEVEN

The chronicler finds this just the time to get back to those stirring days when the Dutch sailed in and decided to give the Portuguese the heave-ho. The history books will tell you how the Dutch commander, Rycleff van Goens, led quite a venomous force of trained Sinhalese to Mannar where he routed the Portuguese in 1658. The Portuguese, it is recorded, fled, honking like geese, to Jaffna, and those who thought better of the whole boiling, went to India which was infinitely more comfortable in the circs.

It was a sort of Ides of March business. On the 20th of the month van Goens entered Jaffna and terrible things began to happen. Laying siege to the Jaffna Fort seemed a textbook exercise, but the Portuguese held out grimly enough. It took van Goens up to three months to dislodge them, bury many and send the rest pelting into the sea. So, on 23 June 1658, the victorious van Goens who, no doubt, used the flat of his sword on many Portuguese bums, encouraging them to 'Goen! Go on!' held a thanksgiving service in the Portuguese church and set about being a good Dutch uncle.

This, impatient reader, must be said. You may wonder how Jaffna became so Tamilian in character. Well, blame the Dutch. Van Goens needed to show the natives that, as a conqueror, he had their interests at heart. Land needed to be cultivated and there had to be enough of food. The problem was a labour shortage and a population which got by in that lotus-eater style so characteristic of the breed. So thousands of slaves were shipped in from India, each with the V.O.C.[1] mark branded on them, who found the land to their liking and fornicated furiously and bred fearsomely.

Oh, the Dutch were cagey enough. They looked upon Jaffna as a splendid retreat—a second capital and with a 'safe house' status in the event that things in Colombo got too stroppy.

British Captain Robert Percival, who wrote a most disparaging book about the Dutch,[2] remarked that he had found oodles of Hollanders living in Jaffna and that when the British took Colombo, the civilian Dutch packed their pots, pans, wives and daughters and fled to Jaffna.

(A remarkable point, actually. When the Sinhalese made things hot for the Tamils in Colombo in recent years, the Tamils, too, were evacuated to Jaffna. They actually sailed to the peninsula in small ships chartered by the government. Jaffna, historically, has always been a place of both sanctuary and internal pyrotechnics.)

Getting back to the van Goens era, the Dutch accepted that with Jaffna being a 'faire countrie' it was eminently politic to have a strong Dutch population there. The problem was the acute scarcity of Dutch women. But there were, in compensation, bounding quantities of Portuguese and these continental women were deemed more than worthy. Dutch soldiers were encouraged to marry them, which they did at the drop of a pike. Great days, to be sure and a marvellous progeny came forth, full of dour Dutch blood and continental fire, a penchant for wicker-clad flagons of sweet wine, desperado eyes and broad Dutch shoulders.

Also, the Dutch encouraged other European settlers into this stew-pot. Emigrants from Europe were given passage on the regular East Indiaman fleets. They came in droves. From Germany, the Hannoverians, Brandenbergers, Bavarians; and

---

1. *Veeringde Oost-Indische Compagnie*—Dutch East India Company.
2. *An Account of the Island of Ceylon*—Percival 1803.

there were Danes, Swedes, Austrians, the French, a few brash Londoners, a sprinkling of Scots, a roister of Irish and even a few Poles who found their winters very unpleasant. The ships of the Dutch East India Company would bring in these emigrants twice a year and they all settled down or ran amok as inclined and became 'Burghers'. You see, the Dutch wanted a cohesive European population. The community was made up of many nationalities, true, but the generic was important as well as administratively convenient. Without distinction, they were nominated 'Hollanders' and more conveniently 'Burghers'.

Jaffna, let me tell you, has many islands scattered around it like breadcrumbs brushed off a mother's lap. The Dutch set about making themselves at home and what better way than the names of those old familiar places? Thus it was that Jaffna and the many islands around the peninsula became as Dutch as could be. The island of Kayts was a storing place for goods and armaments. The name comes from the Portuguese cais or warehouse and sharpened to suit the Dutch. But this island was always Velanativu[1] and the Dutch preferred to call it Leyden Island. Nainativu (also known as Nagadipa[2] by the Sinhalese) was dubbed Harlem, and Karaitivu was called Amsterdam, Punguditivu was Middelburgh, Analaitivu was Rotterdam and Nendutivu was Delft. Today, only Delft remains Delft, and Leyden Island continues to be the easier said Kayts. Thus did the Dutch 'set up house' and it was universally acknowledged in all the island that to be the best of the Burghers, one had to be born in Jaffna! Quaint? Yes, but very true.

It is somewhat sad to think that today, no Burgher in Sri Lanka can ever imagine the northern peninsula as home. It is almost unthinkable. But in the 1700s Jaffna town was

---

1. Tivu is Tamilian for island or islet.

2. Dipa or dwipa is Sinhalese for island. Naga is the serpent, in this instance the cobra—hence island of the cobra. This strays into the realms of Buddhist legend and pertains to a particular visit of the Buddha to Sri Lanka. The author will not dwell on this further, but Nagadipa is a place of Buddhist pilgrimage.

the Burgher Pettah (market town) and its fair-skinned denizens beachcombed in Mandaitivu (Harlem) and went hunting in Klali (Kilali today) and Carlmone (Kalmunai). Today all that stands to remind us of the Jaffna Burghers is the old lighthouse at Kalmunai Point, the toll gate over the road at Point Pedro, Kruys Kerk and naught else (but oh, the memories!).

The Dutch, naturally, entrenched. They strengthened the Portuguese forts of Jaffna and Hammenheil and put up another stockade at Pooneryn which became in turn a resthouse and then seemingly dissolved into nothingness. Beside the causeway was an elephant path, so the causeway became Elephant Pass. It is the present intention of the rebel Tamilians that no elephant should pass,[1] but that is another story I shall carefully avoid!

Another fort was built in Kovilkyal, proudly named Beschutter (the defender) and Vettilekerni—the forest of the betel vine—was, for a time known as Pass Pyl after the Commander, Laurens Pyl.

Even Sonnaboy could not know of Jaffna's Dutch connection. But he knew a very old, coppered man who claimed to be a Burgher but who walked the streets with a black cigar between the yellowest teeth and even his lips were burned black in the torrid sun. The only hint of his Burgherness lay in his very light, watery eyes and he hobnobbed with the engine drivers and hobbled along the platform as though it was a corridor in his own home. He would also undo his baggy pants to urinate against the platform railings and not mind the fact that he was regaling many women who looked quickly away.

He spoke of the Burghers of Jaffna. 'I am Isaacs,' he wheezed. 'All our families from here, no? Real Dutch we are.'

---

1. A fierce rebel war goes on in Sri Lanka at the time of writing. The LTTE (Liberation Tigers of Tamil Eelam) are fighting for a separate northern state. The Sinhalese government, at the time of writing, has as its emblem, the elephant—the symbol of the United National Party.

Carloboy was surprised. The man was as dark as an overdone kettle and as sooty as an unscrubbed one. He dragged cracked leather slippers on his feet and the white hangout he wore had been white perhaps a dozen years ago. 'Over two hundred years can trace,' he intoned, 'You like to see?'

Carloboy gave his father a quizzical glance. Sonnaboy grinned. 'You and your bloody family. Who cares, men, if your great grandfather was so and so. See your state? You ate anything today?'

Isaacs looks hurt. 'So big my people an' you're always talking like that.'

'Balls! Here, take this and go and eat rotti.' Proffers a one rupee note—a small, tatty bit of paper with the face of King George VI looking quite debonair. Old Isaacs takes the note. 'Your son? Must tell about our people to him. Must know, no? In old days had all Burgher peoples all over here. You didn't know?'

Carloboy shook his head.

'Come go,' Sonnaboy said. 'There, signal is down. Oi, Isaacs, must go.'

'You bring and come to Jaffna one day. Tell him about my people. Your people also can be. Had Krauses and Schneiders and von Haghts here. German names, no? Von Bloss don't know but good to know these things.'

'For what?' Sonnaboy grinned, swinging aboard.

'And Heynsberg.'

Sonnaboy hung on the whistle cord. The stationmaster had stopped his preeping and with a long-drawn chug-a-chug, the big locomotive glided forward. Carloboy, quite grimy, watched the fireman dish in the coal and stood at the left rails, watching Jaffna spill past. The train, near empty, bucked along.

'Hungry?' Sonnaboy called over the roaring of the rails, 'Can do a seabath at KKS[1] before we eat. Never mind you bathe in that trouser. Have another one in my bag.'

---

1. Kankesanturai. Sri Lanka's most northern small port.

Old Isaacs was not wrong. Many German 'Burghers' had also lived in Jaffna—and the usual mixing that had produced the Greniers and Toussaints, the Vaderstraatens and Keegels, the Thiedemens and Rulachs, the Speldewindes and the Ebells.

The Portuguese mixture also lent much to the overall colour, both in speech and style. A kiss was *cheraboca*[1] and a dish was a bandeya and oli riccini was castor oil, no doubt liberally spooned down young throats after such periods as the Christmas festivities, where Anna's love cake would have been called Bolo de Amor and nothing else!

As said, Robert Percival described the Burghers of Jaffna with much derision (the chronicler has been accused of doing the same) and even wrote that the Burgher's day began with tobacco and gin and ended with gin and tobacco. Be that as it may, Carloboy—who had taken to pinching his father's Three Roses cigarettes (to which he graduated from Peacocks) and had surreptitiously taken a swig of arrack and ran to the bathroom, gasping, holding his chest and wondering who was applying a branding iron inside his throat—standing in the slow-lapping water and squirming his toes into the soft grey sand, felt at peace with the world.

There would be many such trips before it was time to return to school: to Talaimannar where Sonnaboy would uncouple and shunt his engine to the rear of the train and then push it slowly onto the pier. There the ferry steamer from Danushkodi, India, would disgorge its passengers, through the Customs checkpoint into their compartments for the overnight journey to Colombo. The family would also come at times—to the Kinniya hot springs, or to Tholagatty where Rosicrucian monks made excellent table wines. At times his aunts, uncles, cousins would also come for the holidays and they brought with them the faintest breath of Colombo and all it stood for. The cousins couldn't enjoy themselves. Marlene and Ivor, Leah's children, were quite unmoved by outpost

---

1. 'Smell the mouth.'

charm. It was necessary, even, to save Ivor from a certain watery grave when the family picnicked by the Tissa Wewa[1] one day. While the adults ate hard boiled eggs and bananas and Beryl's roast beef sandwiches and grew quite limp in the warm breeze, the boys cast their lines.

'Have crocodiles here,' Benno said.

'What? Here?' Ivor asked.

'Yes. Two three days ago took a child and went.'

Ivor, perched on a rock, busily tangling his fishing line, stared into the water. The breeze raised frenzied little waves that dashed energetically on the rock-pile bund. When Carloboy pulled in a magura,[2] Ivor rose to remark on it, tread on a patch of slime and fell over, sinking so rapidly that it was barely time to fling rod and fish away and grab an ankle. Leah's shrieks scared every crocodile for miles, it was later said with much merriment, while Marlene wrung her hands and stood up to allow the wind to raise her dress and show a bemused world her bright red knickers.

Carloboy hung on and Benno hung low over the treacherous rock to seize another foot. Sonnaboy sped down the slope, hauled up the boy and dragged him up the bund where he collapsed and gagged and was thumped so lustily that everything that had achieved a liquid state inside him was expelled.

'Enough for you?' Marlene scolded. 'If Carloboy hadn't caught you . . .'

Beryl scowled. 'Caught? That devil? Don't know if pushed even!'

Yes, Anuradhapura was taking on an acid flavour. A flavour of Beryl von Bloss whose one wholehearted resentment was that here she was, at twenty-three, with four children and being quite smothered with children, led by Carloboy whose birth had seemed to open the floodgates for the others who followed, thick and fast.

Sonnaboy handed over his son to guard Lucas. 'Put him

---

1. The tank of Tissa—a large irrigation reservoir.
2. Cat fish.

at the Mount Lavinia bus stand,' he said, 'he can go to Wellawatte. Now go carefully, you heard,' he told Carloboy, 'and go straight to Aunty Leah's. No going anywhere else. And see to your books and pipelay your tennis shoes.' (People rarely said it correct. One always 'pipelaid' tennis shoes—never pipeclayed them!)

'Then Diana?'

'Diana I'll bring and come to Granny's. Can't send both alone.'

So Carloboy chattered all the way to Colombo and Lucas went back to tell his wife, 'My God, that boy. Bright is not the word. Telling about planets also. And can play the piano. Must ask to come and play our piano to see.'

Lucas had two stunning daughters. Claudette and Rosemary. They giggled and Claudette said, 'Must see him loafing all over. Must be telling fibs. He to play this?' But they did call him during the August holidays and Carloboy played and Claudette was enchanted and Carloboy said he was in love with her and took to running over every day to meet her until Mrs Lucas took Claudette by the ear and screamed at the boy. 'You wait, I'll come and tell your father!' and Carloboy ran out to stand by the gate and catcall and sing, 'Tell, tell and go to hell!'

Oh, he was at that age—that age when falling in love was as easy as falling, like Ivor, into the wewa. He was in love with cousin Marlene, with Sheilagh Mortimer, with Yvette Raux, with Diedrie Ratnayake, with cousin Shirley da Brea and another cousin Elise da Brea. Maureen Koch was another and Thelma Jobz yet another. They all blazed like comets for a week, a month, then were forgotten. Drena Swan held him for a while but wasn't sister Yolande more promising? And this time there was no Sonnaboy to whale the tar out of him.

He arrived, quite breathless, at Leah's and was welcomed with his aunt's half-smile and a disparaging sound from Uncle George. He was shown the store room with its tiny wall cupboard and the bed and an old table at which he could sit and study. The bathroom was dark and dingy with large moisture sores on the walls. His uncle Dunnyboy was there, too, visiting it was said, while Leah prayed silently he would go. Dunnyboy stayed, however, and was given a mat and pillow and shown the store room floor. 'Uncle Dunnyboy also will sleep here today,' Aunty Leah said, and Carloboy, hiding his catapult under his mattress, nodded and paid scant head.

It was a shock to find his uncle, quite naked, clasping him urgently that night, dragging down his short pyjamas. 'Uncle,' he breathed, 'what?'

'Wait quiet,' Dunnyboy said in his half-whine, gripping him, thrusting against him. Carloboy felt a big penis press urgently against his buttocks, then settle between his thighs. He tried to fight against it but the man was strong and hard arms pinned him while large fingers gripped his cock and shook it, willing it to grow hard. There was no effusion. Just that big organ creasing through his thighs and the prickles of the old man's chin on the back of his neck and those insinuating fingers working back and forth. Dunnyboy heaved, thrusting him against the wall and ceased, breathing heavily and Carloboy felt a sudden jerk within him and a thick salve that shot out of him. The fingers scooped at it, spread it along his penis and under his testicles. Carloboy lay tight-lipped in the darkness. He had never felt like this before—that blinding sensation of release, that fierce ejaculation that seemed to propel his very spirit into his uncle's gnarled hand. And the feeling. Yes, that feeling of being drawn like a bow which suddenly, blindingly released an arrow from deep inside him, an arrow of sunfire and silk. He found he was breathing heavily and his uncle still clutched him, rubbed him, and squeezed him. 'I want to do pippie,' he whispered.

'Then go and come.' And the man waited and embraced him again and it was towards morning when Carloboy ejaculated yet again and, unheeding allowed Dunnyboy to keep slapping against him until he heard the sound of tea cups and running water and knew that Leah was up and it was morning. Dunny went to his mat, pulled up his baggy trousers and lay there. Within minutes he was asleep. Carloboy stared at his rumpled sheet, a few grey hairs on his pillow, ran a finger along his penis. The stickiness had dried. He trotted to the bathroom, dragging his towel.

'What, child, so early you're bathing. Hurry up and come, right? Now George will come to wash and go to work,' Leah said.

Yes, he thought, it is all too right. I'm in Colombo. Here it is like this. Not like Anuradhapura. And under the shower he recaptured that tremendous sensation of orgiastic wonder, masturbating with a sense of dire urgency while George de Mello yelled to him to hurry up and come out. He did, towel around him, and Leah said, 'Didn't wipe your head properly, no? Go to the room and clean and put the towel on the line to dry.' Dunnyboy slept on. Hurriedly he dressed and mocked himself in the mirror and admired the puff of hair he made on his head. It was the style of the times and boys would remark of another, 'How the puff? Like Elvis Presley, no?' Comb the hair back, then push it forward from the centre of the head to form a rise over the forehead. That was how it was done.

'Wear your home clothes,' Leah would call, 'and don't go anywhere, you hear? Your tea is on the table.'

Breakfast was on an old table in the rear veranda and all other meals too. The large dining table was only used when there were visitors or on special days. Marlene would whine constantly. She battled her father all the time, for George was the mingiest of men and railed incessantly when called on to fork out.

'So what, Daddy, told to bring five rupees for the class trip to the Museum. From last week I'm asking,'

George would scowl. 'Your mother hasn't five rupees to give? Coming to worry me.'

'So Mummy only told to ask you.'

'Museum. Damn nonsense. What for going to the Museum. Because nuns don't know that trying to take and go to show. And so much? Go in a bus and come asking five rupees?'

Marlene stamps a tennis-shoed foot. 'You want me to go and ask all that. What they are asking I told.'

George's scowl deepens. He goes to his almirah and

unlocks it. That almirah is the repository of a great deal of pilfered goods, smuggled out of the port of Colombo. Nobody really knew what George squirrelled away and why. He came home with parcels of this, that, or the other effectively disguised in heavy wrapping, locked the contraband in and there it stayed.

His keys, on a strong chain, are tied with pyjama cord around his waist. Marlene follows and is waved away. 'You go and wait. I'll see if have and give. But don't come every time to ask like this. Can see the price of things these days,' and he extracts a five-rupee note, crackles it between his bony fingers to make sure it is just one and grudgingly gives it to Marlene.

George liked to 'dole out.' Leah would place a hand against her cheek. 'What is this? Only twenty rupees. To buy meat and vegetables and kerosene oil and coconut oil enough? Kitchen soap also and dhoby woman will come tomorrow.'

'So then how much?'

'Give about another twenty.'

'You're mad, men? This way if going to spend, how to manage?'

'Spending *thamai*, spending on whom? Five mouths to feed, no?'

'So anyway must be careful. If go to spend like this where we will end up? Just think and see. Here, have 'nother ten. See if you can manage. In the port using that ball soap to clean. I'll bring and come big lump. No harm if use instead of this bar soap.' It was then that Carloboy talked Ivor into raiding his father's almirah . . . and that scheme, pretty unreal à la Carloboy, nearly introduced Uncle George to the joys of a first heart attack!

It was novel, to say the least. All they had to do was lift off the top board which was of very heavy wood. That was a bit of a struggle and Ivor smashed a thumb and Carloboy nearly fell off the dining room chair on which he perched. Cautiously, and with much huffing, they slid the board away and peered in. It was the long empty section where George hung his Christmas suit. Below, piled quarter of the way up were all manner of stuffed bags, parcels, boxes and tins, the latter making the boys' eyes sparkle. 'Cadbury's Roses!' Carloboy hissed, 'and Bluebird toffees! Sha! Should have had a fishing rod . . . I'll tell you, you get in and pass to me.'

Ivor looked doubtful.

'You're thinner, men, and not so heavy. Have to climb out also, no? If I try whole side may come out.'

A reasonable argument . . . So Ivor climbed, banged his knee and gingerly lowered himself into the contraption.

'You pass out the tins. I'll take,' and a large tin of Cadbury's Roses hove into view. Carloboy placed it reverently on the floor.

'These boxes,' Ivor said, husky with excitement.

'What?'

'I'm trampling, all getting smashed. Don't know what have inside even.'

'Don't trample them. Where? Give some more!'

Leah and Marlene had told the boys, 'Going to Claassens close by. You two sit and play quietly.' One should never ask boys to sit and play quietly on a Saturday morning. And then Carloboy heard his aunt come in and Marlene saying, 'Why you told to put lace round the hem I don't know—' obviously referring to a dress Mrs Claassen hoped to sew for the girl.

Carloboy whipped back the big board, kicked the tin of Roses under the bed and pushed the two chairs out of the way. 'Stay quiet inside,' he said, 'don't make a noise. Try to sit or something.'

Ivor gave a dismal 'ooohw' and Carloboy moved the chairs.

'Where, child, taking the chairs and going? Where is Ivor?'

'Must be plucking mangoes in the back.'

'Go and tell to come inside. Throwing sticks and eating green mangoes. Tell to come in at once.'

Carloboy shrugged and went, shinned up the mango tree and pondered his next move. Of course, Ivor could suffocate and there would be a funeral and he hadn't a black tie even, but sundry things like that could be remedied. Leah

busied herself in the kitchen and Marlene lolled in the hall
to read (a great reader, was Marlene) and it was only when
lunch was served that Leah began to regard her husband's
almirah with deep suspicion. She told Marlene, 'Come here
child and see. Funny noises inside. God knows if rats have
got in even.'

Marlene paid scant regard. But when Ivor shifted and
there was that distinct sound of a small wooden thump and
crumpling cardboard and the rustle of paper, Leah gave a
little yelp and retreated to the safety of the rear veranda. 'Let
eat anything inside,' she muttered. 'Bringing God knows
what and putting. Won't even tell what.'

Ivor, too, seemed to have vanished—a fact which
Carloboy gave valiant explanations for. He's in the next
garden . . . he's playing cricket . . . calling, calling won't come.
And then, it being Saturday, George came to lunch and was
quite disturbed at the way his almirah door creaked and
swung loosely open which was only to be expected since the
heavy top board, quickly shoved back to give an appearance
of being as normal as ever, was not notched in place. 'Whole
almirah is shaking,' George growled, must have knocked it
or something. Leah came up. 'Shaking not, rats full inside.
Noises can hear up to the kitchen and—'

'My God!'

George reeled back, purpling gloriously. Ivor's head was
buried behind the Christmas suit. But his legs and midsection
were there and his feet were buried in a mess of mangled
parcels.

Leah shrieked, Marlene ran in, George sat on the bed
gasping and outside, Carloboy reached the highest branch of
the mango tree where he perched and decided that all the
uncles in the world would never get him down.

Ivor emerged and was immediately cradled by Leah and
George kept imitating a dying puffer fish and kept saying,
'Never in all my born,' in a voice that would have delighted
any tragedian. Ivor snivelled, said Carloboy put him in and
where, demanded Leah, was that devil?

'Don't give to eat!' George roared and Ivor was hauled
to the kitchen and Leah shouted, 'What for going to beat?

Not his fault, no?' and fond mother that she was, firmly believed that her son had been seized and bodily thrust into the almirah, although how this had been done she couldn't imagine.

Marlene spotted Carloboy and said, 'You come down, you'll get it.' But he came down and slunk into his room and listened to a long sermon and the threat of a letter (and bill for damages) to his father: 'And if come and skin you even, not going to lift a finger, did you hear!'

Sonnaboy laughed. 'Damn good for the bugger,' he chortled. 'Robbing from the port and bringing. What, men, a slab of chocolates even won't give the children. Only bringing boxes and boxes and locking up.'

Beryl was peeved. 'And if Leah won't keep, then what? Write and tell to behave, men. Tell that Father Sebastian even to catch and talk to him.'

Sonnaboy said it was a good idea. 'That St Lawrence's has a club for boys, no?'

Beryl said she didn't know and added, 'Who knows if going to church even? Who's going to see? Just dancing the devil. That's all he knows to do.'

So Sonnaboy went to Millicent, Beryl's spinster sister and a 'church pillar', as everyone called her and Millie said that Carloboy needed to be 'channelled' and how can anyone blame a boy who had no family around him. 'Lot of things he can do if he likes,' she said. 'Can be an altar boy also. He comes here in the evenings sometimes. I'll catch and talk to him.'

Sonnaboy was relieved. 'One thing, likes to learn things. And to put on uniforms and all. Was a wolf cub and scout and very proud when became sixer leader. That all gave up when went to Anuradhapura. Might like to serve at Mass.'

'I'll talk and see, you don't worry,' and Millie gave Carloboy *Lives of the Martyrs* and said, 'read and see how even boys and girls died for the Church. If you also be good and strong you will also be not afraid to say you are a Catholic to anybody. How people suffered those days. Burnt them, killed them, gave to the lions to eat but they were not afraid. Even boys like you. And today all are saints. You go and read. I'll get some more books like this. You see what a big thing it is to be good and listen to God and keep the Commandments and all. So close, why you cannot come for daily mass? After mass you can come and have some breakfast here. Early morning five-thirty mass you come and see. Only few people and no sermon or anything. I'll tell Father Sebastian you like to be an altar boy. Learn the prayers in Latin only. You like?'

Carloboy leafed through the book. Why, this was another world entirely. He nodded and ran off—to his storeroom bed where he devoured the book and gave way to a riot of images that danced in his mind. Leah was startled to find a neatly-dressed Carloboy stealing out of the house at five a.m. She clattered back to bed where she prodded George in the ribs (an easy thing, that, since the man was, as far as she knew, all ribs).

'Garrumph,' said George.

'Early morning went to church!'

'Growwxk!'

'You're up?'

'Up I am. How to sleep with you coming and waking? What church? Who?'

'Said going to church and went. Myee, child, like a miracle, no?'

'Don't talk nonsense, men. Look at the time!'

A little while later George understood that Carloboy had actually gone for morning mass and snorted uncharitably.

'You went to church?' he asked Carloboy unnecessarily.

'Yes, Uncle.'

'For why?'

'Just I went. Everyday must go.'

George gaped. Later he told Leah, 'If police come and say anything happened in Wellawatte at five o'clock don't go to say anything.'

Carloboy had discovered religion.

Father Sebastian was intrigued. This was the boy who had, with incredible venom, killed his laying hens. That had been in March, when he had come to the mission house after evening benediction to be told by an agitated Sacristan that two of his hens lay dead. 'To the head have been hitting. There, dead and waiting. Father come and see.'

Later it was learnt that a boy had been seen, perched on the grey church wall and this boy had a catapult. Two and two were put together. 'What boy?'

'*Lansi* boy. Others everyone church inside. This one wall on top sitting was.'

There was no help to it. The parish had its share of ruffians too and Father Sebastian sadly instructed that his hens be interred and delivered a scorching sermon on delinquency and parents who didn't seem to give a fig about what their children were up to.

To a boy who 'saw the light' a good confession was imperative. So Carloboy knelt before the ratanned screen with its dark curtain, crossed himself and said, 'Bless me, Father, for I have sinned.'

Father Sebastian made appropriate murmurs and inquired about the last date of unburdening, and which Carloboy hazily recalled was for Easter Sunday mass in Anuradhapura. He then launched into a long, fascinating account of his many transgressions, being very thoughtful and very thorough and including the stirring news that he had, in a lighter moment killed the mission house hens.

The priest made a strange, strangled sound, then shot out of the confessional to seize the penitent by the collar. 'So you're the rascal!' he said fiercely. 'Ah, von Bloss, no? Only yesterday your aunt was telling about you.' He shook the boy, then stared into those large eyes that seemed to hold all the fears and joys of boyhood in them. The priest frowned, scratched his head and returned to the confessional. 'Say your other sins,' he said, and Carloboy, quite disturbed, said that was all, unless tormenting masters in school needed to be listed, although that could hardly be considered a sin, that being a sort of God-given right to every boy.

The penance was heavy. He was told to say three decades of the rosary, five Our Fathers, five Hail Mary's and five Glory be's and may God have mercy on his soul. 'Now make

the Act of Contrition,' the priest said and listened dully as
the boy intoned 'O my God, I am truly sorry for my sins of
thought, word and deed . . .' and made a muttered *In nomine
Patris* and mumbled 'Go in peace . . . and don't let me catch
you near the mission house again!'

It was a good feeling. Carloboy felt that a lot of lumber
had been cleared along with the cobwebs of his mind.
He stepped lightly and felt quite light-hearted too. Millie
was proud. She gave him scapulars and a handsome Missal,
all black and grainy covered with a cross embossed on
the cover. There were gold, silver, crimson and powder-blue
silk page markers. He learnt how to find and mark the
epistle and gospel of the day, the particular Saint's day
mass and to tread surefooted through the Festive Calendar.
These were books of litanies and special prayers which the
Church decreed, gave indulgences. 'Say this prayer twenty
times and you will get an indulgence of 365 days,' Millie
told him.

'What's that, Aunty?'

'That's for helping you to go soon to heaven, child. We
are not without sin, no? So we will all have to go to
Purgatory and suffer before we are taken to heaven.'

'But why? Can't go straight to heaven?'

'Can, can, but must be like a saint for that. Not a single
sin. Spotless you must be. That's not easy, no? Any amount
of small small sins people commit every day. Even a tiny lie
is a sin. Venial sin.'

'But venial sins you won't go to hell, no?'

'No. God knows we are all making mistakes. So he
sends you to Purgatory to be clean and when you have
suffered a little there he will take you to heaven.'

'So this indulgence, then?'

'Ah that is what I'm trying to tell you. If you have to go
to Purgatory for thousand days then if you say this prayer
twenty times, will cut off 365 days. Like that by saying the
prayers in this book daily all the time in Purgatory is
reduced. Quickly you will go to heaven.'

'So can even go straight to heaven, no?'

'Yes, child. Pray, pray. That's what God is asking us to

always do.' This as we know now, is a load of tripe and has long since been scrapped. Readers will recall that King Henry VIII clashed with the church on the sale of indulgences. One could put down cash and buy one's way out of confinement in Purgatory. This was later watered down to the recitation of long prayers which earned reprieves. All this is, thankfully, over. Indeed, today there is a lot of doubt about the existence of Purgatory, and anyway, don't we make our own heavens and hells and God, sadly, is nowhere around to make reference to?

Father Sebastian was adamant. 'Let him be an altar boy, but can't allow to wear cassock and surplice. If he learns can serve at daily mass. But Sunday Mass can't allow. Going to non-Catholic school, no?'

Carloboy was indignant. He had taken this altar-server business to heart. His quick mind grasped the Latin prayers, and he was spouting them as easily and flawlessly as a star seminarian. He followed procedures, the changing of the big Missal, the ringing of the bell, the holding of the paten under the chins of those who came to the rails to receive the Body of Christ, the prayers at the foot of the altar, how to hold the hem of the celebrant's chasuble at the elevation of the bread and wine . . . he knew the different procedures for a High Mass, the mass of the pre-sanctified, the dead mass, the wedding mass and later, even the Episcopal High Mass. But his first venture into the sanctuary was at that everyday five thirty morning mass where he wore his school clothes and held the communion plate under the chins of old Mr Capper and Mrs Redlich and Aunty Millie and Mrs Toussaint who stuck out a very blue-flecked tongue and whom everybody said had a very evil mouth and anything she said was sure to happen.

Aunty Millie was delighted. She pressed a rupee into the boy's hands. 'One day you can become a priest if you want. Never had a priest in the family also.'

Carloboy thought about it. Why not? He could be a priest. He could be a priest at war, blessing dying soldiers, going into danger with God to keep an eye on him. Leah was stirred. She wrote a near-hysterical letter to her brother, and Sonnaboy wisely said, 'All this nonsense will stop soon. Not doing anything bad, no? But don't allow to sit the whole day in the church. Tell to study also.'

There were several other Burgher boys at Royal. There was Alan Bartholomeusz, fair, curly-haired, a hint of blue in his eyes, and Haig Siebel who was called Kossa because his father was an inspector of police. Oh, Royal had, of old, boasted a creamy crop of Burghers, each distinguishing himself in one way or another. Even in Carloboy's time there was Desmond Van Twest who was on the cricket team and played rugby as well—and Wilhelm Woutersz (who is, at the time of writing, in the Sri Lanka Foreign Office) and Eric Labrooy who had the makings of a fine batsman and had a baby face. There was also Rankine and Van der Gert (Rodney, his name was and he had an elfin face and a most impudent grin and is a Permanent Secretary today).

Royal, like many other colleges, was proud of its Burgher students who, though quite exotic in manners and temperament, were excellent playing field material. None of them hailed from the affluent backdrop of Colombo 7 society yet, in those vintage years, there were the Roberts, the van Geyzels, the Raaffels, (Douglas Raaffels was a great hunter and explored the Ruhuna jungles of Sri Lanka and also did things of instant distinction during the war), and the Kelaarts and de Saras and that scintillating character Elmer de Haan who claimed Belgian blood and superiority over the 'third rate' Burghers!

Colombo 7, originally 'Cinnamon Gardens' is where the rich and the upper-crust live. Peculiarly enough, while a few important Britishers also hang out here, the majority of this society are the rich Sinhalese—the landowners, estate owners, big businessmen, leading professionals. Colombo 7 society in this plush residential area is very real to this day. Within its confines are many foreign embassies as well as the sprawling mansions of ambassadors, gem merchants, politicians, bankers, etc.

The Burghers, however prominent they became, never really claimed the wealth of the country. They lived and died ordinarily enough, eschewing pomp and fine feathers. Indeed, the author claims just one friend in Colombo 7 today and that is Arthur C. Clark, MBE of *2001 Space Odyssey* fame who resides in Barnes place. But then, the author is a Burgher too, so a Colombo 7 milieu is very distant from his own carefree state of being.

Carloboy fared in the best Burgher tradition. He livened up Royal, and the new spirit of 'godliness' which surged through him had to battle hard to keep a grip on his naturally rebellious soul. There was 'Bruno' who was a Burgher too, and taught English, both grammar and literature, and was tall, lanky, quite bony-faced, and a superb sportsman. True, he quit eventually, but he was a strong influence on Carloboy who discovered much of the glory of the English language and Literature under Bruno, whose drawling voice, wisecracks and wit was much appreciated by even the most pagan of souls.

Schoolmasters are quickly categorized and, obviously, it were the madcap Burghers who drew the lines of definition. Men like Baldsing and Perimpanayagam and 'Jowl' were not to be trifled with. Those like Eddie and 'Cowpox' and 'Penda' and 'Pocket Billiards' were mere players who fluffed and bluffed their hours on the stage and then retired to the staffroom to drink tea. 'Lapaya' and 'Connor' were pushovers; 'Cupper' was to be kept at a distance and so was 'Bella' and 'Gon' who flared up for the strangest reasons. Naths and 'Bruno' were the delectables, while principal J.C.A. was tolerated on the basis that, left alone, he would in turn leave you alone. J.C.A. occupied the same status as God in his heaven. As long as God stayed there, all was right with the schoolboy world.

Pushing a working knowledge of Sinhala down Burgher gullets was a trial. It was all well and good for the Sinhalese boys. They had their Sinhala lives at home and their Sinhala ways, manners and customs. It was, after all, their mother tongue. The Tamils too, had their Tamil language periods and were not considered, even remotely, for Sinhala education. The Burghers had no such luck. There was no education system which catered to their mother tongue—

English—and they had to study Sinhala![1] This would give
'Lapaya' many painful moments. Carloboy, especially, seemed
to loathe Sinhala, sat at the back of the class and was, to
both master and classmates, a persecution of major
proportions.

'Von Bloss! Today studying you're going to do?' (All
said in succinct Sinhala, of course).

'Yes, sir.'

'Then books open. Homework you did?'

'No, sir.'

'Why? Homework giving, must do.'

'Will do, sir.'

'What day? Next year you're going to do?'

'Time hadn't, sir.'

'Madness don't talk. Time haven't, time haven't. Where?
Your book bring to see!'

Carloboy makes a great show of rummaging in his desk.
The lid is raised, banged down several times. The class
explodes in titters. Lapaya gets furiouser and furiouser. 'Get
up!' he screams. 'Get out outside! Stand outside! If work
won't do, outside you wait!' and Carloboy saunters out to
stand in the corridor where he makes terrible faces through
the glass and very obscene gestures and even stands on his
head to the hysterics of the boys inside until he is hauled in,
given a chit and banished to the headmaster's office for the
customary six of the best.

Eventually Lapaya resorted to a measure of sheer
desperation. It began on the day that he was nearly skewered
by a pair of dividers. It had been a hair-raising battle. Little
demons like Farouk Abdi and Doyne Jaya, and Milton Amera

---

1. This system naturally catered openly to a polarization of sorts. The
Tamils became a separate entity. The Sinhalese accepted the Burghers.
Strange, when one considers how well the Burghers lived in the Northen
Peninsula and how those who drifted to the central plantation areas also
spoke fluent Tamil. In most schools of the Forties and Fifties, this policy
resulted in the Tamils ganging together socially and academically, only
mixing at sports and other extra-curricular activities. It is true to this day
that all Burghers are fluent in Sinhala but there are Burghers who have
no knowledge of Tamil!

and Ravi and Linton Jayasekera and Alan de Sara began the
war. The idea, as Carloboy explained, was to range on either
side of the class and sling dividers at each other. Whizzing
through the air like dinky stilettos, this was no game. It
could mean murder, but who gave a damn? The dividers
flashed, spinning to stab into desktops and bounce into walls
inches from heads. More nervous souls took cover. Edward,
whose father was a minister and was thus a timid little
fellow, bolted to the safety of the corridor. Lapaya checked
at the sight. With an enormous scowl he stood at the door,
was taken note of with short barks of 'there, Lapaya is
looking!' and with the deadliness of a final arrow, a pair of
dividers cut a dizzy arc and buried its head in the doorpost
half a centimetre from Lapaya's arm. The man wobbled
visibly, speechlessly, and while in this state of extremis,
there was a rush for chairs and, an instant later, a class that
sat silent, clear-eyed, guileless and as well-behaved as pats
of butter. This, the man decided, was too, too much. And if
he shoved them all out, who would he have to teach? With
some dignity he sat at his desk and crooked a finger at
Carloboy. 'Here, you come!'

Carloboy trotted up.

'This thing is whose?' indicating the pair of dividers.

'Mine not, sir.'

'You didn't throw?'

'No, sir.'

'Then you were doing what?'

'Looked and waited, sir.'

'Only looking?'

'Yes, sir.'

'And these when throwing, you did what?'

'Ducking, sir.'

'Ducking?'

'Yes, sir.'

'So you looking and ducking, ah? Then who was throwing
like this.'

'Some boys, sir. Who, I don't know.'

'Ah! You don't know?'

'No, sir.'

'Why? Like this if throwing, you don't know who?'

'I'm ducking, sir, so can't see.'

'Just now said you were looking!'

'Yes, sir.'

'So if you're looking how you didn't see?'

'Dividers from behind coming. So to see couldn't.'

'Then what looking-looking and doing?'

'Just, sir.'

'Just!' Lapaya had this feeling that he was wrestling with a big blob of mercury.

'Today but for you good caning!'

'Sir, why, sir?'

The master blinked. It was a difficult position and he was basically a fair man. And being caned had little effect on this terrible boy. Also, many others would have to be caned too. True, he would make 'Jowl's' day but it had to be considered that any master who kept sending boys up for a whacking were also admitting to a lack of control. A master should be able to take command of his class.

'Your homework you did?' he asked.

'Some I did, sir, but not right, I think.'

Lapaya sighed. Then a shaft of light from some schoolmaster's heaven seemed to speak to his soul. He produced a large coin. 'You go to the tuckshop. Here, this you take. Go and something eat and wait. Bell when it is ringing to the class come back.'

Dumbly Carloboy took the rupee and went. Quite unreal, this freedom, at eleven in the morning. Enough time to use his catapult on the droves of mynah birds who squawked and shrilled in the trees behind the tuck.

And so, despite his Catholic God and the feverish recitation of prayers to circumvent the discomforts of Purgatory, Carloboy remained the boy he was expected to be, a fighting, shouting, riotous creature, and was surprised for stock still seconds when he saw old 'Pol Thel' of St Peter's bowl through the college gates.

'Migorsh,' he told Christopher de Saa (who was called Hakispuruss for reasons to be given shortly), 'you know who he is?'

'Who? Who came on that autocycle?'

'St Peter's geography master. Shout *Pol Thel* to see.'

'What for?'

'Shout, will you. Shout loud.'

And thus was Baptiss welcomed to Royal and the word spread like a thin silk sheet and boys of all ages thumped fists into palms and chortled and greeted the new master with the words POL THEL chalked boldly on the blackboard of the first classroom he entered to take his first lesson. The man, let it be said, hadn't a prayer.

'Hakispuruss' had the dubious honour of unleashing the first catcall. This pleased him no end. He hated his nickname, quite onomatopoeic, and bestowed on him on the day he broke wind loudly in class and covered the sound with a sneeze. Or so he thought. The trouble was the sneeze came first . . . and the fart breasted the tape a close second. The result: first the hakiss of the sneeze and the puruss of the fart!

Millie, sensing the threat of an undisciplined school life a certain obstacle to Carloboy's spiritual progress, exhorted Sonnaboy to take the boy in hand. Sonnaboy did much better. He took his son to All Saints Church in Borella and paused thoughtfully at the storm drain and then grinning to himself,[1] introduced his son to Father Boniface whose father, too, was a railwayman and who knew Sonnaboy very well.

'Taking to Anuradhapura tomorrow,' he told the priest. 'Came to ask you—this bugger wants to be a priest ipseems. Going for daily mass and all. Serving also. You think this is some nonsense or what?'

Father Boniface twinkled. He had said his first Mass at the Kotahena Cathedral barely six months ago. He had fought tooth and nail with his burly railway father to leave Wesley College and enter the Borella seminary. He placed a hand on Carloboy's shoulder. 'Come to the parlour. So you want to be a priest?'

The boy liked to get things straight. 'Aunty Millie also

---

1. I will not explain this further. Curious readers will find the answer in *The Jam Fruit Tree* (Penguin 1993) p. 112.

said can become.'

'But if you become a priest, what do you want to do?'

'I want to go to people in the war and fight also and even if the Germans are dying can bless them and give them communion and go to Russia and open the churches for the people even if nobody allowed to pray there. In my book Catholics are very brave—'

'What book is that?'

'My aunty gave. About martyrs. She said all Catholics must be like soldiers.'

Father Boniface chuckled. 'But you have to be a good priest.'

'So I'll be.'

'And if the Bishop says no war. You stay in the church and say mass and keep quiet?'

'Why?'

'That's the trouble. Priests have to be obedient. Whatever the Bishop tells they must do. And did God tell you to be a priest?'

The boy pondered. 'I don't know. Even if telling how do I know?'

The priest leaned forward. 'You know, sometimes the devil also comes and puts ideas like this. Become a priest, he tells. And you know why? Because he knows you will be a bad priest. So that is the way the devil is playing tricks.'

Sonnaboy grunted. 'What to priest! Shooting birds, hooting masters, tormenting his aunty, getting complaints from everywhere. Got together with the cousin and robbed the uncle's almirah also.'

'How if all this is a trick? Trick of the devil? You go and become a priest and if you are not good biggest shame is for you, no?'

Suddenly Carloboy found it all too much. All his earnest attempts at being good were now making him the devil's plaything. It was all beginning to get beyond schoolboy comprehension. There were more practical things to consider: (a) a bad end of term report with the most charitable remark being 'can study but does not apply himself'; (b) that tomorrow he would be in Anuradhapura and (c) that if his luck held, a tin of Cadbury's Roses still skulked under the bed and which he had completely forgotten about in the stirring events of the moment. This had to be retrieved and surreptitiously packed away. He would give the chocolates to his mummy, he thought, and maybe the holidays would be happier.

George and Leah wanted to do a little jig. They waved their charge away with relief writ in wood type capital letters on their faces. Sonnaboy stopped at Florrie da Brea's to pick up Diana. 'You two sit in the brake van and come,' he said. 'Sit here until I bring the train to the platform. And don't run to the edge, you heard? Watch your bags and wait.'

Carloboy pouted. 'Because of you have to go with the guard. Otherwise Daddy will take me in the engine.'

Diana tossed her head. 'So you go if you want. As if I can't go alone.'

'Huh! You alone? Why do you think I have to go with you?'

'Why?'

'Because you're a girl, that's why?'

'So?'

'So alone you want to go with the guard? If catch and do something to you? As if you don't know.'

Diana shuddered. 'You wait I'll tell Mummy what you said. Always talking things like this.'

'Big people you must be careful, men. Because you're small I'm telling you. You don't know these big people. "Hullo son," they say and buy and give toffees and very nice. You can see, no, that Uncle Clarence next to Aunty Anna's. When coming to talk always catching you and putting on the lap. And what did Aunty Anna say, "Don't go, child, near even when call," and telling to go to the room. You thought I did not notice?'

All this was pretty unreal to Diana who was only ten, still wet her bed and looked for sympathy wherever it was manifest. She protested weakly that Uncle Clarence was nice. Very black, but nice.

'That's all you know. I'm bigger so I must look after you. That is why I must also be in the van. To see to you. Only thing I'm telling don't go too much with big people. Daddy an' Mummy never mind, but anybody else be careful. Uncles also don't know what will do.'

Diana sniffed. She decided that her brother was becoming worse with each passing day. Also, she couldn't believe a word of all this, 'Everybody?'

'Yes.'

'Priests also? And Uncle Edema next door and everybody.'

'Yes, and Hitler also and Churchill and everybody.'

'Pooh! Talking nonsense. Just trying to show off.'

'You wait and see will you. Don't come running to tell if anything happens. I don't care. Let them catch and do anything. Then you'll know what I said is true.'

Sonnaboy strode up. 'Come go. Had to bring to the other platform.'

And long minutes later, after Diana had been taken to the Ladies and guard Francke had beamed and said, 'So, holidays, eh? Here, put the bags in that corner,' and Sonnaboy went to the big, seething locomotive, the stationmaster sounded his whistle and Francke blew his and waggled his green flag and they began to edge away.

'Pukka driver your daddy,' Francke said, 'like a baby takes the engine. Not a jerk or anything. Only thing won't reach till midnight. If sleepy or anything tell, right? I'll put in a first class to have a nap.'

'Uncle, this is KKS mail, no?'

'Yes?'

'Don't know if told Mummy to keep dinner, also.'

Francke grinned. 'You go and raid the kitchen. Anyway, at Maho have to wait for a crossing. Daddy will give you something to eat in the canteen.'

And Daddy did, of course, and Beryl had sandwiches and tea and Carloboy gave her the purloined Roses and told how Ivor was stuck in the almirah and everybody laughed and the beds were ready. Outside an owl said ko-ko-kouee, ko-ko-kouee very plaintively and a big moon was doing business very low in the sky. Carloboy lay awake, face turned to the door leading to the balcony. The curtain moved lazily. It was hot and even the fan spun warm air against his face. He slipped to the cooler cement floor and lay there, sans shirt, waiting for his eyelids to shut out the world.

CHAPTER TWELVE

Bertram de Sella was a railway Foreman Plate Layer and he lived in a small house in Kandy next to a girl's school. It skulked behind a tall screen of wild hibiscus, facing the Peradeniya Road and in it lived Betram, his homely wife Agnes, their two sons Maurius and Quinny and three very attractive daughters Carmen, Maureen and Audrey. In distant Anuradhapura lived a bachelor relation who was also an F.P.L. and who was known throughout that sacred city as 'Homo' Direcksze.[1]

'A bloody boy king,' Sonnaboy would say, but Direcksze was accepted as one who, whatever his quirks 'wouldn't shit on his doorstep,' which was the homespun way of saying that the man pursued his deviations on those outside the society he moved in and thus, could be trusted far enough. The family knew this too. However depraved the man was, he selected his victims from ruder circles—village boys, servant boys, the chance encounters of boys who came to holiday with friends and who would consider such brief encounters as more or less an occupational hazard of living away from home and something to be chalked up as a blur of unpleasant experience.

---

1. The man figures quite prominently in *Yakada Yakā* (Penguin, 1994).

Which was why Bertram had no fears about sending his children to holiday with Direcksze in Anuradhapura. For one thing, the girls would be very safe since Direcksze had no time for girls whatsoever. And the two boys of twelve and ten were never looked upon as objects of the man's gratification. They were, after all, family.

Carloboy, rising early and shooting downstairs to race into the garden and streak through the gate, stood, curious at the little band of people, sling bags on shoulders, carrying suitcases, coming in a noisy wave past the pilgrim's rest. He grinned and said 'Hullo' and the boys grinned and Quinny said, 'Where's your shirt?'

'Here,' said Maureen, 'Direcksze's is number 42, no?'

'You're going there?'

'Yes. You know the house?'

'Yes. I'll show you.'

'You're coming like that?' Quinny asked.

'Like what?'

'Without the shirt even.'

'So what's the harm?' He looked at Audrey, a beautiful eleven-year-old with a donkey fringe of dark hair and expressive eyes. The girl coloured visibly.

'Came for the holidays?' he asked unnecessarily.

'Yes,' said Maurius. 'Damn, these bags are heavy.'

Carloboy was moving as in a dream. 'Here,' he told Audrey, 'I'll take your bag,' and he did and he caught the girl's eye with the corner of his and she bent her head quickly. There was such a quicksilver quality about it all. Inside him, a rhapsody seemed to swell and keep bursting in ribbons of song.

'What's your name?' he breathed in the confusion of the welcome.

'Audrey,' she said.

Carloboy put down her bag. 'I'll put a shirt and come,' he said and she said, 'yes,' and he ran, oh how he ran, rushing indoors to look swiftly in the mirror, rush to the bathroom, wash, scrub and wonder why the heat of his exertions made the sweat bead out on his forehead even after he had washed. Sanity prevailed. He sat on the edge of

the large   tank, allowed himself a breather, then
washe   owelled and ran upstairs to change. Soon, in
a li   hirt and well-starched trousers, and even a pair
o   noes, he sauntered out while Beryl, quite overcome,
          ied, 'Where are you going, good trousers and all.
    pers are still on the table.'

Carloboy said, 'I'll eat a little later. Going up the road a
little.' He was wise enough to leave out mention of Direcksze.
Despite all evidence to the contrary, railway town mothers
did not encourage their sons paying the man visits. Beryl
hmmmed and went indoors. 'Started now, the dance,' she
muttered, 'never thought of bringing leaves for the rabbits.'
But she was intrigued to see her son, a large gunny sack of
leaves slung over his shoulder, lead in three strange children,
through the house, past the rear veranda, into the yard
where they sat among the rabbits and Carloboy took up a
kicking bundle of black and white and gave it to a girl who
held it close and stroked it between the ears and smiled
sweetly.

'From where did you get the gunny?' Beryl asked, saying
'hullo' to the children.

'From Direcksze's. They have come to stay there for the
holidays. We went and got leaves.'

'Still you didn't eat. There have extra hoppers also. All
go and eat. You like that rabbit?'

Audrey smiled. Carloboy blushed—yes, actually blushed,
and Beryl noticed and said nothing. Yes, it would be
a peaceful holiday, she hoped. Put a girl into a boy's life
and he will be on his best behaviour, or at least, he will
try!

Of course, the rest of the gang were quite furious. Benno
was quick to condemn. 'How the bugger? Won't even come
to go fishing or anything. Whole time in that house. Going
with them. That day I asked where and telling going to
show the place. What to show? Trees and thorns?'

'An' talking to that girl. Asked who and telling that's not
my business. Then asking if can give the pony to ride.'

'You gave?'

'Mad? Said can't. For him to take and go. Next time will

165

say want to teach those fellows to ride. Who are those fellows? Came from where?'

'If you ask me, going behind that girl.'

So the jilted boys tried to make Carloboy uncomfortable and there were catcalls from the protection of fences and things like 'Hoo! Audrey!' (somehow they had found out the girl's name) and even more unkind remarks like, 'You're going to Homo's house to give your back to him?' and the tussles became frantic with fists, sticks, even the poles used to push water barrels being used.

Within a week a goodly crop of lumps, bumps, bruises and contusions were spread pretty evenly among the juvenile male population with the cream reserved for the Berenger boy who had to have stitches in his foot because, in the hurly burly he had leaped aside and tread on a broken bottle. Audrey, bless her, recognized that a lot of the skirmishes were due to her hold on this boy. She smiled wisely and held his hand. 'I love you also,' she said simply and that was enough.

Peace came eventually. Carloboy, although with no training to be any sort of diplomat, just went among the gang and said how. They scowled, each in his own way. 'So what are you fellows doing?'

'Nothing. You have other things to do, no?'

'Yes. And one day I'm going to marry her. She also loves me. She told me. So what's the harm?'

The conversation became excited in nature. There was much ribbing and joshing but Carloboy was special now. He had a girl! 'So what are you doing tomorrow?' Benno asked.

'Nothing. They are all going to Mihintale. Going by car. Will come in the evening.'

'So you won't go?'

'Asked me to come also but no room, men. All bundled up inside. But Homo said will take only Maurius and Quinny and Audrey and me to Kekirawa. Taking his gun also to shoot some *korawakkas*.[1] Will give us also to shoot. Anyway I'm taking my airgun also and 'pult.'

1. Teal.

'Nothing like the 'pult, men. By the time taking aim and all we can kill two birds with the 'pult.'

Everyone agreed.

'So come go to the Tissa Wewa tomorrow. Good time for fishing now.'

'Right.'

'Right? Everybody?'

And all said right and all was right again which was a mercy since the 'internecine warfare' was getting on every railwayman's nerves.

It's a peculiar thing about holidays. They begin with a yawn. Days are slow, each hour dawdling along like a slow moving ice-cream van. Half way through Time seems to wake up, does twenty push-ups and begins to canter. Carloboy, sobered in love and desperately dismissing all thoughts of parting, was pained deeply. Elder sisters Maureen and Carmen ribbed him, but gently, and seemed to accept that their little sister (who had grown up a year ago and had small rounded breasts) liked this boy and was happy in his company. Of course, they frowned when he said 'bloody' and 'damn' and said he spoke too many bad words, but Audrey must have seen more in him. Yes, she said, she loved him very much, and they walked to the banks of the Malwatte river and Carloboy said, 'Let's cross to the other side. The water is very low today,' and slippers in hand they stepped into the chocolate-green water which had marzipan flecks of sun in its slow roll onwards.

'My dress will get wet,' Audrey squealed, 'here, hold my slippers, ooh, it's slippery on these rocks,' and Carloboy, surefooted as a goat, caught her hand, then held her very close and they stood together, looking into each other's eyes in the middle of the river.

'I love you,' he said simply and she dimpled and her dark eyelashes fell, screening her eyes. All she said was 'yes' but she allowed him to hold her and then gently touched his face. Her fingers brushed his lips and suddenly he had dropped the slippers and kissed her fingers and she whispered, 'Always?'

He put an arm around her. 'What?'

'Always you'll love me?'

He nodded and she made a soft sound, a dove-like murmur. 'I love you also . . . always,' and he kissed her cheek and then, for the first time, found his lips against a girl's lips. It hadn't been easy, he thought later, hugging himself in a dreamy daze. Her nose and his nose seemed to get in the way, but they kissed and kissed again and drank deep at each others lips and the water soaked the hem of her dress and the legs of his trousers. Far down the river two pairs of rubber slippers floated merrily away. They didn't give this a thought, even when barefooted they roamed the banks, pausing ever so often to kiss, to touch each other, to seek out promises, and as they came together he felt her small breasts against him and he knew that he was hard too, and surely she could feel him against her. He was surprised and shy to notice the patch of wetness on his trousers. She saw and said nothing, then with the wisdom of the girl-woman gently took his hand.

'No one has touched me like this before,' she said. 'Only you. Only you I'll allow,' and they lay together under a big tree, his hand nestled in her, and they kissed and kissed and they both wanted desperately to tell the world to stay still.

They never came to the river again. Maureen, more mother-henny, declared that they should never have gone wading and losing slippers and all that sort of thing. Also, who asked them to go off alone like that? Maurius and Quinny were looking all over! And suddenly Time began a madcap gallop and it was devastating to learn that the de Sellas were returning to Kandy. Everything blurred into an awful sense of misery, of an ache that churned from the pit of the stomach to the chest and then probed the mind with spaghetti fingers. Carloboy went to the platform, hung at the carriage window, touching her fingers, willing her to stay. But she was going. A long journey, too. All the way to Polgahawela. Then change trains for Kandy. Her face, her dark hair, her bright eyes fixed on him. As the train moved out, he ran as far as the platform took him, and then her face looked out and a hand waved and he stood, watching, mixed in a whirl of empty wind. The face stayed out, grew

smaller, more indistinct, a tiny brown-black dot. Carloboy
stood. The train had gone and suddenly Anuradhapura was
the loneliest, most desolate place on earth.

He went home with a sense of deep dejection. His
holiday, too, was coming to an end. 'Come and see me,'
Audrey had pleaded, and he had promised, as blindly and
as earnestly as all lovers do. In the veranda that evening
there was much talk about the war. What did he care about
war? He strolled past Direcksze's bungalow, then went to
the river—their river, where they had stood, locked in that
first starry kiss. 'I must go to Kandy,' he muttered. An
iguana slunk in the watergrass, its long tail twisting as it
clumped in an ungainly fashion. He touched his pocket and
thought, 'Forgot to bring my 'pult.' It had to be true love! He
had even forgotten his catapult!

In many Burgher homes—and the homes of all other
nationalities for that matter—the Americans were the heroes
and America the custodian of the most terrible weapon of
the age. Even with a sort of terrible lovesickness which
swamped him, Carloboy was as agog at the war news, the
war stories, as anyone else. The war comics flooding out of
America were food and drink to thousands of starry-eyed
boys who revelled in the exploits of that new breed of men
who were the famous Carrier pilots and struck deadly blows
at enemy bases after launching from aircraft carriers.

'Big, men . . . mus' be like football ground, no, the deck?'
Sonnaboy would say and driver Edema would whistle and
say, 'Such huge things how going in the sea even can't
think.' After a bottle of arrack the carriers got bigger,
naturally, and the fighter bombers they carried increased
dramatically.

There was much technical (and rapidly slurred) talk
about Landing Signals Officers and the Hellcats and how
they had their own private call signs and this worrisome
business of 'controlled' crashes.

'No! You mean after they bomb and come they have to
come to the carrier and crash?'

'No, men, you don't understand? Coming fast, no? And
ship also not just sitting and waiting. Going up and down

and this way that way in the waves. So have to make like crash landing.'

'My God. Nothing happens to the planes?'

'Who knows? But anyhow they go and come, no? It seems have big wires and under the planes in the back have big hooks. As plane comes down hook catches the wire and pulls the plane to stop.'

'My God, like a catapult or something?'

'Yes, men. Like that have four wires. Sometimes in the dark pilots are missing all the wires. If they don't put speed and go up again, fall straight into the sea!'

'Holy mother of God! Pour, men, another drink. Must give these buggers to drive an engine to see.'

'Hah! Pukka that will be. Will climb the bloody platform and go through the station!'[1]

The defeat of the Third Reich caused church bells to be rung vigorously and the atomic strike created universal awe. So this was how it all ended. A single plane in a grey, battle-clouded sky and a projectile that shredded the land into crimson, blood spattered dust, bearing down with all the lust, the vehemence of war. There were no people—just a gravy, a thick oily sludge that was once a metropolitan population. Who, then, could comprehend such an obliteration? Carloboy couldn't. He was just a boy, wasn't he? He returned to Aunty Leah's, wrote long letters to Maurius and Quinny and volumes to Audrey. Even Marlene who liked to spread her brown legs, then place an ankle on a knee and relax while she read, held no special interest for the boy. He had been very taken up with the way Marlene sat. As she cocked up her leg, bent over her books, her skirt would fall away and a fat thigh would be revealed all the way up to where her knicker cut into her flesh. He never knew it then, but it was Marlene's 'come hither' gesture. Yes,

---

1. Inebriated summations notwithstanding, readers will agree that carrier pilots had to be a daring breed of men. The author is reminded of the World War II pilots' ten commandments. With typical gallows humour, he declared: *Check frequently thine airspeed lest the ground rise up and smite thee.*

Marlene was interesting, and very beautiful too. He had loved her. . . when? Oh, that was a light year ago. He had even slipped a note among her books one day and yet, the girl gave no indication that she had seen or read it. And she was older, too, and thought much of her studies and looked upon the world with too much seriousness for her age.

The first wet dream made Carloboy feel that he was growing to be quite depraved. He woke up, hazily recalling that somewhere, a naked girl had figured in his dream. But he was wet and the stickiness on his pajamas made him get up hurriedly. This was awful. Who was that girl? And were there other people, too, in his dream? He went to the loo, passed urine, washed himself and came back to bed, yawning. He felt very tired.

In school he told Alan Bartholomeusz: 'I say, hell of a thing happened. Last night when I was sleeping, dreamt I was landing a girl and had a leak.'

Alan grinned and yelled: 'Hey, you heard? Von Bloss shot in his sleep.'

Abdi chuckled, 'Must have been putting a shake in his sleep.'

'No, men, it was a dream,' and Carloboy explained.

'Sha, if I also can dream like that. You can remember the girl?'

'No, men. But in the dream saw the cunt an' all and I was landing and suddenly I got up spill all over the sheet also.' So, gradually, school claimed him and the pang of that platform parting became duller and duller and when Sonnaboy announced that another brother or sister was now shaping up in his mother's womb he just nodded, while Leah looked quite startled and said: 'One in the hand, one in the stomach. How going to manage like this God knows.'

George grunted, 'Took and went there, no? If stayed with the mother no problem.'

'Yes, men, but living in that tiny house. There even nice upstair house and all.'

'When is the baby coming?'

'December, I think. You heard?' she told Carloboy. 'Good Christmas present for you.'

Carloboy scorned reply. The postman had brought him a letter from Audrey who said she was going to act in a school play and why couldn't he come and see her perform? Also, she said, her brothers both wished to become doctors and what would he be? And she wished to be his wife and that was enough, wasn't it?

'One thing, quite quiet now he's becoming,' Leah said and George rubbed his beaky nose.

'Don't even say like that,' he warned. 'Can see the father, no? If quiet also don't know what will do next.'

'Uncle George, for this art competition need fifteen rupees.'

'What? What competition? And from where money to give like that?'

'See in the papers have. Bluebird Art Competition. Have to send drawing or painting of a child in a flower garden. Entrance fee is ten rupees and see the prizes. First prize hundred rupees, then fifty rupees, like that. Have to send by post the picture.'

'Just keep quiet, men. I haven't money.'

'So what, Uncle George, if I win?'

'Rubbish. Waste of money all this.'

'I drew the picture also. And next week closing date.'

'I haven't I told, no?'

'But Uncle—'

'Don't come to worry like this! Your father never gave money for all this. Only for your food and bus fare giving something.'

'Huh, if Daddy was here would have given.'

'So then write and ask your bloody father!'

Carloboy stormed indoors, brought out his picture, crushed it into a ball and flung it in the garden. 'There! That's what you want, no! You wait I'll write and tell what you said!'

'What did I say?' George hooted. 'You think you can show your temper here? This is my house, you heard.'

Leah tried to pull Carloboy away. He jerked free and his eyes blazed. 'Telling bloody father! Why? You're not a father? So you re also a bloody father, no?'

George shot out of the lounger. Leah wrung her hands. Carloboy recklessly glared at the man. 'You think I want to stay here? Bloody miser, won't give five cents to a beggar even!'

'Get out at once!' George roared.

'Now bloody father! When we were in 34th Lane nicely came to drink my father's arrack and eat and go!'

'Arrack! Your father gave arrack? Your father gave piss to drink, you heard? Piss!'

Carloboy said, 'We'll see. We'll see what you'll get. Catch and kill you, that's what my father will do. You can tell anything, I don't care!' and he banged into his room, trembling in the fever of the moment and refused to eat. He didn't know how Leah took up the crumpled picture, carefully opened it, gently releasing it crease by crease. She took it inside, showed it to a wide-eyed Marlene who whispered, 'It's nice, Mummy, in vain he spoilt it, no?'

Leah laid a thick napkin over it and plied the smoothing iron. Slowly, the sheet of drawing paper was restored, although colour smudges did lie in lines where the creases had been ironed out. She checked the newspapers, then rummaged in the Cream Crackers tin in the kitchen for the money she carefully hid away. 'Don't tell,' she cautioned Marlene, 'we'll send and see.'

It was an all-island competition and Carloboy was startled one morning by a summons from the principal. J.C.A. no less. Even Pol Thel throbbed visibly. 'What have you been doing this time?' he asked.

'Nothing, sir.'

'Nothing? Then go to the Principal's office. Here's the chit.'

The class buzzed. Carloboy rose slowly, then swaggered to the door. The swagger was essential. What the devil could the principal want? But J.C.A. had a smile on his chubby face and asked why Carloboy paid such little attention to Art, and anyway congratulations were in order, weren't they? Carloboy blinked.

He hadn't the foggiest until Corea told him that he had won fifty rupees being the second prize in the Bluebird Art

Competition. Carloboy's hands shook and for a minute amazement washed over him. Corea gave him the page from the *Ceylon Daily News*. Yes, it was there in bold black type. 'Second prize Rs 50—C. P. von Bloss' and the information that winners would receive their cheques in the mail. Corea smiled slightly. 'You see what thought and application can do? You have the makings, boy and you are, I feel, sadly misguided. *Mens sana*—you know what that means? *Mens sana in copore sano*—a healthy mind in a healthy body. That's what I want of my students. You insist on playing the fool. Why?'

Carloboy groaned inwardly. Why not? Life held too much for a twelve-year-old who had lived through such things as an atom bomb and kissing a girl knee deep in the Malwatte river and living in an Anuradhapura railway bungalow which everybody called 'Monkey House'[1] and ogling Marlene's fat thighs each time she cocked a leg in his presence.

Why? The whole damn world was playing the fool! The civics periods had degenerated into long discussions on events leading to the Second World War—interesting enough, if only 'Gon' didn't make it so utterly boring. Why, the ribald roistering conversations between railway cronies at home were more colourful, interesting and eminently listenable. He had thrilled to the gory renderings of Pearl Harbour and how the Japs and sunk HMS *Prince of Wales* and HMS *Repulse*. Rommel's capture of Tobruk had been another high point, and again how Montgomery had brought Rommel to his knees.

'How dew like!' Sonnaboy had exulted. 'Finished for Rommel. Whole army surrendered. Quarter of a million buggers!' That was May 1943 and North Africa was rid, finally, of the Axis forces. Hitler was, as Edema had said, 'getting it tight from all sides, serves the bastard right!' But Hitler didn't seem to care, or did he?

'Three hundred thousand buggers gone!' Totoboy would cry, waving a small Union Jack. He loved waving the flag

---

1. Why this is so is detailed in *Yakada Yakā* (Penguin, 1994).

even if he had poked it into Iris' eye one day and had to take her to the Eye Hospital in Darley Road.

'Gone? Gone where? What the devil are you talking about?'

'Gone! Finished! Russians killed 300,000 Germans! And how? 'Nother 100,000 surrendered!' It was the great Stalingrad victory. And the war got closer to Ceylon too. The Japanese tried to launch an attack on India but were defeated at the battle of Kohima and America began its long-range bombing of Japan from the Marianas. And then came D-Day and the liberation of France and that famous Channel crossing by the Allied Armada on 6 June 1944. All the world was in a ferment. So was every home in Sri Lanka, and for sure, every classroom in every school in the island.

Old 'Penda' gave his boys a graphic description of the debacle in France. 'You know-um-Hitler is not listening to advice. He won't even allow his generals to retreat. So a lot of men are being trapped and killed.' He outlined how a group of German military leaders had tried to assassinate Hitler. 'The man was lucky and see what he did? Executed everybody. Even Rommel was caught.'

'But, sir, Rommel committed suicide.'

'Yes, yes, but only because Hitler said, commit suicide or I will have you shot. So what to do? Rommel killed himself.' He rose to write on the blackboard. 'Take down these dates and notes. These are the most important dates in the world. Always remember them.' And 'Penda' catalogued those stirring times and when La Brooy, who was monitor, wanted to wipe the blackboard after the bell had rung, Carloboy said, 'Don't do that? Let it be. You don't understand, men? These are what have happened now. This is our time also, no?'

And 'Penda's' potted history of German and Japanese surrender had remained and been remarked on by every successive master in every successive period except, of course 'Cowpox' who received his charges in the chemistry lab and had his own daily battle of the Bunsen burners.

Years later, when Carloboy had been sacked from the college and been well pummelled by Sonnaboy for this 'disgrace to the family', he had sat morosely over his monitor's exercise books and come across 'Penda's' notes:

GERMANY:

April 25, 1945:	Russians entered Berlin and advance units of the Russian and American forces met on the River Elbe.
April 30, 1945:	Mussolini captured and shot by Italian partisans. Hitler committed suicide in his bunker and his body burnt in the courtyard of the Chancery.
May 7, 1945:	Hitler's successor, Admiral Doenitz, surrenders.

JAPAN:

August 6, 1945:	Atom bomb dropped on Hiroshima by an American Superfortress bomber. 78,000 people killed in a single blast.
August 8, 1945:	Russia declares war on Japan. Invades Manchuria.
August 9, 1945:	Second atom bomb dropped on Nagasaki.
August 14, 1945:	Japan surrenders.

It was all so unbelievable that he, Carloboy, had lived through all this. How many hours had he spent poring over the many shocks and aftershocks of this massive show of human hatred—the destruction of the Japanese navy at the battle of Leyte Gulf, the decimation of the Japanese airforce at Iwo Jima and Okinawa, those ghastly concentration camps of Belsen and Buchenwald and the grim extermination of millions of Jews at Auschwitz. And what about the Battle of the Bulge and Hitler's famous Siegfried Line? And those terrible V1 flying bombs and those silent, deadly V2 rockets. What, he thought could any boy of twelve do when the whole world seemed intent on slaughter, offence and defence?

All he did, as Corea said, was play the fool! At least, in this, he excelled and became a quickly identified plague to his mentors.

It was so easy to make 'Cowpox' a victim. The master (who always slapped his boys according to Geometry) would sit in the lab, keep his pipe on the desk, and after detailing a simple experiment which would not result in any terrible aftermath, relax, read a book, nod over it and even doze off for a few unguarded minutes. It was the work of an instant to push a few crystals of iodine into his pipe, burying the crystals in the Three Nuns tobacco the man relished.

The staffroom had never known anything quite like it. 'Cowpox' came in, put down his books and clip file, shrugged off his twill coat and lit up. There was a teeny-weeny crackle and then, a horrified man, eyes bulging, flung down his pipe and rubbed at his lips before rushing to the water filter. A thick thread of violet smoke curled out of the bowl of burning tobacco!

Caning Carloboy became the pastime of every master. 'Bada' would glower. 'What is this? Again? In the morning I gave you six cuts. Now what?' Later he didn't even ask. But one day the wily man checked after the fourth cut and gave his victim a quizzical look. 'You know, von Bloss, I don't seem to be making much of an impression. And you know something, boy? I like to make an impression! But you seem to be determined to deny me the satisfaction. Take off your trousers!!'

'Sir?'

'You heard me! Take them off!!'

When Carloboy stood in his underpants, the headmaster chuckled. 'Aha! I thought so. Very ingenious. Now take that off and stand still!'

Carloboy unhitched the padding of motorcycle tube rubber he had cleverly wrapped around his bum. The six cuts, vigorously applied on his thin underpants, smarted like the devil. 'Bada' dropped the rubber into his wastepaper basket. 'You may go,' he said with deep satisfaction, 'and this trophy,' indicating the rubber which he prodded with the end of his cane, 'will be exhibited in the staffroom for the edification of the whole staff.'

Ruefully and with much rubbing, Carloboy went back to class, then cheered himself at the thought that he had weathered many such sessions and there had to be more ways, surely, to upholster (if not skin) a cat.

But the mayhem continued and it infected others too. Athula, would have none of it. A podgy, well-built thick-lipped and wide-mouthed boy he was well-liked by his cronies and much disliked by those who thought him very much a damp squib. Athula was also an ambitious fellow and to boys like von Bloss who were seemingly born unambitious, there was little in common between them. They tolerated each other, being classmates and Athula would dismiss Carloboy's many peccadillos with that superior sniff that said: 'What can you expect. He's a no-class Burgher and we are from good families.'

Athula in turn was scorned by Carloboy who watched him waddle, quite fat-assed, his posterior masquerading as a bowl of jelly and hissed: 'Copacabana!' A delicious name for a boy whose arse moved to the rhythm of his soul. Athula, as would be expected, was sorely disturbed. He dared not challenge Carloboy who had no use for the Queensberry rules. Also, as was constantly demonstrated, the boy seemed to have fists of iron. It had happened, quite naturally, one day. Each boy had a little wooden locker in which he kept the usual rubbish and what was better kept away from class for fear of whatever it was being confiscated. Interval time saw a stampede for lockers where such strange items as three-days-old chewing gum, pen knives, etc., were extracted. Ashoka Madanayake had a pet squirrel in his locker. Ranjit Jaya, who was a roly-poly with calves in keen competition with his thighs, had cake and a bottle of strawberry jam while Doyne had a policeman's hat and a bottle of ammonia! (The author couldn't explain why—the mind truly boggles). Farouk Abdi, who was proud of his biceps and had begun weight training had a poster which read:

Cows may come
and cows may go
but the bull in this house
goes on forever!

(Later, he had set this same poster, ornately framed, inside
the door of his bachelor apartment—his only souvenir of
madcap college days.)

On the day Carloboy mislaid the key to his locker, he
didn't fret. He just grinned, swung a fist and split the door.
Soon, he was designated emergency locker-opener and when
this reached the staffroom, Danton Obeya, who was the
boxing master hmmed and said that a pair of fists like that
belonged in the gym. Also, shrilled 'Bella', the boy should be
dissuaded from going around, destroying school property
and what next? I ask, what next?

So Athula accepted 'Copacabana' in good grace, and
Vishva, who had collided painfully with those fists, vouched
most fervently that it was wisdom to stay three metres out
of reach.

Thus did the months flit by and December holidays saw
Beryl von Bloss at Leah's from where she was rushed to
hospital to deliver her fifth child, Michael Granton Duke[1]
and it was transfer time, too, and Sonnaboy descended on
Anna *en masse* where the entire family squirrelled into a
single room until negotiations for a house in Saranankara
Road, in Kalubowila, were completed.

Carloboy was disgruntled. There was, he thought, nothing
to look forward to. He had endured Uncle George, passed
his time smirking at Marlene's legs, written fervently and
faithfully to Audrey, done his best and worst at school. And
there was, half a day away by rail, that jewelled land of
gleaming stupas and silver-swept rivers and vacant-faced
tanks and clamorous jungle. In transferring Sonnaboy, the
railway had slammed the door on a boy's wonderland and
tossed away the key.

---

1. Details of this Boxing Day delivery are elaborated in *Yakada Yakā* (Penguin, 1994).

Nobody cared tuppence for what a thirteen-year-old thought or did not think. Germany swept into centre stage and the Burghers, all Christians, had a new whipping boy— the great Godless Russia. Father Sebastian would get all worked up at Sunday mass and thunder on and on at sermon time until he grew quite hoarse and croak through the offertory. A draught of mass wine put him right, however, and he would eventually leave the sanctuary, altar boys leading, well satisfied that he had given Stalin and Lenin and Trotsky and other unpronounceable blighters what for.

Father Sebastian held strong views. He declared that the radio was the work of the devil and foamed at the mouth when he heard, at a St Lawrence School Carnival, a group of boys singing a hot favourite of the times.

I, I, I, I, I, I like you very much,
I, I, I, I, I, I think you're grand,
Why, why, why, why, why, why, when I feel your touch
My heart starts to beat, to beat the band.

This was vile, lewd, all this feeling and touching. 'Don't sing these I, I songs!' he screeched, importuning parents to protect their children from these sinful modern songs. He also detested that rousing 'Pistol-packing Mama' which was always bounced around at parties together with 'She'll be coming round the mountain when she comes' and to which strange new verses had been added—verses like:

She'll be sucking my banana when she comes

and:

She'll be wearing pippie knickers when she comes.

Indeed 'she' could be relied on to be doing the damndest things whenever she came, and as the arrack level lowered her accomplishments became more outrageous.

Father Sebastian warned his parishioners that these were surely the Signs of the Times. 'Think about what is happening today!' he would bellow. 'Pray! pray! See what Russia is doing! In Poland they have abolished the Holy Father's administration. Now even the priests there are appointed by these Communists! But is our Catholic spirit broken? Never! In Hungary also this has happened. And you are having parties and singing dirty songs?'

Yes, *Communism* was the new dirty word of the times. The Catholic Messenger spewed forth virulent attacks on this anti-Christ—the red machine that destroyed churches and hounded the faithful. When Cardinal Beran was expelled from Czechoslovakia in 1951 there were yips and yaps of horror and Father Sebastian declared that 'Martyrdom was upon us'.

Carloboy didn't pay much heed to the deterioration of Germany which began like a hoof-and-mouth disease in 1948. At thirteen years he had (a) brought a mynah bird into class and caused a hellish uproar and (b) nearly broken the vice principal's neck. As a result of (b) he had been caned and embarked on (c) which was to report his caning to the Cinnamon Gardens police. This caused more complications involving an inspector who was determined to do his duty and Sonnaboy who wished to flay his son preferably before the whole school and the vice principal who complained long and loud that he needed a surgical collar.

Masters met in hushed conclave. How can one little demon cause so much trouble in two days? One even ventured that the problem was glands. But Bruno said he has the only pupil he had who could recite the whole of Gray's *Elegy* by heart and didn't this mean anything? Pol Thel snorted and said, 'Decidedly not! The boy's a menace. See what he did—' and produced a map of Ceylon which Carloboy had drawn and proudly labelled MY MUMMY GOING TO HAVE A BABY—and couldn't understand why Mr Anghie laughed till the tears rolled down his cheeks. The author would like to reproduce this map which he was able to secure and which gave Pol Thel a nervous tic for the rest of the day.

Let us unroll (a), (b) and (c) in order that it be forever on record, shall we? What else could a boy, to whom

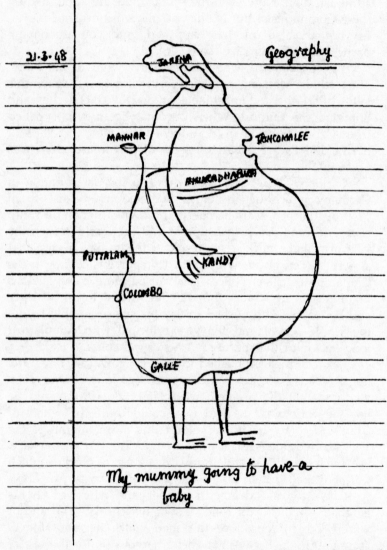

Carloboy's map of Ceylon. This was secured from the home of
Mr Baptiss, given to the author by his widow. This good lady, too,
died in 1993.

Anuradhapura was so special, do but carry his catapult with him wherever he went? It was a symbol. Hadn't he brought down a bronze pigeon with it before Audrey's admiring eyes? The 'pult stood for a glorious boyhood, unfettered, unconfined. He winged the mynah bird while chewing on a sugary bun in the tuck shop. He used glass taws as ammunition, better than any pebble. And he aimed carefully to stun. The idea was to take the bird home, cage it, teach it to talk. In class, he popped the irate bird into his desk where it sulked, having no doubt the mother of all headaches (*Saddam Hussein, please note!*).

Besides the usual stalwarts, the class also held a tall, dark gawky boy who walked quite disjointedly and was, alas, an epileptic. Bassie, as his name was, was a mass of nerve-ends, had a sort of internal lever movement all his own, tended to drool and was painfully ignored by masters as a dangerous commodity. One never knew with Bassie. He would be perfectly normal, then his eyes would glaze, cross, and his hands would begin to twitch. Then his legs would begin to kick out and his head would begin to assume an angle that 'Cowpox' would have given him a medal for. He would foam, too, and emit strange garroty noises while Abdi would leap on his chair and gleefully announce that Bassie was having a fit.

Yes, Bassie was the beloved of the class. Abey would note that there was a History test on Thursday. '*Adai*, Bassie, can you get a fit in third period on Thursday?'

Bassie would smile weakly, say something like gobble-gobble and frown at his Hall and Stevens *Algebra*.

When Carloboy opened his desk to check on his mynah bird which was scrishing and scrushing madly inside, the bird gave him a baleful look, then made its dash for freedom. It also gave vent to a stream of Mynah Billingsgate, both irritable and indignant, and flashed across the class, whooped over Pol Thel's head, swerved inches past Bassie's nose and rollicked around, scolding incessantly and demanding to know where the tuck shop was.

The uproar was only to be expected and yells of 'mad bird! mad bird!' and more personal remarks like 'catch and put some pol thel' and all to the accompaniment of falling chairs and thumped desks made the scene pretty frenzied. Bassie, too, obliged, and by the time the mynah gave a last hair-raising screech and shot through an open window into the quadrangle, boys were shoving wooden rulers and pencils into the epileptic's mouth and Pol Thel had rushed for help and the row, Jowls said, quite paradoxically, was 'unspeakable'. Well, perhaps he was right. It was more of the 'yellable' quality. Bassie's parents were summoned and the boy taken home in a limousine. Oh, very rich were they. Old man Bassie had a bookshop and they lived in a plush home in Bambalapitiya. Carloboy, needless to say, was whacked and Pol Thel shakily declared that he had aged ten years and demanded that something, anything, be done about that boy!

Jowl selected his longest and stingy-est cane for the occasion. It was new, and seemed to have been saved for a very special purpose. Carloboy stared. Never had he seen such a long, malevolent cane. With a quick intake he positioned himself. Six may be of the best, Jowl had said, but twelve were infinitely better.

Canings in the Forties and Fifties were accepted, hither and yon, as standard tactics. Children, looking for a crumb of comfort would go home to say, 'I got a caning in school today. Not even my fault. That behind fellow pulled my chair and I upset the ink and got a caning.'

Daddy would look at the dishevelled ink-stained figure. 'Very good! Go and rub a limeskin on those ink marks and put your shirt to wash!'

However, ply the rattan as one wills, one was not expected to draw blood. Teachers could be pretty sadistic at times. The old and beautiful technique of giving a child a *kanay* was frowned upon. A master had allowed his enthusiasm to get the better of him once and burst a boy's eardrum. Knocks or carefree swats across the head were better and the edge of a ruler on the knuckles very satisfying. This time, however, Jowl drew blood. The end of the cane, curling lovingly round, split the skin on the boy's forearm. Every successive blow sent that same cane end burrowing into the wound. Twelve cuts later, Carloboy stood, face twisted in pain while blood dripped down his hand and onto the floor.

Jowl blinked. Should never have used such a long cane he thought. 'Go and get something put on your hand,' he said sharply. Carloboy grimaced, spun on his heel and walked out, out of the college, marched along Racecourse Avenue and straight to the Cinnamon Gardens police station. His lower arm still bled. 'I want to put a complaint,' he said breathlessly and the desk sergeant who only wrote complaints in Sinhala and couldn't make out what, bounced the boy into Inspector Patternot's office where Carloboy said his vice principal had assaulted him.

Patternot was a Thomian—he had been educated at St Thomas' College and as everyone will tell you, Royal and St Thomas' are deadly rivals. Patternot clucked, examined the hand and clucked again. 'Your dadda knows you came here?'

'No.'

'When did you get caned?'

'Just now. If one boy gets a fit in class I must get caned?'

'So if cane pricked your hand why didn't you take your hand away.'

'Won't allow. Must hold the table and wait. If try to move will cane summore. I know, no, everytime I'm the one he's caning. Can't even pass his room. If see me calling and caning.'

Patternot chuckled. Bugger must be turning Royal upside down. 'I'll tell you what? You go and tell your dadda. If he wants let him come and put a complaint. Now you came from school without telling anyone, no? When you go back might ask where you were and give another punishment. So what are you going to do?'

Carloboy stared. 'If beat me like this why I cannot put a complaint? Useless telling Daddy. Just he'll say very good and keep quiet.'

Patternot grinned. It struck him that here was a swell story for the club. 'I'll tell you what? You go home. I'll go and put the fear of Moses into your vice principal.'

Carloboy doubted this very much. Moses and all his Israelite brickmakers couldn't faze old Jowl but the idea of going home appealed. All he had to do was get his bicycle out of the shed and pedal away. Which he did.

Patternot, pulling a very serious face, called on Jowl and had, as he later said, words. He assured the man that he had not entertained a complaint but took a most serious view of the matter. The boy's father, he said, had every right to prosecute. Shylock, he reminded, was entitled to his pound of flesh but what had Portia decreed? 'Shed thou no blood . . .' wasn't that so?

Jowl nodded dumbly. A police inspector who quoted Shakespeare! It was all too much for the poor man.

The next morning he asked gruffly about Carloboy's arm. The boy informed him, stiff-voiced, that his mother had dressed it.

'I'm excusing you from cadet drill for a week.'

The boy said nothing.

'Now look here, von Bloss, I'm sorry about this. But it was an accident as you are plainly aware of.'

No answer.

'I understand that you went to the police.'

'Yes, sir.'

'Was that really necessary? You were punished for the uproar you caused in class.'

'Yes, sir.'

'Anyway, we will say no more about this.'

'Yes, sir.'

'What happened was an accident.'

'Yes, sir.'

Jowl meditated for a moment after Carloboy had gone. The boy was a menace. Ease off for a week, he thought, then I'll clout him again . . . and he cheered up considerably. That afternoon he bustled out of office and 104 pounds of boy fell on him!

It was Malin Abeya who looked down the school building from the second floor and noticed the stout wire, stapled into the red brickwork. It disappeared near the steps at the tennis court end, lodged in a conduit of sorts. The wire connected to the lightning rod.

'If you're so big,' he said, curling his lower lip (which always made him look like some galactic life form), 'why don't you climb down this?'

Carloboy peered over the side. 'Pooh! Anyone can do that!'

'So you do to see.'

'Wait, I'll take off my shoes.'

Malin scoffed in a nasty way. 'Shoes? You're calling those old cricket boots shoes?'

Carloboy crimsoned. The cricket boots were also a punishment. A week ago he had stopped on his way back from school at the Wellawatte canal. There, barefooted, near the Kinross Avenue railway bridge, where the canal met the sea, he had spent a very wet evening catching guppies which he transferred into a jam jar. And he lost his shoes. He stood, nonplussed. There was nobody in sight so all he could gather was that a stray wave with a fondness for shoes had nipped up and seized his.

He had found it quite tedious giving explanations. Why was it that boys were always asked to explain their every thought, word or deed? Also, these explanations were never believed. So he told his mother: 'I went to catch fish and my shoes went.'

Beryl glared. 'Went? Just like that went? What? Somebody wore and went?

'No-oo, must have gone in the waves.'

'Very nice. Your only pair also. Wait till your father comes home!'

Sonnaboy looked his son up and down. 'When you're going to behave yourself I don't know. Bigger you get the worse you're becoming. Now you wait till payday, you heard. You lose your shoes go barefoot to school!'

Cricket boots were all else he had. He spent some time with a pair of pliers, wrenching out the hobnails . . . and he hoped, quite foolishly, that the school wouldn't notice, which hope was dashed the instant he entered.

'*Adai*, von Bloss is coming in cricket boots. Oy, von Bloss, where's the match?'

Anyway, Carloboy tossed aside his footgear, dangled over the second floor ledge and tested the wire. It held. Thus assured he began a cautious descent. Malin fled. He wasn't going to witness this. The stapled wire held, and Carloboy found it tolerably easy although the wire cut into his fingers and the top of his palm. He was over the ground floor arch and the wire turned left to follow the huge pillar, and that's where the weak spot was. A staple gave way with a crumble of red dust and Carloboy clawed up to seize the upper section of wire. His feet slipped on the smooth crenellation of the arch and as the wire took his weight, another staple popped. It seemed to the swaying boy that thousands of boys were congregated below, hooting, whistling, cheering. His palms burned. Another staple tumbled from way up, bouncing on his shoulder. Jowl strode out. Above Carloboy let go, kicked out and fell. He hoped to clear the steps. He didn't. He landed like a sack of spuds on Jowl, who collapsed.

When the vice-principal rose, having assured himself then he had not been hit by an atom bomb, he gave Carloboy, quite unhurt except for deep blue wire scores on his palms, a terrible look. The man was hurting. His neck was stiffening, his shoulders seemed to have had a quarrel with his breastbone and emerged losers, his ribcage seemed to have made a bad impression on his lungs. He hobbled away, rubbing a hip that had suddenly begun to ache, and wrote a letter. It was to be delivered, by messenger, to Sonnaboy von Bloss.

It was an end-of-tether, very final sort of letter. It reminded that the Royal College had produced generations of the island's finest citizens and sportsmen. It also said that many of the country's most notable Burghers, the cream of the crop, so to say, had graced the hallowed halls, corridors and study rooms of this College whose houses honoured Hartley, Harvard, Marsh and Boake. It described Carloboy as an infinite pain in the Royalist butt. It admitted, albeit grudgingly, that boys in whatever form, would be boys, but the College was comfortable in the thought that boys could be defined, their needs anticipated, their moods met, their peculiar temperaments kept in check. The College prided itself on refining the crudest, polishing the roughest, bringing up those gems of purest ray serene from dark caves of ocean; unfathomed or whatever. Something had to be done, the latter insisted. In this case, the College needed help. Sonnaboy had to enforce what the college decreed.

Sonnaboy did. He gave a bellow of rage that rattled the neighbours' windows. 'Go and cut me a stick!' he thundered and Carloboy did just that. There was a large jak tree[1] in the garden. He tied his son to that and belaboured him until the boy's shirt was in bloodstained tatters and the neighbours rushed out to cling to him and drag him away and Orville Ludwick narrowly escaped being punched by a flailing fist.

It was the end of a madcap chapter. Carloboy spent two day at home. Beryl drenched his weals with Dettol and tended a split upper lip and dosed him with venivelgeta and, for once, looked white-lipped at her son. The long crushed-skin vents scabbed over and the boy found it uncomfortable to even take a deep breath. He avoided his father and turned his face to the wall when Sonnaboy entered the room.

He returned to school, swotted to catch up on a lot he had lost or blithely ignored. He sat the Junior School Certificate and passed commendably enough. Yes, 1948 hadn't been such a bad year after all.

---

1. *Arthocarpus heterophyllus.*

CHAPTER THIRTEEN

All things considered, 1948 had, to repeat our previous sentence, been quite a year. Among other things, it was a year of independence and thus a good enough occasion to impregnate the wife yet again . . . which was what Sonnaboy did.

This was accepted by all the family as more than natural and Carloboy and his sisters and toddler brother found an old familiar mummy with her old familiar big stomach, also most acceptable. Little Heather Evadne Maryse had howled in fear when Mummy came back with baby David Stefan Lance. It took a long time persuading the child that this was the same Beryl and that she was slim and most unusual because she had just brought forth David.

Perhaps, for Ceylon, 1948 will always be remembered—not because Carloboy nearly flattened his vice principal, but because, at long last, the British said 'nuff and hauled down the Union Jack.

Oh, there was always the agitation to be free. The British faced a rebellion in 1818 and another in 1848 and wrote home to say that these Ceylonese were most revolting. Certain local stalwarts even formed a Sinhala Maha Sabha[1] and

1. Sinhala Greater Council.

demanded Dominion Status. The Council, headed by a leading politico who was later bumped off by a Buddhist monk, actually demanded on March 26, 1942, that the British Secretary of State quit stalling and give an assurance of Dominion Status. The motion read:

(a) The British Government should give an assurance to the effect as has been done in the case of certain other British possessions and

(b) That Sir Stafford Cripps should be instructed to extend his Indian visit to Ceylon also in order that he might discuss the matter with representatives of the people.[1]

The National Congress also got into the act. In this body however, members held conflicting views. The D. S. Senanayake clique were all for Dominion Status. Wasn't it just right? D. S. for D. S. A made-to-order manifesto which had quite a ring to it!

J. R. Jayewardene, however, had different views and this led to the usual in-fighting. Long years later J.R.J. with great shrewdness of manner and force of personality became the island's first president, but it will always be remembered that he held a maverick stance when all others thought that freedom was all. In fact the infighting became so pitched that D.S.S. broke away from the National Congress and having sulked for the appropriate time, re-joined to put the J.R.J. clique in disarray.

The British hemmed and hawed. They were reminded of the Atlantic Charter. They also knew that the forces of nationalism were not lightly brushed aside any longer. So 1948 saw the end of British control in South Asia. Unlike India, Ceylon made a peaceful transition to self-government.

HRH the Duke of Gloucester strode in to read the Speech from the Throne and open the first session of the

---

1. Tabled by Mr A. P. Jayasura and seconded by Mr H. W. Amarasooriya. The former was member for Horana, the latter member for Galle.

Dominion Parliament. It was a neat record of British stewardship, actually:

> . . . After a period of nearly a century and a half, during which the status of Ceylon was that of a colony in My Empire, she now takes her place as a free and independent member of the British Commonwealth of Nations.

> It was in the year 1796 that the Dutch Governor of Colombo surrendered the town and all Dutch territory in Ceylon and under the terms of the Peace of Amiens of 1802, the Maritime Provinces of Ceylon became a British possession. In the year 1815, in accordance with the terms of the Kandyan Convention, the dominion of the Kandyan Province was vested in the Sovereign of Great Britain and the whole island thus became a part of My Empire.

> . . . I have given over charge of the conduct of all relations between my Government of the United Kingdom and My Government of Ceylon to my Secretary of State for Commonwealth Relations.

> I have also, on the advice of My Prime Minister in Ceylon, appointed Sir Henry Monck Mason Moore to be the first Governor General . . .

All very stirring of course, but the chronicler must record the feeling of regret that pulsed in many Burgher homes as the old order changed. Not just Burgher homes, true, for many Sinhalese and Tamil homes also felt that things would never be the same again.

'But we are free!' one would exclaim.

'How? Now can wear a sarong and go to Governor General's house?'

'Now our people in charge. Our people running our country!'

'Our people running. That's true. Already putting big

arguments. All the bloody cooks trying to make one big soup.'

'So what to do, men. So much to do, no? You think it's easy after so long? Have to try, no?'

Oh, there was much misgiving. 'Left us in the soup and going, that's what. You think it will be the same?'

'What, men? Our country, no? You wait and see, will you. We can do anything now.'

The Burghers, let it be said, were quite distressed. They had always held that edge under European rule. But the twinge passed quickly enough. Still under a British Governor-General, still a part of the British Commonwealth, they remained an essential part of the island's fabric and found that their services were as wanted as ever before. And the British, too, didn't just up and quit. Many remained on the tea plantations, the rubber estates, in the Port, the Oil Facilities offices, the shipping, brokering and freighting companies, in banks and merchant houses. At least, there was no Iron Curtain as forecast by Churchill that would descend through Europe.

Carloboy, of course, couldn't have cared a snap. In his new home in Kalubowila, he found an interesting set of new friends and new territory to explore. Things happened, of course. New neighbours reached that stage where they woke up each day to wish that they hadn't. Winston Dias, who was so proud of his king coconut palm would foam at the mouth each time he emerged to find that the best of his pink-orange crop had emigrated. Honorine van Sanden would blanch and scream to her children: 'Royce, Therese, Marlo, come inside at once!' and once her indignant litter came in with general remarks like, 'What, Mummy, won't allow to play, even,' Mrs van Sanden would grind her false teeth.

'Play? You're going to play with that nex'-door garden devil? Told, no, not to encourage? Saw what did to Mrs Lisk's windows? What were you doing in the corner there?'

Royce made a face. 'Nothing.'

'Nothing? You want a slap from me? What is that you're holding behind your back?'

Royce produces a catapult. It is in an embryonic stage.

'Give that here! Who told you to make this?' snatches the weapon away and marches to the kitchen. 'Coming to make catapults and give. Not enough breaking other peoples' windows. Now you want people to come here also and complain?' tosses the half-done 'pult into the fire, 'Next time he comes I'll give him with the broomstick! Not enough what he's doing, now coming to make and give here also? and what are you also going to do with the boys, miss?' this to Therese who is only nine and as mischievous as a parcel of monkeys, 'Told, no, to take a broom and sweep the house?'

Therese gives her famous hangdog look.

Fascinating, too, was the Dutch canal that skirted Saranankara Road and carried household rubbish in festering piles—empty Kotex boxes, coconut shells, rotting banana leaves, shreds of sacking, empty sardine tins, old bandages, shredded bicycle tyres, whatever. This waterway looped around like a spineless knicker tape on a dirty midriff. On the Wellawatte bank was a colony of squatters in cadjan huts who ripened the air with their everyday chatter and, in lighter moments, kept threatening to fuck each other's mothers. This, if taken seriously, would immediately classify this lower stratum of Sinhala society as a bunch of evil-minded mother-fuckers who also wielded knives and clubs with gusto.

The neighbourhood girls, too, were interesting and quite appealing to any hot-blooded boy. There was, above all, the Swan's little beauties, Marianne and Rosabelle, who considered every boy for miles around their personal property and were, as a result, much detested by Sonia Beekmeyer, Maryse Lisk, Carla Gray, Menik Wijesinghe, Barbara Fernando, Renee Ludwick, Nirasha Amerasinghe and Janine and Josephine de Kretser.

The boys, in lazier moments, bunched under a cashew tree in old Boteju's garden, would discuss the merits and demerits of the girls around them.

'*Machang*,[1] Tony, your sister is looking nice these days.'

'Why? You're getting interested? So put a cap[2] if you want,' says Tony Gray expansively.

'So just put a word, will you.'

'You're mad? She'll eat my head. 'Nother thing I think that Tudor Wijesinghe is interested in her. When go to Sunday school whole time he's talking with her.'

'*Adai*, Merril, fine one you are. What about Sonia, then?' says Malcolm Morrel.

'What about her?' asks Merril de Kretser.

'Just see this bugger,' Malcolm says, 'only last week was running behind that Sonia Beekmeyer. What? She gave you the boot or what?'

'Yes, I also noticed,' Carloboy says, 'now suddenly he's interested in Tony's sister.'

Anil Fernando, the smallest of the gang pipes up. 'That Menik is also not bad, no?'

The boys stare and guffaw. 'What do you know, you small bugger? How the bugger? Menik! Pukka one you're saying not bad. Half the buggers in the bloody Polytechnic must have landed her already.'

Carloboy jostles Anil and grins. 'See your size. She'll eat you, you go close. Why don't you put a cap to Therese?'

Royce van Sanden would snort. 'You don't come to try even. My mother will kill you.'

Carloboy stretches. 'Hot, men, today. You heard what happened to Maryse? Big row. Father caught and hammered the tuition master also.'

'I say, yes, men. Not to be seen now, no?'

'Keeping in the house. Won't allow to go anywhere. These days even Ivor won't come to play.'

'Why, what happened?'

'Pukka thing, men. Tuition master used to come, no, to

---

1. Sinhala 'brother-in-law' but universally used as a form of friendly address. A sort of acknowledgement that we are all brothers under the skin, perhaps.

2. Sort of like 'throw your cap in the ring'. To cap a girl was to show, in various ways, that one was interested in her.

teach Sinhala? Mrs Lisk caught, men. Master's hand under the dress.'

'No!'

'Yes, men. An' she's also nicely squeezing his cock. Hell of a row there was.'

'Bloody wretch. How the parts she's putting when going on the road? One day I put a whistle and should have seen the face. Now how?'

'Wait, will you,' says Alan Ludwick, 'she'll come one day, no. Must put a hoot and say how the tuition!'

All most entertaining of course and Carloboy would go to his room to write many sheets of undying love to Audrey although he had, as he admitted, 'other fish to fry', one being Carla Gray who accompanied him to the mosquito-laden, untenanted, overgrown, tree-peopled garden that lay beyond the fences and an abandoned rice field and there, snug and unseen in the confines of a thick hedge, allowed herself to be kissed and have her knickers yanked off and lay on a pile of damp straw while Carloboy rode her, spent himself and dusted away the black ants that ran along her thighs. He comforted himself in the thought that what Audrey didn't know couldn't hurt her a whit, and, surely, he didn't love Carla, did he? Quite the man of the world was our Carloboy becoming!

Audrey, however, was becoming more insistent. Couldn't he come for the holidays, for a week, for a weekend? Didn't he care anymore? Shrewdly, the girl also wrote that if she were he, she wouldn't care what anybody said. 'I'll just take the first bus and come,' she wrote, adding reams of gushes, undying love, and wilily enough, how the thought of that eternal morning on the banks of the Malwatte river still made her tremble at the knees and give her that very warm feeling in places she was too shy to mention.

In college, too, Bruno took up the *Adventures of Tom Sawyer*, and Carloboy revelled in the high jinks on the Mississippi. Would he ever have such freedom, he thought. And thought again, 'Why not?' That evening he cycled to Maradana, circuited the junction, the railway station and followed, along Drieberg's Avenue, the railway lines, noting the direction. He came upon the black iron Victoria bridge spanning the Kelani river. Crossing this, he followed the road. It branched. Roundabout signposts said Negombo to left, Kandy to the right. And farther along another branch with a feeder road to the Kelaniya Temple. He followed the main road and was satisfied to see the railtrack running right. Yes, he had his direction. He pedalled along and ahead, still to right, was the Kelaniya railway station. With a sigh of satisfaction he turned and went home, was stormed at for returning so late and went in to prepare for his own Tom Sawyer adventure. Money, he told himself, was important. He broke his till and counted thirty-one rupees. He decided to boost the kitty.

'Give my lunch money now,' he told Beryl.

'What for?'

'Father Sebastian said to come and serve mass tomorrow. Other altar servers can't come.'

'So? Go and serve and come.'

'So no time, no? Straight from there I'll go to school.'

'Without eating even?'

'I'll go to Granny's. Will give to eat something.'

Beryl considered for an instant, then gave him a rupee.

'Give a little more, will you? For one rupee nothing proper to eat.'

'So all these days giving a rupee?'

'Yes, and just eating buns and plantains. Have to inflate the bike also.'

Beryl, exasperated, flung another rupee at him. 'Here! Take and go!' But Carloboy knew where to look. Mummy always had money in her machine table draw. He nipped in, pushed away a pile of sewing, tried the draw. He took the neatly folded ten rupee notes. Ah, thirty rupees. He felt no qualms. His mother sewed, took in sewing, and hid her earnings. Beryl always maintained that it was what any wife would do. 'If know I have a little money, will take and go and buy a bottle,' she told Mrs Ludwick and that worthy would heave and say, 'One thing, these men!' It was just as easy to cadge another two rupees from Aunty Millie who smiled fondly when she spied him at five the next morning.

'Going to mass?' she asked.

Carloboy nodded. If he did, he would be in the presbytery where the altar boys knelt and not seen by the congregation anyway. He swung around the church, dumped his schoolbooks at his aunt's home and pedalled away.

Morning was sneaking in from every direction. It usually does when the day promises to be hot and the sun turns baker. Crows had begun their kwa-kwow and the shadows on the road began to dissolve.

'Von Bloss!' called Perimpanayagam and looked up, scanned the class eagerly and marked the boy absent. He also cheered up considerably.

At five that evening Beryl put down what she was embroidering and went to the kitchen. She had engaged a servant that morning, a well-rounded, young Sinhalese woman of twenty who lived on the canal bank. 'Now five the time,' Beryl said, 'big baby still coming not. Flask inside his tea keep.'

At six-thirty Carloboy was drinking a cup of incredibly weak tea in a small kiosk at Kegalla. A lorry drove up and the driver shouted: 'This bicycle whose?'

When Carloboy came anxiously out the man said, 'Ah, baby, a little move it. To park can't.'

Carloboy obliged. He had come a long way. Seventy-seven kilometres, to be near-exact, and another thirty-nine would take him to Kandy, but the worst, as the man who served him the tea had said, was ahead. The man had raised an eyebrow. 'Kandy going? On bicycle? What for?'

'Just.'

'Baby from where?'

'Dehiwela—no, Dehiwela not—Kalubowila.'

'*Ammo*, mad work, no? So far to go on bicycle. So incline to climb also you're going?'

'Incline?'

'If not. Feet almost one thousand to climb must. See will you these children,' he told others in the kiosk, 'bicycles climbing Kandy going. How? From Colombo coming.' The lorry driver eyed the boy. 'I also Kandy going. Baby want lorry inside come. Bicycle in the back can put.' Carloboy eyed the man. It was a tempting idea but he knew how easy it was for a boy to get himself into a corner. At least, he could be robbed of his bicycle. And wouldn't he be at the complete mercy of the man—no, two men—for he had noticed that there was another when the lorry parked. He shook his head and another thought struck him: the borrowed bike and that crazy career along the Galle Road, clinging to the tailboard of a lorry. Well, why not? He'll be more careful this time.

'I'll come,' he said, 'from the back, catch and come.'

'Baby mad?' the hotel man said. 'Those bends just catching and going can't.'

The lorry driver laughed. 'Let's see, will you, like that going if want, catch and come. If can't, let off and go.'

By now a knot of loafers had gathered to give advice. 'Night time road to see even can't. This devil at speed if bend taking for baby *thoppi*,' one said. Another told the driver, '*Ado*, you just go. Other people just into trouble trying to put.'

The driver shrugged. 'Just said, no?' and to Carloboy, 'Baby you want anything do. *Habai*,[1] on bicycle incline climbing can't. Get down and bicycle push-push and walking have to go. I'm but going. Straight Kandy I'm going.'

It was growing dark and lights had long since sprung up in the town. Carloboy straddled his bicycle, swung around and caught the tailboard of the lorry. 'Right,' he called, 'you go!'

Sonnaboy, too, was on his bicycle. He had told Beryl, 'Bugger must be in some house or the other. I'll go and see.'

Neighbours had ventured to suggest an accident. Freda Pereira told Mrs Pat Silva, 'You wait an' see if double decker didn't run over or what. My Romaine also asking to go on bicycle to school. I won't let!'

Old Mrs Ludwick told Beryl, 'Go, child, and pray. Ask God to send home quickly.'

Beryl glared. 'Let him come!' she snapped. 'Not enough

---

1. Sinhalese—loosely, 'in truth.'

he's getting, still dancing the devil. Only know to worry, that's all he knows to do.'

Meanwhile Carloboy was speeding through Kegalla town, past the police station. The road was broad and riddled with pot holes and broken metal but he found that the lorry's headlights, picking out the verge and the long puddles of water he was forced to splash through, allowed him to see what lay ahead and take, where necessary, evasive action. Then street lights thinned, buildings grew far apart and night fell with a thud. He whizzed on. If only those namby-pambies in his class—in the whole school—could see him now. From Hingula the real climb began and the lorry slowed to a crawl, belching puffs of exhaust smoke, clashing gears, whining around Z-bends. The eyes of dogs flared green in the headlights. He hung on and shifted his handlebars a fraction, this way or that to avoid a pile of stones, a long rut, a deep puddle. The trouble was the twists to the right when the headlights swung away and the darkness dazed him. He couldn't see a thing. Only the red glow of the tail light that drew faint threads of pink on his spinning wheel spokes. They climbed and climbed and then there were hairpins to navigate and the road narrowed with tall rock walls towering at his shoulder and the sounds of water like crumpling tissue paper and an entire orchestra of insects whirring about him. At seven forty-five they lumbered through a rock tunnel and laboured up a steep rise, cleared the crest and with a stutter of gears, rolled speedily into Kadugannawa. A shout from a patrolling policeman went unheeded. The town flicked past—the railway station, the rows of ill-lit boutiques. Then the lorry slowed, stopped and a few urchins in torn, sagging trousers congregated to stare. Carloboy put a foot down and eased his right hand. It had begun to ache. The driver grinned.

'Just came to see baby here or not. Somehow came, no?' and told a fat woman whose jacket could scarcely contain her breasts, 'See, will you, from Kegalla hanging and coming. Kandy going. How the job?'

'*Arr-ney!*' the woman said, '*haberta?*[1] From where coming? Kegalla?'

'No, no, Colombo from coming. Kandy going telling.'

The urchins had crowded around to touch the bicycle, exclaim at the cable brakes, notice the gear lever on the bar. In the hubbub Carloboy heard the woman say. 'From home jumped and come must be. To the police if catch and give good.'

The boy edged his machine back. 'If staying, I'll go. My Kandy uncle looking and waiting must be.'

'No, no, now going,' and to the woman, 'There, heard? Like this *lansi* children jumping and going won't.'

Which was an observation worth remarking on. Whatever the social attitudes of the times, it was a common belief of the Sinhalese that the Burghers kept nice little homes (be they ever so humble) and dressed well enough and were comfortable enough. There was quite a bit of 'colour envy' too which can be noted to this day. Any Sinhalese mother in any Sinhalese village would be proud to call her baby *sudhu* or *sudho*,[2] and every family had its *sudhu nangi*[3] and *sudhu akka*[4] and even a *sudhu maama*.[5] It was necessary to stress the fact. It was a mixture of mild resentment, true, and tolerance as well. Burgher children too, most gregarious, invited friendship. There was a hardiness in them that invested that spirit of getting on, making the best of any situation, any social environment. Right now, Carloboy was a 'stranger in a foreign land' but even the ragged urchins who surrounded him had nothing but admiration for him, his bike and for the fact that he had clung grimly on, all the way from Kegalla, mind, all the way up the Kadugannawa incline . . . and in the dark too.

The woman, whose name was Jossie, asked him if he'd like some tea. 'Come, come, tea a little drink and go. For what like this Kandy going?'

---

1. Sinhalese: 'Is that true?'

2. Sinhalese: 'White or fair-skinned'.

3, 4, 5. White younger sister, elder sister, uncle.

'Uncle's house I'm going. To come said. Father said if like on bicycle go if like.'

'*Arr-ney*. Father is mad? So much distance? So baby came?'

Carloboy nodded.

'Come, come. I'll some tea make. *Habai*, just tea, right? Baby's home milk and all putting, no? We are poor, no?'

'That never mind,' Carloboy assured.

'Here, boys, the bicycle touching not! You all what doing here? Get out home!'

Eight o'clock. Sonnaboy was at the Wellawatte police station. Inspector Orr tapped his teeth with his pencil.

'Any idea where the bugger might be? I phoned around and checked the hospital also. Nothing. Bugger must have gone somewhere. Outstation, must be.'

'Outstation?'

'Obviously, men. If anywhere around here you think will allow to stay so late? Anyway, still only eight, no? Don't know if went to some schoolfriend's house and putting dinner there.'

'Yes, must be. But must inform no? I'll give the bugger when he comes home!'

At home Beryl discovered the loss of her sewing money. She gasped, quivered and slapped Marie who rushed in to complain about what Diana was doing. 'Who took the money from this draw?' she demanded, and twisted Diana's ears for good measure. Sonnaboy returned to the sound of two wailing daughters and a wife who stalked the house pantherishly.

It was almost nine when Carloboy gave up on the lorry, swung away and braked alongside the narrow kerb. He was in Kandy and the streets were peopled and the lights of hundreds of shops flared and winked in the crisp air. He looked about him. He had never been here before. He asked a man, 'Where is Peradeniya Road?'

The man laughed. 'Here, here. This is Peradeniya Road. Why?'

'Number 528 is where?'

'I don't know. Who are the people?'

'De Sella. In the railway he is.'

'Better if you go to the railway station and ask.'

'Where?'

'That also you don't know. Where you're from?'

'From Colombo. Have to find the house. Now late also.'

'So then go back and see the numbers. Whereabout you don't know?'

'Near a school, said.'

'No school anywhere here. Have that side. You go back and see.'

It took time, but suddenly there was a church and a school and Carloboy sucked in his breath sharply. Yes, there it was. Number 528 . . . Audrey . . .

At ten o'clock, a distraught Sonnaboy was searching his son's cupboard in which he found a stack of letters. 'Here! come and look at this! Who is this girl, men? Kandy address.'

Beryl stared. 'My God, don' know if went to Kandy. Last week also he said if can go to Kandy for holidays. Said he had some friends there.'

'So postman comes and gives like this and you won't even go to see what?'

'What to see? I'm in the back cooking, no? Now even have a servant. Going early to school also. Must be catching the postman top of the garden and taking.'

Sonnaboy thought a while. 'Must have gone to Kandy. And where the till? No till to be seen. Took the money, must be.'

'Never mind that, had some sewing money in my machine table draw. That's also vanished. Don't know where put the bike and went.'

'Wait. I'll teach him a bloody good lesson. God knows if went on the bike even. I'll go to the police station and come.'

'Again?'

'Put a bloody complaint. Give this address and tell he stole the bicycle.'

'My God, will catch and lock up, no?'

'That's what must do. Teach him a bloody lesson.'

'Dinner also served and getting cold.'

'Damn the dinner. You eat. I'll go and come.'

Beryl sat, reading Audrey's letters.

The de Sella's gave the tired wanderer a riotous welcome. Mr de Sella looked the boy up and down through his reading glasses and accepted the tale that Carloboy had come with a group of his classmates.'We are on a cycle tour. Going to stay tomorrow in Kandy. Then we are going to Nawalapitiya.'

'So where are the other boys?'

'All went to one boy's house. He is from Kandy. So I also kept my things and said I'll come and see Maurius and Quinny. Uncle, I can stay here?'

Maurius insisted. Quinny whooped. Audrey, at the curtain smiled and smiled and Carloboy felt he was treading air. Why, she had grown! She was lissom and her hair shone and her gathered skirt pinched around her waist. Her soft blouse embraced her breasts and his hands ached to reach out, touch her.

'Did you eat anything, child? Cycling all the way. Must be dead tired, no?' Mrs de Sella said.

So Carloboy went in, washed, was given a change of clothes and Audrey said, 'My, your shirt is filthy. Smelling of sweat,' and Mrs de Sella took away his clothes to wash and he sat to a meal of rice and cold curry while the boys talked incessantly and Audrey sat across the table. He reached out with his leg and touched her shin and she ran her feet alongside his, her toes brushing his ankles, lower calves. Maureen and Carmen said, 'From where did you appear? Came from Anuradhapura? You're still saying dirty words?' and everybody laughed.

There are those all-too-short days every boy remembers. They are days filled with a special magic. No, not ecstasy, just a special magic when one feels that one is very much loved, very much wanted and that every hour is suffused with its own special colour that starts as a pinpoint inside one's head, then grows and breaks through in a starburst of red, silver, violet, magenta. This was such a day. While the morning sped by happily enough—they went to the Kandy lake, roamed the town, ate mangoes in the Kandy market— Audrey said she had to show Carloboy the wilderness of their own back garden which melted into the backyard of the untenanted house next day. At its boundary stood a long dormitory-like building, a part of the school's complex, also empty and quite broody looking in the afternoon sun. They walked with the carelessness of the innocent, exclaiming at the fruit-laden jak trees, the big green lizard on a fence post. Maurius and Quinny knew, of course, and kept away. They took the bicycle instead, screeching along the road and the red gravel path beside the house.

Maureen asked, 'Where are these fellows?'

Mrs de Sella looked up from the kitchen hearth, 'There, playing in the back. Real tomboy that Audrey is also.' Carloboy and Audrey were seated, close together in the rear veranda of the empty house. A wall, moss-grown at the base, hid them. Their own grotto, and there they kissed and clung to each other and feverishly discovered each other. Undying love was sworn, thirty times a minute and her mouth was minty sweet against his and he demanded urgently to come to her at night.

'Can't,' she breathed, 'I'm sleeping with Maureen and Carmen, no?'

'So say you're going to the bathroom. I'll go and wait there.'

'Can't. Gosh, if we get caught.'

He ran his hand down her, touched her small breasts, hugged her. She held him fiercely. 'I'm scared to allow,' she said in a small thin voice.

He nuzzled her. 'Don't worry.'

'I'm scared. I know, no, other girls also telling can get a baby also.'

His hand was under her dress, fingers digging under her knickers. 'That is only when doing inside, no?' He placed her hand on his cock. 'It's all wet again. You remember in Anuradhapura?'

She squirmed and said, 'Wait, I'll take out,' and coloured richly when he asked to see.

It was very uncomfortable. His knees hurt on the cracked cement and they were cramped, sweating, and her dress was in the way and his trouser zip pressed rudely into the top of his penis, but he spent himself between her thighs and she rose, bent over carefully to keep the cover of the wall and said, 'That's all? I'll put the knickers?'

Carloboy, breathing heavily, rose, 'Wait, let me clean,' and with the tail of his shirt wiped the inside of her thighs. He dropped to his knee to look at her, the soft down that curled, brown, the curving lips of her labia. His hand cupped her sex, squeezing it, then he ran a finger along the brown crevasse, upwards to touch the throbbing clitoris. Audrey made a soft cluck-like hiss. 'Don't,' she said, 'feel funny when you do that.' He rose to embrace her, kiss her and his cock was hard again and he wouldn't let her go. Her hand took hold of it, tucked it between her and they stood together, belonging, belonging and that was all that mattered.

In the Kandy Police Station, Sub Inspector Wijesinghe called a constable. 'Here, there's a report from Colombo. Boy stole a bicycle and came to Kandy. What nonsense is this? Can just come cycling to Kandy?'

The constable tittered. '*Apoi* sir, these days boys Jaffna even will go.'

'All nonsense. What are you doing?'

'Now must go to Suduhumpola, sir. I and P. C. Perera, Some *gori*[1] there,' he sniffed, 'everyday *gori* there, no?'

'Then on your way back just go to this address. Peradeniya road close by Number 528. Just ask if have a boy there with a bicycle. If have, ask the name. Here the name. Von Bloss. Burgher boy. If there, catch and bring here.

'Bicycle also bring?'

'Saying stole, no? So bring and come.'

The constables, P. C. Mendis and P. C. Perera made the necessary out entry and left the station.

'What nonsense, no? *Lansi* boy from Colombo bicycle stealing to Kandy come,' Mendis said.

'Who knows? Now we are where going?'

'Suduhumpola. Other thing afterwards will see.'

Which was just as well, for the Suduhumpola fracas was

---

1. Sinhalese: loosely a 'fight', a disturbance, a breach of the peace.

bigger that they had imagined and a particularly repulsive neighbourhood thug who fancied himself the King of Clubs had broken several heads before being set upon by screaming men and women who had quickly converted him into a pincushion of sorts. Lots of blood, hysterical women and knives and crowbars and the necessity to dispatch the immobile to hospital and chase those who suddenly remembered urgent business elsewhere. P. C. Mendis said, 'Tomorrow we'll go that other thing to see,' and Perera nodded. So nothing, not even Perera and Mendis, spoilt that magic day. The gods must have known that, as far as Carloboy and Audrey were concerned, it was the last day they would know together.

Carloboy had to stick to his story. Accordingly he rose early, drank tea and informed the family that his friends would be waiting to proceed to Nawalapitiya. Audrey was sad, but cheered up when he announced that the boys would return to Kandy the next day and remain in Kandy for some time. The lies fell easily, so naturally that old de Sella, emerging in green-striped pyjamas and a banian that rolled up his belly, said, 'Then come for lunch tomorrow, right? Who is in charge of you boys?'

'Two prefects.'

'Good, good.'

He gaped when, at ten, two constables came to his door.

Carloboy reached Nawalapitiya quickly enough. He bounced over the railway lines that sliced across the road, swung into the ill-kempt town with its dirty kerbs and toppled dustbins and said to himself, 'Now what?'

He was hungry. He was also tired. He hadn't reckoned on the slow, wearying climb. The pot-holed road through Gampola had been a nightmare. He could, of course, go to any of the railway bungalows. Why, even the Running Bungalow, but he quickly dismissed that idea. My God, Daddy might be there . . . and the sudden reflection that Daddy could be at Nawalapitiya spread the seeds of unease, even panic. How if Daddy had worked train to Nawalapitiya? He could be anywhere. In that railway bungalow, drinking with a friend, maybe. Or in town, coming to buy a pint from the liquor shop . . . in town? Carloboy looked around uneasily, then turned his machine, anxious to pedal away, and slammed a front wheel into a man carrying a large bunch of king coconuts on his gunny sack draped shoulders. The boy lost his balance and so did the man. They both fell as did the bicycle and the coconuts, and the man howled wrathfully and as is the custom, a perfectly unpeopled road suddenly bulged at the seams. Boys, men, urchins, dogs, women billowed in to make comments, judgements, shout advice or just stare. Cyclists rang bells and a carter stopped prodding his bull's anus with his toes[1] and declared that bicycles should not be allowed to attack pedestrians with nuts of any variety. Into this strode a policeman with a quick, eager air. Life had been pretty humdrum of late and he cheered up when the man groaned and said that the boy had, very vindictively, waited until he had approached and then swung his bicycle wheel which had done dire things to his testicles. 'To me with the bicycle hit!' he bellowed. 'Just on the road I'm going. To go when tried he also fell!'

Another asked: 'Who this boy?'

And a woman advised: 'To the police take and go, *ralahamy*.[2] This way with bicycle to hit can? To harmless men this way can do?'

The policeman seized Carloboy's shoulder. 'Where your house? Come go station.'

The man who had dropped his coconuts and insisted that other nuts which were his pride and joy had also been frontally attacked, suddenly forgot what had troubled him. He rose, looked around, found a gap in the crowd thicket and darted through, shifted gear and streaked away. His nuts lay where they fell. So did the gunny sack. This caused more confusion and the policeman, nonplussed, hung on to Carloboy. 'Where he's running?' he demanded and old Babanis cackled and said, 'Why *ralahamy* don't know that Lokuvijay? From somewhere king coconut bunch cut and

---

1. The accepted way to goad the animal into second gear.

2. Sinhalese colloquial: 'Policeman.'

taking. His job that is. King coconut bunch anywhere have cut and take. King coconut rogue!'

The policeman was annoyed. Eventually Carloboy found himself in the Nawalapitiya police station, telling Inspector Mendis that he lived in Kandy and had just come for the ride. Mendis was a nice man. Too nice to be a police inspector, one would think. He chuckled. 'Anyway, no harm done, no? That man must have stolen those king coconuts. So, young man, you're going to Kandy? Just came riding, ah? What can you see here? At least today there's some sun. Raining, raining otherwise, whole time its raining here. What about your bike? It's all right?'

The right pedal had been dented and kept brushing the gearcase. 'That's a small thing. There, take it to that place there, where all those tyres are piled up. You can see? Go and tell to straighten the pedal and give. You have money?'

Carloboy nodded.

'Give fifty cents enough. But stay and tell to do. Don't leave the bike. Will take out the saddle bag or the dynamo and lamp or something.'

When the phone rang and the Kandy police told Inspector Mendis that there was a boy on the loose, possibly on his turf, the man whistled, said, 'hold the line' and roared for a policeman. Sergeant Nonis came in, chewing a thumbnail.

'That boy! There is the bicycle shop. Bring that bugger here, and stop biting your fingers!'

'Sir, yes sir.'

'So go!'

Nonis went.

It took time, naturally. Kandy demanded that Carloboy be sent there. Mendis asked how and was surprised to learn how choleric the range inspector could get at midday.

'You still didn't eat lunch?' he asked.

'What the hell is that to you?'

'Then why you're shouting? Boy is here. Whacked a *thambili*[1] rogue on the balls also. How to send there? Haven't policemen here to come on bicycle all the way.'

---

1. Sinhalese for king coconut.

'Don't talk cock, men. Put on train and send.'

'Bicycle also?'

'Yes. That is stolen bicycle, no?'

'Real damn nuisance. I caught here, can put charge and produce here if want. My lockup also empty.'

'No, no. Father also came and waiting here. You send.'

So Mendis put down the phone, glared at it for ten seconds and spent the rest of the minute glaring at Carloboy. 'Sit and wait!' he shouted. 'If you get up I'll handcuff you to the chair! You heard?'

Carloboy nodded. He wasn't Tom Sawyer or even Huckleberry Finn. He was just Carloboy von Bloss and his father was at Kandy and he was, as is said, in deep shit. And on the way up, at Ulapane, he had sat by the side of the road and actually written a letter to Bruno where he had given as address: *Sitting on a rock, somewhere near Nawalapitiya*, and informing his Literature master that he was having a wonderful time and was very much alive and well. He had posted it and had been very pleased with himself. The guard eyed him with deep suspicion.

'What's this? Police taking to Kandy in my van with bicycle? What? You're von Bloss' son? What the devil are you doing here?'

'From home jumped and came. Bicycle also stole,' the policeman said. 'To Kandy taking. To police there giving and coming.'

It was a short walk to the police station from the Kandy railway station. The policeman wheeled the bike and Sonnaboy rose up to seize his son by the shoulders and shake him until he felt he was trapped in a giant winnow.

'You know the trouble you have caused! Police cars going all over Colombo, people praying in church for you, everybody upset. I went to Sellas! You go there again to see what you'll get! Girls! What girls at your age! You think we don't know? Small bloody wretch writing love letters. Mother gave her a good hammering. You come home and behave yourself, you heard?'

So the prodigal returned and was beaten and given a flurry of slaps by his mother too, for stealing her sewing money and the neighbours came to look him over and exclaim and say, 'Some dance you led everybody,' and Mr Dias swayed in to say that, 'If my son will tie to the lamp-post and hammer,' and tell Sonnaboy, 'Yes, men, thash what'll do. One thing no bluddy nonsense with my buggers. You have drink? Put two shots at that Vihara Lane joint. Buggers mus' be mixing an' giving.'

And so were Carloboy and Audrey parted and both children brooded and decided to call it a day. Kandy and Colombo, no longer connected by bicycle became isolated, receding into a mist so unreal that neither place mattered. Carloboy found this business of undying love and its many hazards too much to handle. What was the use? All he got for his pains was a beating, a soreness of loss, an emptiness of spirit and, as the popular songs proclaimed, a broken heart. He decided to circulate. Saranankara Road was full of girls. So what? The whole world was full of girls. And years of agonizing over one was, he decided, an appalling waste of time. Where had it got him? By the time his fourteenth birthday came around and two Germany's had been established and NATO had come into being, he had become almost predatory in his relationships with a long line of girls with whom he took his satisfaction and then abandoned. Some of them clung on, refusing to accepted rejection. Monique Ludwick would creep around the house and climb in through the store room window. She would leave her knickers at home.

Cindy Perera would always go to the outhouse servants lavatory when Carloboy came in to play carrom with her brothers. It was a signal for him to break away. 'Wait a bit. I'll put a pump and come,' and he would race round the house and tap and dart into the lavatory where they would clutch at each other and kiss and he would satisfy himself, standing up, and say. 'I'll go. You wait a little and then come out.'

'You love me?' she would ask.

He would nod. 'Of course. Now wait quietly. I'm going.' No, he didn't love anybody, anything. Love meant beatings, ridicule, shame, torrents of rantings and ravings and those fierce slaps only his mother could give. The world, he decided, was a foul, rotten place. Uncle Viva would come, humming hymns through his nose, whining insistently about the evils that beset all mankind. 'Now we are in end time,' he would bleat, 'destruction! destruction! The Lord will smite the sinners!'

Sonnaboy would yawn. 'Don't talk bloody nonsense, men. Smiting! If smiting then Russia also can make the atom bomb? If Russia is so bad why did God allow?'

A fierce argument would follow which raised many issues, all half-cocked, half-baked, of use only because they contained some merit in keeping the crosstalk going.

'See will you, even our Dutch buggers. Where all their *pakkum*[1] now? Japanese pushed from East Indies and now Indonesia came. Where the bloody Dutch? Gone. Did the bolt!'

Viva would dig his nostrils, 'Wickedness!' he would trumpet. 'Pray, men, pray. Whole world is going to damnation. Ah, how, men, Beryl? How the children? Carloboy is studying? My three are doing all right, praise the lord, learning well in Bandarawela school. Now Claude is fifteen almost sixteen, no? Winston and John also OK only Winston likes to joke too much. Told him only las' week, ask God to help, son, not good to make jokes everytime and must be more serious, no?'

'How are the girls?'

Viva sighs. 'Patricia is at home. Left school also and in the house with Opel. Little lazy, men and Opel always grumbling. Praying for good husband for her. From Diyatalawa navy camp sometime fellows coming on the road and have nice Burgher boy also always looking when pass the house but all in God's hands, no?'

Carloboy, listening, would grin slowly. What a load of rubbish this uncle talked. God's hands, Praise the Lord. Pray, pray, pray! 'Penda' was agog in class with the Cold War in Asia and how the Communists had chased Chiang

---

1. Sinhalese colloquialism—pride, swagger.

Kai-shek into Formosa. And here was this uncle with his big nose in his Bible, praying that someone will marry his Patricia! Marry! 'Marry for what?' he told his cousin Ian de Mello who, although much older, lived a sad, befuddled life under his tyrannous mother.

Ian would look sheepish. 'If not how? To have a girl must arrange and get married, no?'

'Aha! You're thinking of landing a girl?'

Ian would ripen redly. He stuttered when he grew excited. 'Then how?'

'What madness, men, just catch and do. I'll tell? You come home. Our servant woman not bad, men. You like to put a try?'

'Mad? As if your mummy won't see.'

'She won't see. Whole time sewing. I'm also thinking, one day I went to the kitchen. Had a 'pult in my pocket and it was sticking out in my trouser. She gave a funny look and said, "Baby, in pocket what?" and came and caught it and I said, "That's my catapult," and she's laughing and saying, "Ah catapult only? I thought something else." How? I asked "You thought what?" and she's just smiling and looking. Easy to catch and do, men.'

Ian grew redder. 'Ma-ma-my gosh. Yu-yu-you shure? What about . . . what about our servant?'

'*Apo*, old no? And if put a shout or something . . .'

'Ma-ma-my God. Ma-ammy will kill. But here. I-I-think Dunny Uncle . . . Dunny Uncle, he-he's doing men. Ki-Ki-kitchen he's going when Mummy sleeping e-e-in the afternoon. One day I went-went to the ba-ack to drink water. Kitchen door clo-closed but when I'm ca-ca-coming door open and Dunny-Dunny Uncle coming out.'

'That old bugger. Anything for him. Enough he landed you? Now also you're going?'

'No-no-now I won't. Wo-won't call also.'

'Old bugger!' Carloboy says again. 'Did to me also one day, and I know, no, how he came and did to Marie and Heather also. I tried to tell Mummy and got a slap only. One thing useless going to tell anything. In the room, men, and Heather is small also.'

Poor Ian. He hung on Carloboy's every word and fantasized immensely and masturbated with a diligence that should have earned him a knighthood. But the conversation made Carloboy think more about the woman so conveniently at home in the kitchen and he took to hanging around the rear veranda and brushing against her at the door and, growing bolder, coming up behind her one day as she stood at the kitchen window, to press against her broad buttocks. She stood still for a second, then pressed backwards into him and breathed, 'Baby go. Mummy if come?'

He walked away, hard, throbbing, sat on the old rattan chair in the veranda and pretended to read a Sexton Blake. It was, for him, a mid-term holiday. The girls were at school. Baby Michael crawled around a mat in the hall, Beryl was big with child and had taken to sleeping in the afternoons. Long hours at her sewing-machine gave her, she said, a pain in her back. She called to Soma: 'This child for a little look after. What big baby doing?'

'There backside chair a book reading. Asleep falling I think.'

'Here a little come and wait. I'll nex' door go and come this dress fit-on for next door lady and come. Kitchen door close and come and here wait.'

Carloboy dropped the book on his face and breathed evenly. Beryl came. 'How? Asleep fell. Like that let be. I'll go and come.'

Carloboy heard the kitchen door being closed and the sound of his mother's slippers on the front step, heard her say, 'This door also close. If anybody comes I'm next door say and afterwards to come tell.'

Oh, Carloboy knew where and why his mother was going. Next door, of course, where Bunty and Dora de Kretser were not at home and their boarder, Kinno Mottau occupied a room and Beryl would creep in and Kinno would come to the hall windows and draw the blinds. It used to be different before Soma was installed. Kinno would come home then. He would sneak in through the back door, coming around the common well. Beryl, because of her stomach, chose to go to the front door.

Carloboy rose, went to the hall. Soma looked up. 'Baby got up?'

He nodded. 'Mummy went?'

The woman nodded. Carloboy sat beside her, looked at her. Funny, he thought, one never notices servants. She was young, soft-lipped, large eyes, beautiful eyes, he thought. Yes, she was so black-haired, so pretty. He took her hand. Soma moved urgently. 'Mummy if come . . .' He assured her that Mummy won't come. He knew she wouldn't. Mummy was being fucked by the lodger next door. He knew it. He hated it but now he had Soma to himself. He pulled down his trousers zip. Soma nuzzled him and embraced him and he found that she wore an undercloth too. 'Take out, will you,' he said and she pretended to struggle as he undid her wraps. When he pushed her down, her cloths lying in a heap against her, her dark bush, her brown thighs, her long legs, her cleft of navel were like a poem of exceeding grace. Gently he mounted, pushing his knees between her. His mouth touched her chin. He felt himself rigid, pushing, brushing, seeking entry and her hand helped him enter. He buried himself in her and she gripped his buttocks. He pushed and they were one. It was such a sensation. He arched and pushed, then moved and her feet, firm against the mat, raised and lowered her lower body to his rhythm. He felt a warmth grow and he moved quicker, quicker and he heard her breathe in a strange, whistling way, mouth open. Suddenly it was a delirium of sensation and spending, spending and he felt as though she was draining him of life. Orgasm clutched at them with a single, grasping hand. He lay over her, head in her shoulder and she pressed her lips to his forehead, his ear. 'All inside went, no,' she whispered.

He nodded.

'Baby quickly get up. I'll wash and come soon, before too much go in.'

'Why?'

'Baby if get? Good thing from hospital pills some kind bringing and giving. Anyhow careful must be, no?'

Carloboy watched her drape her cloths. 'Come soon,' he said and looked down at the dampness on the front of his trousers. 'Trouser must change Mummy coming before.'

When Beryl returned, Carloboy was cleaning his bicycle. 'Anyone came?' she asked.

Soma said no. She then went to the kitchen, slyly touching the boy's head as she passed him. That night he thought about her and pressed his hardness into his pillow and stroked and stroked until he spent himself.

At fourteen, going on fifteen he had fucked his first woman.

CHAPTER FOURTEEN

There is little left of the Burgher community in Sri Lanka today. Many have adapted, or left, and yet, a few remain to cling to a vanished past. The erosion of emigration and inter-marriage began a long, long time ago. In 1796 when the British took over the island, the Burghers were given a choice. Stay and be ruled or go to Indonesia.[1] Those who stayed became quite passionate about all things English, but for years and years after the British take over, the Burghers still celebrated St Nikolaus Day on December 5 although many sent their children to be educated in England. Let it also be said that the Burghers became so attuned to their colonial rulers that they actually fought in South Africa against the Dutch in the Boer War. Strange? No, just the quirks of happenstance. British education, British standards, were the stepping stones to a good future in Ceylon. Those who rose to eminence orbited in their own social plane. In the 1920s six of Ceylon's nine Supreme Court judges were Burghers.

But—and aha! there's the rub—the great commingling and feverish intermingling produced a Burgher community which, with its many gradations of colour, raised its own

---

1. It was Batavia then.

snobberies. All Burgher families have had mixed marriages, and yet at the gateway to the fashionable part of Colombo there still stands a white and gingerbread house which is the Dutch Burgher Union where records are kept, which trace each Burgher family to a European ancestor. Here, the snobbery begins. The community becomes classified. 'Top quality' are they who can show an undiluted paternal European line. And what makes all this so special? As Sonnaboy, after his fifth arrack would have said, 'Balls!' which, as a juicy expletive, covered everything. The Dutch East India Company, when it took control of Ceylon in 1665 found the island a convenient staging post between the Cape of Good Hope and Dutch possessions in the Far East. What came in thereafter were company employees and fortune seekers from the rough and tumble of Europe. No bluebloods, mind. One saving grace, it could be said, was that, unlike Australia, there was no 'ball and chain'. As mentioned earlier, especially of Jaffna, intermarriage was the done thing (apart from a frenzied screwing around which was a pleasurable pastime) so where does that leave us? And where does it leave the author who is also a Burgher? Why, one piteously pleads, this snobbery?

Carloboy, at fourteen, found another edifice to this hardcore Burgherness rise very near where he lived. Saranankara Road accepted the establishment of St Nikolaus Home—a home for elderly Burgher ladies who had lost everything: their homes, their families, their ties. Although Burghers maintained strong family ties, this was a phenomenon of the changing times. Children, grandchildren, even great-grandchildren quit Ceylon, migrating to Australia, England, Canada, New Zealand, the US. Old women, bereft of all they had queened over, were stranded. Families sent money for their upkeep, true, but they sat in the home, quarrelled incessantly (which was their only real entertainment) and memories and their rosaries were their talismans to fight the awful loneliness that enshrouded them.

Carloboy was quite taken up with the home. Relics in a house of relics, elderly women seated, cooling themselves with small hand fans, eating home-made toffee, yearning for someone, some fair-skinned, brown-haired visitor to march in, say 'hullo aunty' or 'hullo granny' and place a parcel in their laps and say, 'Look what I brought for you.'

It took just eight years, eight years after Independence, for the cosy world of Sri Lanka's Burghers to collapse. Once again the choice: adapt or leave . . . and most left. Carloboy found this all quite unthinkable. He would argue with old Mr Young in Pereira Lane, who, with his lank wife who had a candlestick complexion, and his children Daryll and Claudia, were preparing to leave for Australia.

'So what for going, Uncle. Can stay here, no?'

'And do what? No future for our children now. You tell your daddy also to pack up and go.'

'Never mind going. But see will you, all the grannies and old people dumping and going.'

'No, son, you don't understand. These countries only want young people who can work. Can't carry old people and go.'

'But that's not fair, no?'

'Why not? There I can still work and Darryl also get a job and Claudia can go in an office and Mrs Young also can take a job. So all four will work.'

'Just they give jobs when go?'

'Plenty of jobs, men. And everything have there. Not like here.'

'So why can't take old people also? Can keep at home when all are going to work.'

'Who's going to look after if all go to work? There also will have to put in a home. And new place, new things, won't even like. They are used to here, no?'

Yes, there seemed no way out. Dump the old, the frail, the feeble. No future for them. Only the whitewashed walls of a home, the dreary wait for death. As American actress Celeste Holm once said: 'We live by encouragement and die without it—slowly, sadly and angrily.'

And who was there to encourage the old ladies of St Nikolaus Home? Rather, it was the universal opinion that Carloboy, like a lot of heedless Burgher youth, was driving his schoolmasters and others in authority into premature old age. 'An early grave,' 'Connor' would intone, 'that's what I'll get because of you,' while 'Pol Thel' who loathed the boy, swore fervently that he had more grey hairs on his comb each morning. 'Lapaya' had to leave. He couldn't take it any more. He never brought a pen to class, anyway, and the boys were quite fed up with the way he would say: 'One of you give me a pen.' The problem was he would stick the pen into his coat and carry it away.

'Sir, my pen, sir.'

'What? What pen?'

'My pen, sir, you took.'

Sometimes he would give it back with an 'oh' and an 'ah' but one day he just glared at Abdi and said, 'Nonsense. You must be dreaming,' and walked away with a nice Parker 41. Abdi was annoyed and boys put their heads together—an occurrence that bodes no good for anyone.

Lapaya beetled in the next day. He set the day's lesson. Apparently the man had other things to do. He could be writing his autobiography. All he did was say: 'Read chapters six and seven. No noise. End of period I'll ask questions.' And he would begin to write. It had to come. He raised his head. 'One of you give me a pen.'

Forty-two boys form a sizeable class. When this number, in seven half-dozen knots, suddenly stampede all else is chaff. Lapaya yelped. Boys surged, chairs banged backwards, glad cries of 'here, sir,' 'here my pen, sir,' and the poor man cowered, eyes popping as his whole class milled around his desk, brandishing fountain pens. His desk was showered with pens, the noise was deafening, the hoots, cheery cries, laughter and rousing, roistering roars ran outdoors to echo down the corridor. Forty-two pens. Who the blazes wanted forty-two pens? Parkers, Swans, Watermans, Shaeffers . . . Lapaya windmilled out of his chair with a strangled scream. His first blow took 'Bull' de Sara on the ear. He swiped at Doyne, missed and caught L. M. Perera on the side of the neck. Bassie, mercifully, didn't get a fit, but Lapaya seemed to be in the grip of something more vast than epilepsy. He seized handfuls of pens and hurled them out of the window. The row sucked back, inward. Boys stood, gaping, as their pens vanished. They were two floors up and outside it rained pens on old Kadalayachchi[1] who gave a sharp scream and plucked her basket of pickled olives out of the way. The uproar of dispersion became a crescendo of deprivation. Lapaya broke and ran as grim-faced boys advanced on him. It took three masters and a co-opted prefect to restore order. Some pens, when recovered, were in writing order, many had to be scrapped. Lapaya decided to leave. To join a nunnery, maybe, but never to face that hideous class ever!

Those tender years were not so tender any more. Life twisted, turned and sometimes the pace was giddy. Carloboy discovered the charms of Big Match days. Royal College always played St Thomas' College—arch rivals, and at these annual cricket encounters there was, to borrow a common phrase, hell to pay. Girls' schools and convents declared a state of emergency. Some even closed on a Big Match Day. Mother Gonzaga of Holy Family Convent, Bambalapitiya would do no such thing. Riotous boys, waving flags, whirring infernal wooden clappers and blowing whistles were not going to intimidate her. It all began with the waves of bicycles, naturally, and parents were even advised to send their boys to the Oval—the Wanathamulla cricket grounds—by car or bus and not allow them to roam the streets on their bicycles. Easier said, of course, than done.

Jowl always gave a very threatening talk at morning assembly. The school listened with great respect and rushed out to plan the Big Match mayhem. The need was for about 200 boys on sixty bicycles. Also everything necessary for a blanket disturbing of the peace, flags, cloaks, mummy's kimonos, sisters' straw hats, father's waistcoats, false faces, rattles, bells, trails of empty tins and bits of shrubbery to be

---

1. The old woman who would come to the school each day to sell gram (kadalay) and peanuts, doubtful-looking toffees and other things dear to boy's tummies. Achchi is grandmother. Kadalayachchi, who had served generations of Royalists was an institution. When she died she was sorely missed.

tied behind each bike . . . and so, on a mad March morning, 1950, a wave of bicycles left Dehiwela. Other tributaries poured out of each lane, from every junction. Traffic snarled, knotted and lay palpitating. Policemen, purple-faced, blew whistles. The tide rolled on. St Clare's College was ignored. Chapel Lane was narrow and presented too much of a bottleneck. First port of call was the Milhargiriya—St Paul's Girls School and then Convent—ho!

Mother Gonzaga was fit to be tied. She had closed the big grey gates but hundreds of lunatic boys had climbed the walls, leapt into the grounds and were rushing around singing the most peculiar songs and roaring lustily. Convent girls went into storms of giggles, but they were beyond sight and reach of the demons who had breached defences, opened the big gates and poured through, bicycle bells going bing-a-bing. Mother Gonzaga's rickshawman wrung his hands, gave a wail and bolted. The ruckus was unreal. These weren't boys? Or were they? And what were these uncouth songs and battle cries that threatened to crack the walls, blow the tiles off the roof?

> Hurrah! for the Mary!
> Hurrah! for the lamb!
> Hurrah! for the Royal boys
> Who do not care a damn!
> Oh! everywhere that Mary went
> The lamb was sure to go,
> Shouting the battlecry of freedom!

and then one demon with bulging neck veins would scream: 'Arr! O! Why! Ai! Ell!' and two hundred others would howl 'Ro-yal!' and run into each other waving flags, hats, leap the Convent box hedge and tumble the palm pots. Nobody could fathom what it all meant. Words seemed to have been stung together for the sake of bad rhyme and tolerable meter. Mother Gonzaga was outraged. Desecration of her school was one thing. Who ever said 'the Mary'? And when do lambs shout battlecries, for St Patrick's sake! She stormed out, umbrella in hand, determined to drive every boy out of her gates. She was surrounded, set upon with great shouts of glee, carried to her rickshaw and many hands raised the shafts. Her bearers took off at a sharp trot and behind and beside ran a horde of dishevelled boys . . . onto the Galle Road, down Retreat Road, whooping past the side gate where they laid down their burden, did a war dance of sorts and raced up the road to collect their bicycles, pile up passengers on bar, carrier and handlebars and shoot away, full of jolly good cheer.

Scenes at the Oval, too, grew frantic, billowing, ebbing, as Thomians surged into Royalists, and flag snatching was the name of the game and fights along the boundary commonplace.

Mr Angus of Royal was most peeved when, in 1951, he was duty master in the boarder section and missed the morning session of the Big Match. It was just as well, for by eleven he was rushing to the Cinnamon Gardens police station where an entire mob of hoarse-voiced boys stood amid piles of bicycles and an angry inspector said that all he wished to have was a horsewhip.

'Ward Place!' he thundered. 'Ward Place! All these buggers and their bicycles! Round Lipton's Circus. Riding in the roundabout also. Bus also went on the pavement. Some riding this way, some going other way and hooting. Whole Ward Place they blocked. Next to the hospital, no? Ambulances also stuck. Your school don't know to control?'

Angus sweated. He had, true, quite a graphic description but imagination failed beyond that. He seized Carloboy's ear. 'You are also here!' and turned to glare at pint-sized Thavan. 'And you! Playing for under-sixteen also! Rioting on the road!'

The inspector said, 'Take all and go. But no bicycles. If they want let come with their parents to take the bikes.'

A groan coloured the air. 'But how to go for the match?' Carloboy protested.

'Go by bus! No bicycles! What match? Match started long ago. What are you doing in Ward Place?'

'So we were going. Borella and then Oval.'

'Oh yes? So long you were taking. Got reports here.

Went to Ladies College and Bishops College and playing *pandu*[1] in all the girls schools . . . No bikes!'

Angus, muttering some sort of Chinese incantation, led his boys out. On Reid Avenue he turned on the mob. Those who are going by bus, go! Oh, and by the way, how did you all come to the station?'

'Police said to come,' Brendon Kurups said.

'So you came?'

'Yes, sir.'

It would never do to tell Angus how the police, waving batons and with some actually carrying wicker shields, had routed the bicycle flotilla, threatened to crack heads, smash the bikes, made them dismount and wheel their machines to the station. Shrewdly, they noted that Angus was ready to erupt. But erupt he did, and a punishment, rare and undreamed of awaited them. They were gated for a week, labelled 'undesirable', not allowed to enter the college and confined like lepers of sorts, in a shed where the sternest of the staff set them interminable hours of Maths and cast aspersions on their leprous states, which, if one had a mind to, could have been argued in court on grounds of libel, slander and general defamation.

Just as this master faced his outcasts in the hot, corrugated roof shed, 1950 saw the two Koreas facing each other across the 38th parallel and Carloboy was priming for his Senior School Certificate when America got embroiled in the Korean War. China swarmed in to oppose General MacArthur and the Burghers, who always followed war news diligently, were most annoyed with President Truman who dismissed MacArthur for wanting to take on the Chinese as well. 'MacArthur, men, MacArthur, no? If can just go and land atom bombs in Japan, what's the harm to put one in China also?'

'Yes, men,' George de Mello would say, 'but United Nations scared. How if MacArthur attacks China? Russia will get angry.'

---

1. *Pandu*—ball. In this sense, however, it could be interpreted as playing socks, merry hell, the dickens, the devil, etc. etc.

'So let get,' Sonnaboy would snort.

'Yes, easy to say, but Russia also got atom bombs, no?'

'Then must put in China and Russia also. Damn nonsense. Where will they get another fellow like MacArthur? That's what I want to know.'

'That's true,' George nodded, 'damn shame, no?'

Carloboy conned over his *British and World History*. It did not satisfy him, not when history was being made all the time. Why, his history book came up to the First World War and that was all. But 'Penda' had warned that World War Two would also figure and urged his boys to read every note he had given. Rapid development of technical weaponry was yet another thing to be familiar with. Five subjects—that's all he needed to pass, and Sinhala, English and Maths were compulsories. He added Art and History, and just to increase his chances, English Literature, General Science and Civics. It meant longer hours in the examination hall, but he would get his five, at least.

In 1952, posted results told him that he had his Senior School Certificate. Masters shook their heads wonderingly. Sonnaboy was pleased and more pleased to know that Mr Dias' son had failed miserably. 'Somehow my bugger passed, men. I told Beryl also, with all the nonsense he's doing, still when have to learn, will learn. Six subjects, men, and credits also.'

Dias grimaced. 'My bugger failed men. Saying can't study again. What nonsense? Put him a bloody slap. Go and learn and sit again. If haven't SSC even what he's going to do. Even that new postman who's coming said he also passed SSC. How? And became a postman. Couldn't get a better job it seems. Nowadays even this SSC useless men. Have to go higher, I'm thinking. But where? Will have to send to join the army or something if he cannot pass.'

Yes, Dias was so right. Even a Senior School Certificate was no guarantee of any sort of future in a rapidly changing country. Sonnaboy too, was finding the railway under a new regime quite bloody-minded. He retired, drew his commuted pension and decided to launch a small grocery store. He thought little of Carloboy who, flushed with his exam success, dutifully went into the Upper Fifth and raised eyebrows.

'What?' asked Pol Thel. 'You're going to do your Intermediate?'

'Yes, sir. Can go to the University, no?'

'Good help the University,' Pol Thel said piously.

Carloboy, at sixteen, had begun to find himself. He felt, at last, that he belonged. He had played Royal foul—oh, many times over—but his school still held him, did him proud. He was broad, strong, a trouble-maker and a trouble seeker, but he had seen six merry years at Royal and had watched the college heave in horror and yet absorb the worst and best he manifested.

Why, dammit, he was hardly a boy anymore.

Time to put away boyish things.

Time to be a man!

CHAPTER FIFTEEN

$1$952.

The year of the Upper Fifth. A year to decide . . . the University Entrance, or what?

In Iran they sent the Shah into exile and in Malaya the British fought Communist guerillas. Arabs seethed over the independent State of Israel and masters in Royal College seethed over this bunch of SSC-passed terrors who, relaxing after the rigours of the examination were now apt to run amok at the press of a button . . . any button.

A bad year.

There was Pearlyn, dusky, beautiful, poised like a goddess. Sinhalese father, Burgher mother, and possessed of the best of both, her laughing eyes and rich lips in a perfectly heart-shaped face captured Carloboy. And she was twenty-two and wore an engagement ring and her fiancé, Gerry Waidya was big and sweated and always wore a tie and tight collar. Gerry called on Pearlyn in his car, Carloboy on his bicycle. She was intrigued. Soon they would meet outside the Dehiwela railway station and she would laugh and say, 'But you're still going to school, no? And see, I'm engaged to Gerry also.'

Carloboy was adamant. 'So I'll leave school and get a job.'

'How? You are not even eighteen.'

But she looked on this game and its excitement and felt very satisfied with herself. 'Don't come at five. Gerry will be there. If you like, come after seven.' And Carloboy would go to her little Kawdana home and hold her hand and feel quite breathless.

That, too, didn't last. Gerry would say, 'What is that bugger hanging around here for?' and decided to marry before his girl got any silly ideas. Pearlyn whispered, 'Even if we get married, you'll come to see me, no?'

'What for?'

'Why, you said you love me, so come and see me.'

'You think he will like?'

'But you'll come, no?'

Suddenly Carloboy was tired of it all. 'Oh go and do what you want,' he said crossly, 'if you're marrying him go and marry. Go to hell even! I'm going!' and he went. But nothing ended and the scene shifted and life became a sort of revolving barrel of affairs that blossomed and died in quick succession.

Beryl's brother, Charles, moved to Saranankara Road—a hip-pocket of a house with a doll's house veranda and in which his three lovely daughters and his homosexual son adorned the rooms, positively electrifying the air. The youngest and most precocious was Rosie, who favoured the titillating art of the exhibitionist from an incredibly early age. As frequent family visitors, the da Breas turned many heads as they trooped down the road to Sonnaboy's home. It was so easy to take Rosie to the back of the house, where she would lean against the lavatory wall and Carloboy would bend so that she could rub his cock against her clitoris and squeeze and squeeze until he ejaculated against her. He would go to Uncle Charles' to sit in the little hall, looking through the half-drawn bedroom curtain. In the room Rosie would lie on the bed, open wide her long, white legs and rub and rub and twist her body and turn to show him her trim buttocks. It was a beautiful performance and Carloboy would sit, penis-stiff, and the wetness would mark his trousers. Opportunity took its time, however, until the day he was able to get her alone and he was seventeen and she was twelve and she gave a lip-biting gasp when he entered her and she was tight, so tight that he felt he had impaled her and the head of his penis was clenched inside by a small, urgent vice. And the blood. Oh, he knew, of course. All manner of sex books, surreptitiously circulated in class, told him that virginity demanded sacrifice, offered blood. But her blood was so red and she was so white. It lay in thin lines on his prepuce and around the curl of his foreskin. She said nothing, even when he withdrew, unfulfilled, afraid even of what he had done. The blood fell, a big drop, a crimson tear on the sheet. She rose and walked stiffly to the bathroom.

'It hurt,' she said. 'I tied a cloth but have some blood on it. If wet a cloth and rub will it come out?'

Carloboy stared.

'You go and wash then. I'll clean quickly before anybody comes. Wash and go from the back, round the house.'

He felt shame, shyness, what? He couldn't say. She still came home, chattered her small girl talk, made eyes at him, groped for him, quick, darting, nobody-must-see movements. Even in company. It was all so natural. She would bring a newspaper, squat beside him, spread it open half way across his lap. 'See this, what is this word? Mummy said you're good in English,' and the adults would smile and all the while, under the newspaper, her fingers would press and press and circle around his cock and he would say the first thing in his head and she would lean closer to query and Sonnaboy would tell Hazel, 'If like, men, send in the evenings to learn. Carloboy can teach her a little, no?'

And at his sister Marie's birthday party, while the revels were in progress he put her on his bicycle and they went to her home where he hurriedly entered her, just as hurriedly spent himself and she smiled and said, 'Now we did it properly, no? Other girls in school will be mad when they know.'

'What? You're going to tell your schoolfriends?'

'So what's the harm? All talking only but only that Cora Ohlmus said how her uncle did to her. She also blood came like last time we did. She cried, it seems and uncle held the mouth and said don't make a noise. We'll go, no? Might ask where we are.'

Can one fuck a first cousin? Apparently, in the case of a Lolita, one could? But Carloboy couldn't really contend. The child was so positively nymphomaniacal. And she chattered away so unselfconsciously. 'You must see the size of Geordie's. Huge. Bigger than yours. Bigger than anybody's, I think. Yesterday he tried to put it in. I nearly screamed. My goodness, the size. I said don't and had to shake until like you suddenly that white thing came.'

Carloboy glared. 'What! He's your brother!'

'So?'

'So with your brother also you're going? No shame?'

'So you can also do. There Diana and Marie and even Heather also not small. What's the harm?'

'Brothers and sisters cannot do. It's bad.'

She pouted.

'You're going to be like this I won't come again.'

'So don't then. Who cares? Enough girls I can get!'

And that, thankfully, was the end of that.

Beryl sacked Soma. Soma, she said, had a big mouth. The woman had spread the word among other garden domestics that the mistress was being fervently serviced by the dapper man next door. Beryl had borne Beverley Annette and lost two babies thereafter and with her 1952 abortion the home became a shambles. Carloboy was outraged. It was all over the neigbourhood.

Trevor Dias said, 'What men, should have heard my daddy and mummy talking last night. About your mummy men. My daddy saying damn hore. What's a hore, men? And next door also they're coming to the fence and saying sin for your father and shame for the children and what, your father is blind, he couldn't see what was going on?'

Carloboy nodded morosely. 'Not only that, men, you must see how my sisters are saying. Very good for daddy, only drinking and shouting. Feel like going and kicking all out of the house.'

'What is your daddy saying?'

'What to say. He's keeping quiet. I told him everything. How used to send me long time ago to Bambalapitiya with notes to give someone. I don't know who that man is. Coming and saying here go to that place and give this letter. Will give a reply, bring and come. One day I opened the envelope to see. Had fifty rupees. Just people will give fifty rupees? Must be going there quietly when going marketing.'

'So what to do?'

'I don't know, men. I went to tell Daddy and he's saying I know, I know but she is your mother.'

'And that other bugger put the bolt, no?'

'He has gone. One thing anyday I see him I'll kill him.'

Mrs Van Sanden sniffed. 'Still coming here? Don't step this house again, you heard! Damn prostitute's son!'

Carloboy clenched a fist. 'Who is what? You bloody bitch?'

The woman's screams bring in the garden folk. Pat Silva propels Carloboy away. 'You go home. If not wanting why you want to come?'

Enemies hid behind walls to taunt. '*Ado*! Who fucked your mother? If we come also can do?'

Carloboy was in no mood to suffer 'Pol Thel'. He was asked a question and snarled at the master.

'What? What did you say? Stand on the form!'

This, for an Upper Fifth boy was unthinkable. One told First Formers to do so, even second formers. Carloboy grunted and ignored the man.

'Stand on the form!' Pol Thel shrieked.

'I won't!'

The class cheered wildly. Pol Thel came up, hand upraised. 'I have had enough of you,' he hooted, 'how long do I have to put up with your insolence?'

Carloboy stared at him stubbornly. It was a wild look, a look the master should have taken time to assess. Instead he swung his hand. A stinging slap . . . and something snapped in the boy's tortured mind. He swung out and as Pol Thel turned, the blow took him hard against his shoulder. The class was in ecstasy. Pandemonium peaked as Pol Thel, his spectacles askew, rushed for cover. Carloboy kicked back at his desk, strode up. 'To hell with you,' he shouted, 'to hell with you!' He didn't even gather his books. He stood, a short, fierce figure.

'You will be sacked,' Pol Thel squeaked, 'I'll see that you're sacked!'

Carloboy tossed his head. 'I'm going.' Suddenly there was silence and in the silence he passed sentence on himself.

'Do anything you like. Do . . . any . . . fucking . . . thing . . . you want!' and he strode away.

He cycled home, tossed his bike against the gate. Home was quiet. His mother moved around the house. 'You're early,' she said, 'what happened?'

'That's my business! What do you care what I do?'

'Don't you come to talk like that to me. I'll tell your father!'

'Why my father? Why you won't go and tell that Kinno? Or the baker? Or the vegetable man?'

'You shut up!' Beryl screamed.

'Why? What you do no one can talk about?'

Beryl quivered, even her lips grew ashen. 'You have nothing to talk,' she brazened. 'That's between your father and me.'

'Why? For people in the lane to say things? For boys to hoot when I'm going. Anybody asks I'll say you're not my mummy!'

'What? You want a slap? Trying to be a big man here?'

'Slap to see if you can! Mother? Shame to call you my mother!' and he stormed past a white-faced Beryl who rushed into the room to break into uncontrollable sobs.

Sonnaboy was bewildered. He wanted to kill somebody, anybody. He wanted to take his wife by the throat, choke her till her eyeballs burst and the blood jerked out of her mouth. He wanted to find Kinno, he wanted to walk into Jason Rodrigo's house and smash it to pulp. He wanted, he wanted, and here was this bitch snivelling, snivelling and his son stony-faced, accusing him, him! of being a gutless cuckold.

'I left school,' Carloboy said.

'Why?'

'I hit a master. Sack me anyway.'

'And what are you going to do? Not yet seventeen even. What are you going to do!'

'I'll study at home. Have enough credits to take Varsity entrance.'

Sonnaboy saw red. This was the boy he had beaten, hugged, wondered at, accepted despite everything. All the anger of ages gripped him.

'What did you say to Mummy! What's the matter with you?'

The boy stared defiantly.

'You want to stay here you keep your bloody mouth shut, you heard? I'm the master here. I'll settle things my way.'

'I told the truth.'

'Truth? You'll say nothing! Think you're a big man now because you can hit masters and come? And Varsity! No bloody Varsity! Go and find a bloody job if you can!'

'But—'

The blow caught Carloboy along the side of his face. It stunned him. He couldn't avoid the next that hurt him even more. He cringed, backed into a table. A glass splintered. There was nowhere to run. Between wall and dinnerwagon, which long ago he had scored with the penknife his father had given him, he stood trapped. Over him hung a picture of his grandmother, Maudiegirl Esther von Bloss *nee* Kimball with the legend 'Lest We Forget'. Sonnaboy clenched his fists. 'Nobody comes to try anything in my house! This is my house, do you hear?'

Beryl came through the bedroom curtain. She laid a hand on her husband's shoulder, was savagely pushed aside. Carloboy took a deep breath. 'I'm not staying here,' he said.

'Then get out! Take your things and get out! Now! Go on! Let's see what you'll do!'

Carloboy edged past. His legs trembled. He felt sick in the stomach, dry mouthed. He took some clothes out of his cupboard, stuffed them into a mat bag. His bicycle was still beside the gate. He went round the house, slung the bag. His father stood at the door. He didn't say a word.

Carloboy saw too much hurt in his father's eyes. And an awful loneliness. He wanted to go to him, put his arms around him but he somehow didn't know how he could. 'I'm going,' he said. Sonnaboy just stood. Like some big stone idol. Then as though from faraway he said, 'You come back when you want, all right.'

Carloboy didn't know what he would do, where he would go. He had friends across the canal. Eardley Steinwall and George Saverus and so many other in and around the neighbourhood. He would survive.

'All right,' he said.

'You have money?'

Strange . . . two proud men—yes, men—determined not to budge an inch for the other. Father and son. One bruised outside, both bruising terribly inside. One willing the other to stay, one willing the other to say stay. But they battled on.

'No.'

'You want some money?'

'No.'

And the man pedalled away, and he lived with his friends and would stand at the wall to gaze across the canal where home was. Sonnaboy would cycle past sometimes.

'How are you?'

'I'm all right.'

'What are you doing?'

'Nothing.'

In 1953 Carloboy joined the Royal Ceylon Navy. He was enlisted as a signalman. Kitted out, he rode across the Vihara Lane bridge, into Saranankara Road. In uniform, he placed his bicycle against the fence and walked in. Sonnaboy was in the hall. Beryl sat on the sofa, hemming a dress and there was another baby, gurgling and dribbling on a mat in the centre of the hall. Marie was spreading a cloth on the dining table. She gave a squeak when she saw him at the door. Sonnaboy looked up, rose hurriedly. 'You came?' he said and somehow his voice broke a little. 'Beryl, see, have been joining the Navy!' and they embraced and became one.

Inside each of them the bruises disappeared.